# Private Desires

Mimi Francis

Second Chances in Hollywood

Mimi Francis

Published By: 4 Horsemen Publications, Inc.

4 Horsemen Publications, Inc.
PO Box 417
Sylva, NC 28779
4horsemenpublications.com
info@4horsemenpublications.com

Cover and Typesetting by Autumn Skye
Edited by Blaire Park



*Library of Congress Control Number: 2024935569*

*Paperback ISBN-13: 979-8-8232-0403-3*
*Hardcover ISBN-13: 979-8-8232-0404-0*
*Audiobook ISBN-13: 979-8-8232-0463-7*
*Ebook ISBN-13: 979-8-8232-0402-6*

# Dedication

This one is for my Shih Tzus. If it wasn't for you guys, I would never stay up late writing. Quit barking and go to sleep.

# TABLE OF CONTENTS

# Prologue

## SASHA

Sasha shut the door and leaned against it. She wasn't hiding. She wasn't. After spending the day dragging boxes into the house and unpacking them, she needed a break.

"Sasha?" Sofia called her name from the top of the stairs.

Sasha banged her head against the door, turned around, and yanked it open. "I'm right here," she replied, as she stepped into the hallway.

Sofia skipped down the stairs and hurried toward her. "Are you hiding from me?" she teased.

Sasha laughed. "No. What makes you think I'm hiding?"

"Because after dinner, you darted out of the room like someone lit a fire under you," Sofia said. "And now you're down here. What's wrong?"

"Nothing," Sasha said. "I'm tired. I thought maybe I'd go to bed."

Sofia snorted. "At nine? Isn't it a little early?" She took a step closer to Sasha and bent down to stare into her eyes. "Talk."

"Okay. I am hiding," Sasha mumbled. "From Seth."

Sofia narrowed her eyes. "What did he do? If he did something inappropriate, I will make Chris kick his ass."

"Oh, God, Sofia, stop. He didn't do anything." She reached out and squeezed Sofia's arm. "I swear. He's been a perfect gentleman."

Sofia's eyes narrowed. "Why are you avoiding him? I mean, he's cute and sort of sweet, don't you think?"

Sasha nodded. "I do."

"So, what's the problem?" Sofia asked.

Sasha sighed and shook her head. Despite her interest in Seth, she'd heard the rumors. According to the press, he was a ladies' man who couldn't commit. His life revolved around partying and dating as many women as possible. He took full advantage of his friendship with a celebrity. Deep down, she knew dating Seth—in any capacity—would probably be a mistake. It would be Liam all over again. Thinking about it made her hands shake.

"Earth to Sasha." Sofia bumped her with her elbow. "I said, what's the problem?"

Sasha narrowed her eyes. "Are you playing matchmaker?"

Sofia shrugged. "Maybe. Are you not okay with that?"

"I don't know if I'm ready to date."

Sofia rolled her eyes. "He's not Liam," she reminded Sasha. "And it's been over two years since your divorce. It's time to move on."

"Why do you and my mother keep saying that?" Sasha muttered.

Sofia crossed her arms and stared at her friend. "Because we're smart women. Seriously, Sash, what's the problem? Seth is a great guy. You should give him a chance."

Sasha laughed and shook her head. "If I tell you I'll think about it, will you quit bugging me?"

Sofia grinned and nodded.

"Okay, I'll think about. Now, you were looking for me for a reason. What's up?" Sasha asked.

"Chris is making hot chocolate and lighting a fire in the fire pit. Come outside with us. It'll be fun." Sofia clutched her hands in front of herself and bounced up and down on her toes. "Please?"

"Okay," Sasha said. "Let me grab a sweatshirt and I'll be right up."

Sofia kissed her cheek. "I love you, Sash." She spun around and ran up the stairs.

Sasha ducked back into the bedroom, snatched her sweatshirt off the end of the bed, and tied it around her waist. As she exited the house, music played in the distance. Fuzzy and slightly off, it sounded like jazz, old jazz if her memory for songs was correct.

Down the small hill behind the house, Sasha saw four chairs on the large deck built over the water, a lake the house butted up against. The chairs circled a large fire pit. Flames licked the sides of the pit, and she could hear the pop and crackle of the logs over the music.

Chris and Sofia were on one side of the deck, a box on the ground beside them. Chris crouched in front of it and every few seconds, he pulled out an album and handed it to Sofia. She would either approve or disapprove, which prompted Chris to put the album in one of two stacks.

"What are you doing?" Sasha asked.

Sofia grinned. "I found this old record player in the attic, along with a box of records. We're going through them to see what's good or not good."

"You could just turn on your phone," Seth mumbled.

He sat on the opposite side of the deck, sprawled across the lawn chair like it was a bed or something. He sipped his beer and grinned.

Sofia glared at him. "I like the authenticity of the sound," she said. She stuck her tongue out at him and turned back around.

Sasha kneeled beside the record player, trying to see how it got its power. Seth spoke in her ear, making her jump.

"It's plugged in over there," he said, pointing at an outlet on the deck. "Chris has all the modern amenities."

Sasha's eyes followed the orange extension cord to an outlet on the rail of the deck. She giggled as she got to her feet, tugged on the sleeves of the sweat-shirt tied around her waist, and tried not to look at Seth. It wasn't easy.

His dark brown hair fell over his left eye; he was constantly pushing it off his face, only to have it fall over his eye again. His T-shirt was a little too small and too tight, and, apparently, he was cold, if his nipples poking at the fabric were any sign. Sasha attempted to drag her eyes away, but she only slid them down his taut stomach, admiring the snug fit of his jeans.

*Quit ogling him,* she silently chastised herself.

"Would you like a drink?" he asked. "Wine? Beer? Hot chocolate?"

She focused on his face. "Yes, please. I'll have some hot chocolate," she replied. There was no way she was going anywhere near alcohol. Because she was nervous, she would suck it down, get carried away, and do something stupid.

Seth poured her a cup of hot chocolate from a thermos on the table, handed it to her, and sat down, his long, denim-clad legs stretched out in front of him, head thrown back against the chair, his eyes closed. Sasha walked over and perched on the chair next to him.

"Tired?" she asked.

Seth shrugged. "No, not really. I'm enjoying the silence."

Sasha laughed. "Aw, yes, you're from New York, right?"

Seth nodded. "Yes, so this is … this is heaven."

She closed her eyes and rested her head against the back of the chair. Aside from the jazz music coming from the record player, and Chris and Sofia whispering, it was quiet. No street noise, no people yelling, nothing.

"That is nice," she said.

They sat in comfortable silence for a while, enjoying the cool weather and watching the water lap against the deck.

"They're adorable, aren't they?" Seth whispered.

Sasha opened her eyes. Chris and Sofia swayed back and forth to the music, arms wrapped around each other, lost in their own world. Sasha envied her best friend.

"I'm so happy for them," Sasha murmured.

The song changed, an upbeat tune that had Sasha tapping her foot. Chris hooted and spun Sofia in a circle. They twirled past Sasha and Seth.

"Come dance, you two," Sofia insisted.

Chris snorted. "Yeah, come dance." He spun Sofia away, continuing their circle around the fire pit.

"You know what they're doing, don't you?" Seth asked.

Sasha laughed. "They're not exactly subtle. I know Sofia means well. She wants me to be as happy as she is. You know how it is. When you're happy, you want everyone around you to be happy."

"That must be why Chris keeps asking me if I have a girlfriend yet." Seth cleared his throat. "Would you like to dance?"

"Really? You want to dance?"

"Yeah," Seth replied. "Especially if it will shut Chris and Sofia up." He winked at her.

Seth stood up, took her hand, and, in one swift move, he pulled her into his arms and spun her around. Sasha threw her head back and laughed, dizzy with delight.

The four of them danced around the fire pit, the music coming from the old record player barely loud enough to be heard over the sound of the crackling fire. One song ended and another began, this one soft and slow. Seth's arm around her waist tightened as he hugged her closely. Sasha rested her head on his chest and breathed in his strong, masculine scent. He rested his head on top of hers, and her heart skipped a beat.

They danced until the fire died down and the weather turned. Thanks to the wind coming off the lake, the temperature dropped and made it too cold to stay outside. They cleaned up the empty bottles, glasses, and mugs, then doused the fire and headed inside.

They stopped in the kitchen to put the glasses in the sink. Sofia gave Sasha a one-armed hug and kissed her cheek. "I'm going to bed. I'm exhausted."

Chris and Sofia excused themselves, leaving her and Seth alone in the kitchen.

"Would you like another hot chocolate?" Seth asked. "Or maybe some wine?"

Sasha shook her head. "No, thank you. I'm fine." She leaned against the kitchen counter with her arms crossed over her chest and shivered.

"Are you cold?"

"A little," she whispered. "I think I left my sweatshirt outside."

Seth stepped into her personal space, his eyes never leaving hers. He reached out and rubbed her arms. He inched a little closer, ducked his head, and brushed his lips against hers.

It was the perfect kiss, a light, unassuming touch of his lips to hers. His hand slid up her arm, and he cupped the back of her head, dragging her close. The kiss deepened, and Sasha's heart pounded so hard she was sure Seth could hear it. When they separated, Seth smiled at her and tucked a strand of her hair behind her ear. His fingers lingered on her cheek and slid down to trace the edge of her jaw, his thumb skimming Sasha's bottom lip.

She sighed and shifted closer to him, pressing her body against his as he hugged her closely. She wrapped a hand around his neck and pulled him toward her. Their second kiss was hard and demanding, enough to make her gut twist in anticipation.

"Is that better?" he asked.

"Wh-what?" she muttered.

"Are you warm enough?"

Sasha giggled. "Oh, yeah, definitely."

His lips found hers again, and this kiss was as tender and perfect as the first one. She closed her eyes and let herself sink into it.

They stood in the dimly lit kitchen kissing for several minutes. Heat roared through Sasha's body as her body ached with need.

Seth took her chin between his thumb and forefinger, tipped her head back, and kissed the tip of her nose. He sighed loudly.

"As much as I would like to follow this to its logical conclusion, I think we should go to bed. In separate bedrooms." He beamed at her with a gentle, kind smile, an apology in his eyes.

Sasha's arms dropped to her sides, and she tried to take a step back, except the counter was behind her. "Oh, um, yeah, okay." She stared at the floor.

Seth took her hands. "Hey, look at me."

Reluctantly, she brought her eyes to his. "What?"

"I like you, Sasha," Seth said. "A lot. I swear I'm not blowing you off. I'm exhausted. Chris worked my ass off today, lugging in boxes and furniture. Second, I'm not looking for a one-night stand. Sofia would kick my ass. And there's your third reason. If I hurt you, Sofia kicks my butt. And Chris would help her."

Sasha's gut clenched uncomfortably, but she ignored it and smiled at Seth. "I totally understand. Falling into bed probably isn't a good idea."

Seth chuckled. "Ouch."

"Shit, that didn't come out right." Sasha giggled and shook her head. "It's not that I don't want to sleep with you." She snapped her mouth shut and put her hand over it for good measure. "I have got to shut up," she mumbled.

Seth took her hand and pulled it away from her mouth. "I think it's cute." He kissed her. "Why don't we quit while we're ahead? We can talk tomorrow, exchange numbers, figure out when we can see each other again. Okay?"

Sasha nodded. "Yeah, sure. Go to bed, get some sleep."

Seth raised an eyebrow. "This isn't a brush-off, Sasha. Trust me. I would love to take you to bed." He leaned down and pressed his lips to her ear. "When I go to bed with you, it is going to be an experience you will never forget."

Sasha swallowed, her dry throat clicking. She exhaled slowly as her nerve endings tingled.

Seth twisted a strand of her hair around one finger, leaned down, and kissed her cheek. "I'll see you at breakfast." He turned and walked away.

Losing his body heat made her shiver. Sasha watched him until he got to the top of the stairs and turned the corner. Only then did she relax, slumped against the counter, her hands braced on the counter to hold her up.

*"What the hell are you doing?"* the sensible side of her brain asked.

"Shut up and get out of my head," she mumbled.

*"You kissed him,"* the voice continued.

Sasha pinched the bridge of her nose. The sensible, goody-two-shoes side of her always butted in and ruined her fun. She didn't *want* to be good. She wanted to enjoy herself for once. Next week, she'd go back to being the most responsible person she knew. Right now, she wanted Seth, and she wanted him badly. The sensible side of her could shut up and have some fun. She deserved it.

"Yeah, I deserve it," Sasha said. "So, shut up."

With a grin on her face, she headed downstairs, wondering how long it was until breakfast.

# Chapter 1

## SETH

*Two and a half years later.*

Seth shut down the control panel and jumped off the crane. As soon as his feet hit the ground, the photographer snapped his picture. He adjusted his hard hat and gestured to the reporter from *the New York Times*—Allison something—to follow him.

Inside the on-site trailer he used as his office, Seth poured himself a cup of coffee, then he offered some to Allison and the photographer. They both declined. He shrugged, sat down behind his desk, and leaned back in his chair.

"Did you have questions for me?" he asked.

Allison sat down across from him, set her phone on the desk, and pushed something on the screen. "Just a couple, Mr. Mitchell."

"Please, call me Seth."

Allison smiled at him and popped her gum. "Okay, *Seth*, what do you attribute your success to? Especially at such a young age? People as successful as you are usually much older."

Seth tipped his head back to look at the ceiling. "I've been busting my ass since I was eighteen years old, learning construction from the best in the business. I hired people to help build my business, and they are still with me today. Honestly, Allison, I am good at what I do, and I am not afraid to let people know about it. That's why I got this contract."

"That's arrogant, don't you think, *Seth*?" Allison asked.

Seth cringed. Why did she have to say his name like he'd pissed on her Cheerios? He took a deep breath and shrugged. "You call it arrogance. I call it confidence." He grinned at the reporter. "Whatever you call it, it works for me."

Allison smiled at him. "Yes, it does."

---

Seth stepped out of the shower, snatched the towel off the rack, and wrapped it around his waist. He cursed under his breath as water dripped on his brand-new hardwood floors as he stumbled across the room. He grabbed his phone off the bathroom counter and checked who was calling–for the fourth time–before he answered.

"This better be good, Wyatt," he said. "I dripped water all over my hardwood floors getting to the phone."

"Seth, thank God. I need to talk to you."

"You couldn't leave a message?" Seth asked. "I would have called you back."

"No man, I really need to talk to you." Wyatt chuckled nervously. "It's important."

"So important you had to call four times?" Seth closed his eyes and took a deep breath. He loved Wyatt; he was one of his closest friends and a great guy, though he didn't always think straight. "Never mind. What's so important you had to call so many times in rapid succession without leaving a voicemail?"

"I need you to come to California. I need your advice on my job site," Wyatt said.

Seth laughed. "You need me to come to Cali to give you advice? You're a big boy, bro, more than capable of handling any project your boss throws at you. I believe you reminded me of that when you left me high and dry without a foreman to move to California. Why would you need my help?"

"Because this project is falling down around my ears. Literally. I haven't seen the construction company's owner in weeks. The last time I saw him, he was so drunk he didn't know who I was." A weird, squeaky laugh escaped him. "Please, man? This project is in shambles. I don't know how to fix it."

Seth scrubbed a hand over his face. Despite his reluctance, he knew he would fly across the country. His friends were everything to him. When his best friend Chris's life had been falling apart, Seth hadn't hesitated to put his life on hold and go to California to rescue him. Or try anyway. Wyatt needed help, and Seth couldn't refuse.

Seth sighed. "If I come to California, what do you want me to do?" he asked.

"Come to L.A. and look at the construction site. See if it's salvageable or if I should bail. As foreman, I've got a lot of guys depending on me. If I can keep them from losing their jobs, I will. But if I have to, I will make the tough call to shut us down. I need advice from a true professional."

"You don't have to flatter me." Seth closed his eyes, picturing his calendar in his head. "I can fly out Sunday and come to the job site on Monday. Will that work?"

"Hell, yes," Wyatt replied. "I can't thank you enough. You're a lifesaver."

"Yeah, I'm always coming to everybody's rescue." Seth cleared his throat. "I'll see you Sunday."

Seth disconnected the call and returned to the bathroom. His mind raced with everything he needed to do before he left for California. Calling Chris was at the top of his list. Since he was going to California, he might as well visit his best friend.

---

# CHAPTER 1

Seth spent Saturday morning planning for his trip. He felt confident that his foremen, Romeo and Lewis, could handle the day-to-day details of the current job site while he was gone. That was why he paid them the big bucks. Once he had work straightened out, he booked his flight and arranged for a hotel. His next call was to his best friend Chris to tell him he would be in L.A. He hadn't seen Chris Chandler in two years, not since Seth had been the best man at Chris's wedding. He was long overdue for a visit.

His office phone rang as Seth reached for it. His call to Chris would have to wait. He cleared his throat and snatched the phone off his desk.

"Mitchell Construction, Seth Mitchell speaking."

A deep chuckle came from the phone. "I love your professional voice," Chris said. "It's so sexy."

Seth laughed. "Screw you, asshole. How'd you know I was going to call you?"

"Best friend intuition?" Chris snorted. "We haven't talked in a while, so I thought I'd check in. Why were *you* gonna call?"

"I'll be in L.A. on Monday," Seth replied.

Chris whooped loudly. "It's about time. I haven't seen you since the wedding."

"I've been busy," Seth said.

"Too busy for your best friend, huh?"

Guilt gnawed at Seth's gut. "Cool it with the guilt trip, would you? I'm sorry I haven't been out to California. It's not like you've been jumping on any planes to come home to New York, either. I'll be there

Sunday night, but I'm only staying for a day or two. We need to hang out."

"Come up to the house," Chris suggested. "Sofia would love to see you."

"I would love to see your wife too," Seth said. "I'm checking out a job site for a friend on Monday. I'll call you on Monday night after I get back to the hotel. Are you working?"

Chris was an actor; in fact, he was one of the most popular actors in the world because of his TV show *Hunting the Criminal*, and a series of romantic comedy movies he'd done. Chris Chandler was known worldwide. His show filmed in Los Angeles, at one of the big studios.

Seth's friendship with Chris made him semi-famous, and he had gained a celebrity status of his own: the famous actor's best friend. It had some benefits like easy reservations and female attention, but it was mostly irritating.

"Nope, I'm not working," Chris answered. "We're on hiatus for three weeks. You couldn't have timed it better if you tried."

They chatted for a few more minutes before disconnecting the call. Talking to Chris always made him feel good. After going through hell, the man had a loving partner and a beautiful wife in one. It gave him hope for his own future.

While he'd had his share of girlfriends, none of them had been serious. Because of his friendship with Chris, their early years carousing and raising hell, Seth gained a reputation as a playboy and a ladies' man.

A reputation he sometimes regretted, especially now that he was older. Lately, he wondered if it was time to settle down. His current girlfriend, Allison—the reporter—would jump at the chance to make things with Seth more permanent. His feelings were more uncertain.

Seth wanted a woman in his life but had no time for a relationship. Work didn't leave him a lot of time for romance. Owning his own construction company kept him busy, especially since he was contemplating expanding his business beyond New York. He had been offered several out-of-state opportunities, but he didn't accept any of them. The offers kept coming in, and he wasn't sure how much longer he could say no. The money was too good.

Seth shook his head and pushed himself to his feet. Leaving for California in two days meant he had a lot of work to do.

---

He wasn't even off the plane in California before his phone rang. Wyatt had called to make sure he got on the plane and just before takeoff. He probably would have called while Seth was enroute if he hadn't turned off his phone.

"I'm on the ground, Wyatt," Seth said when he answered. "I'll be there tomorrow, like I promised."

"Let's grab a beer," Wyatt said. "I know a place we can get good food and excellent beer."

"Man, I'm tired," Seth said.

"Too tired to check out Jake's new restaurant?" Wyatt asked.

"What? It's open? I thought it didn't open until next month?"

Jake was another New York transplant. He had graduated high school with Chris and Seth. Wyatt was a year behind them in high school, but he played on the football and basketball team with them. They'd grown close because of their shared love of sports. After they graduated, Seth stayed in New York where he went into construction, while Chris and Jake moved to California to pursue their respective dreams of being an actor and a chef.

"All right, one drink," Seth said. "Only because it's Jake's restaurant. Pick me up at my hotel."

"Turn your head to the left, dude," Wyatt said. "I'm standing about twenty feet away."

Seth turned his head and immediately spotted his friend waving at him. He shoved his phone in his pocket with a laugh.

"I figured I'd save you from a shitty cab ride," Wyatt said.

Wyatt held out his hand and Seth took it, then he pulled his friend close and hugged him tight. "It's good to see you," Seth said.

"Same," Wyatt replied. "Listen, I can't thank you enough for this. You're really saving my ass."

"I know." Seth chuckled. "Come on, let's go check out Jake's restaurant. I'm eager to see the place."

As they drove to Jake's restaurant—Blue Velvet—Wyatt filled Seth in on the multitude of issues at the construction site. By the time they got to the restaurant, Seth's head hurt.

"Damn, Wyatt, that's insane," Seth said. "I'm not sure I'm going to be much help."

"Well, I'm desperate," Wyatt said. "You'll understand after you see the place."

Wyatt pulled into valet parking and handed over his keys. As Seth climbed out of the truck, he noticed photographers—paparazzi—lining the sidewalk on the other side of the street, snapping photos of everybody who visited Blue Velvet. He gestured to them.

"Already?" Seth said.

"It's a popular place." Wyatt laughed. Inside, Wyatt gave the hostess their names. She excused herself and returned a minute later, with Jake following behind.

"Jesus Christ, it's good to see you!" Jake pulled Seth into a hug. "How long has it been?"

"A long time." Seth laughed. "You didn't make it to Chris and Sofia's wedding."

Jake shook his head. "Unfortunately, no. I was stuck working for some bigwig in Anaheim that weekend. I couldn't get out of it. It's one reason I opened my restaurant, so I'd have the freedom to do what I want, when I want. I heard it was nice, though."

"It was. Has Chris been in here yet?"

"Yeah, a couple of times." Jake chuckled. "It's good for business. I wish they'd go away, though." He pointed out the large windows at the paparazzi with their cameras pointed at the restaurant's front door.

"Yeah, they snapped my picture when we came in," Seth said. "Even though I've stayed out of trouble for two years, I still get recognized. They'll put it online with some stupid caption telling the world that me and Chris aren't friends anymore because I'm in L.A. without him."

Jake laughed. "They'll do anything for money. I have to get back to work. You guys get anything you want. It's on me."

"Drinks this time," Seth said. "I had a long flight. I'm exhausted. But next time, I'll go all out."

He slapped Seth on the back. "You'll get the three-course meal, right?"

"I promise," Seth said.

The hostess led them to the bar after Jake returned to the kitchen. He and Wyatt ordered beers and chatted for the next hour until Seth's eyes were heavy. He wasn't sure he could stay awake much longer.

"Time to go," Seth mumbled. "I need sleep."

The paparazzi snapped more pictures as he and Wyatt walked out the door. Seth wasn't even sure they recognized him until he heard someone calling his name. When he turned around, a light flashed in his face, blinding him. He heard the voice of the guy from *The Gossip Monger*, the one Sofia called "the Rat."

"What's up, Seth? You and Chris have a fight? Let me guess, you don't like his prostitute wife, do you?"

Seth clenched his fists and turned away from the Rat. He couldn't let the guy get him riled up. He'd seen Chris lose his temper, and it hadn't led to anything good. Staying calm was crucial.

The valet arrived with Wyatt's truck, and they climbed inside. Seth slammed the door in the Rat's face and gave him a wave with his fingers as Wyatt pulled into traffic.

"God, I hate L.A.," Seth muttered.

# Chapter 2

## SASHA

Sasha pinched the bridge of her nose and closed her eyes as her mother expounded on her daughter's list of deficiencies, in particular her inability to visit her mother more than once a week.

"Yes, Mama," Sasha said. "I know. I will do my best to come over next week."

"Do not interrupt me when I'm speaking, young lady," her mother scolded.

"Sorry," Sasha muttered.

Ophelia, Sasha's mother, lived in a small retirement community near Sasha's apartment building. Ophelia never liked the arrangement. She wanted to live with Sasha so she could "take care of my only child." Sasha had refused, which opened the door to immense guilt. Guilt her mother capitalized on every day of her life.

"Mama, I have to go," Sasha said, when her mother took a breath. "I'm buried in work. Remember, I told you I have a new position in the company with a lot of added responsibilities. I will come over for dinner next week, okay?"

"Fine." Her mother sighed loudly. "Do your mother a favor and call me tomorrow, okay?"

"I will, Mama. I promise." Sasha heard her mother take a deep breath and knew she was about to lecture her again. "Bye, Mama, I love you." She quickly disconnected the call and dropped her phone on her desk. Twenty-seven years old and her mother still got under her skin.

Her entire life has been like that. Sasha was an only child. She had been born to aging parents who thought they couldn't have children. Her father was in his late sixties when she graduated high school, and her mother was only a few years younger. Saying her parents smothered her was an understatement.

Sasha returned to her laptop. She needed to finish some work if she wanted to leave before midnight. Of course, her cell phone rang, interrupting her again. She snatched it off the desk, but when she saw it was her ex-husband, she hit the decline button.

"Ms. Baker?"

A faint squeak escaped her, and her hand hit her cell phone, knocking it to the floor.

The owner of the architect firm, Eleanor McDonald, stood at Sasha's open office door. Sasha jumped to her feet, smoothed her wrinkled skirt, and straightened her jacket.

"I'm sorry, Ms. McDonald. You startled me." She cleared her throat. "What can I do for you?"

Eleanor McDonald gave her a friendly smile, then gestured for Sasha to sit down. "For starters, please call me Eleanor."

"O-okay," Sasha stammered.

"I would like you at the meeting with Phillips Innovations on Monday morning. Their head of company expansion called. He demanded a meeting first thing Monday morning. I'd like you to be there."

"Oh, um, well, that's not my project, ma'am. I believe Eddie is in charge—"

"I'm asking *you* to be there, Ms. Baker." Eleanor cleared her throat. "Edward said you were part of the team that did the designs for the Phillips Innovations project. Is that correct?"

Sasha's mouth snapped shut. "Yes, ma'am, I was," she replied. "Is there a problem?"

Eleanor nodded. "Yes, but not with the designs. We're having some issues with the construction company. Edward has thrown his hands up and taken a step back. I need some answers, and I need someone familiar with the project to help me get them."

"Oh, um, okay," Sasha said. "I can be there."

"Edward mentioned you recommended the construction company. Is that correct?"

Sasha clenched her hands by her side. *Shit.*

"No, not exactly," she said. "I believe the company my ex-husband works for put in a bid after I told him about it, but I did *not* recommend them.

I'm not familiar enough with the company to recommend them for a job. Phillips Innovations made that decision."

Eleanor nodded and tapped her finger against her lower lip. "You're correct, of course. No offense, Ms. Baker, but I don't believe the word of a junior associate would be enough to get her ex-husband's construction company a multi-million-dollar contract. I'm afraid this might be a case of getting what you pay for. Phillips Innovations chose the lowest bidder, and now they are dealing with the consequences." She sighed. "This situation with the construction company won't affect you at McDonald and Skousen."

Sasha smiled, though it felt off, even to her. "Thank you. I'd be happy to sit in the meeting, ma'am."

Eleanor smiled. "Great. I'll have Clara email you the details."

Her boss walked away. Sasha exhaled, pushed a hand through her hair, and shook her head.

*What did Liam do now?*

She leaned over, snatched her cell phone off the floor, and dialed her ex-husband. He answered on the first ring.

"Hey, babe. How's life?" he said.

"Fine." She took a deep breath and refrained from reminding him yet again not to call her babe. "I need to talk to you."

"Always straight to the point with you. So serious all the time." Liam chuckled. Sasha pictured him rolling his eyes and shaking his head.

*At least I'm serious. Unlike you.*

Her ex-husband wasn't serious about anything. He prioritized partying over college, career, and his marriage to Sasha.

Liam rambled on about their past and their marriage. She interrupted him before he got to the "why did we break up" stage. "Liam, listen to me. I said I need to talk to you."

"Sorry, babe. Just reminiscing. I need to talk to you, too. Why don't you meet me for dinner at Rudy's tonight?" Liam said. "How about eight?"

Sasha sighed. Despite her reluctance, she had to have dinner with her ex-husband if she wanted answers.

"I'll see you at eight," she said. "But it's only for drinks, Liam, not dinner."

"Great, babe, I'll see you at eight!"

Before she could reply, the phone went dead in her hand.

"Goddamn it." She resisted the urge to throw her phone across the room. Instead, she took a deep breath and gently set it on the desk. It wasn't her phone's fault that Liam was insufferable.

---

The dark, empty office was quiet. Being alone in the office didn't bother her; she enjoyed working in peace with no interruptions. It was the fifth night in a row she worked late. She prayed her late nights hadn't gone unnoticed.

If what Eleanor said was true, Sasha worried her job might be in jeopardy. Another more experienced architect oversaw the project, even though she had been a part of the team that designed the new, high-tech Phillips Innovations building being constructed in Los Angeles. Sasha vowed to work her hardest until she became the project lead. The issue with the construction company might derail all of her hard work. It might derail the entire company.

Sasha glanced around her windowless, coat-closet-sized office. The space radiated a cozy and inviting atmosphere. She decorated it with two small plants, a picture of her family, and her favorite thing in the office, a painting her best friend Sofia had done of the Hollywood sign.

Sasha glanced at her watch. Leaving now would get her to the restaurant by eight. She took her purse out of the filing cabinet, turned off the light, and locked her office door.

It was a short walk to Rudy's, a small restaurant down the street from her office. She took a seat at the bar and ordered a glass of sweet tea. Alcohol was her preferred drink of choice when dealing with Liam, but it would cause trouble.

Standing up to her ex-husband never came easily. She could not tell him no. It was the reason they had married young and why he was still part of her life five years after their divorce.

Sasha sipped her tea and checked her watch. Liam was late. As usual. If Liam didn't arrive in the next ten minutes, she would place a to-go order and leave.

"Would you like another drink, ma'am?"

She looked at her glass, surprised it was empty. "Yes. More sweet tea, please."

With less than a minute to spare before his ten minutes were up, Liam burst through the door, stopped to flirt with the hostess, then headed in Sasha's direction. She forced herself not to squirm under his scrutiny, though her leg bounced uncontrollably.

"Hiya, babe." He leaned over and kissed her cheek before sitting in the chair beside her. "How's it going?"

"Fine." She pushed a drink menu in front of him. "Thanks for meeting me."

Liam took her hand, intertwining his fingers with hers. "You look amazing."

Sasha rolled her eyes. "Starting with the sweet talk right off the bat, huh?"

Her ex-husband burst out laughing. "No. You're always so paranoid. Can't I tell you that you look good without you thinking I have some crazy ulterior motive?"

"You always have an ulterior motive, Liam."

"Hey, you invited me here. You said we needed to talk," Liam reminded her. "But that doesn't mean I can't say something nice to my wife."

"*Ex*-wife."

Liam leaned in, still clutching her hand in his. "Why is it ex again? We were good together."

Sasha sighed. "No, Liam, we weren't. I worked my ass off in our marriage. You did nothing. While I worked two jobs and went to school, you hung out with your friends from high school, spending every dime I made. After what happened with the—" She cut herself off, swallowing past the lump in her throat. She refused to dwell on the past. "We aren't good together."

Liam brushed a strand of hair away from her face and tucked it behind her ear, his fingers lingering on her cheek. "Maybe we should think about trying again?"

Sasha jerked away from Liam's touch and inched away from him, out of his reach. "There's nothing to think about. Our marriage is over. There's no going back."

"It doesn't have to be over. We should try again and see if it works. We're in a different place in our lives. You've got your job at the architect firm now. Things are looking up for you. I've got my job with the construction company. Things are going great."

"Are they going great, Liam?" Sasha asked. "I mean, with the construction company?"

Liam wiggled in his chair and stared out the window at the street. "What do you mean?"

"It sounds like your construction company is having trouble with the Innovations building. Do you know anything about that?"

"My boss, my *friend*, is having some marriage problems. It's become a bit of an issue on the project."

Sasha's stomach rolled. "Oh God, there *are* problems on site?"

Liam gave a barely perceptible nod. "Some. But it will be fine. I swear. Travis needs some time to get himself together. It should only be a few weeks before we're rolling again."

Sasha put her head in her hands. "Damn it, Liam. This isn't good."

Liam slid his barstool close to her and put his arm around her waist. "It's going to be fine. I promise."

"I'm supposed to go down there and check it out, report back to my boss."

Liam grinned and sat back in his seat. "Great, you can tell her everything is good."

"I won't lie for your friend, Liam. This is my job, my career."

"Not even to help me?" Liam asked.

Sasha snorted. "Absolutely not."

Liam put his hand on her knee and tipped closer. He pressed his lips to her ear. "Hey, babe, why don't you come home with me tonight? We could talk about this some more."

"Are you joking?" she scoffed. She tried to push him away, but he wasn't budging.

"I think we rushed into the divorce—"

"Like we rushed into the marriage?" she interrupted.

Liam cringed, but he pushed on. "We were young and stupid. Everything worked against us. Now that we're older and wiser, we might make it work. Our marriage might be over, but I never stopped loving you."

Sasha resisted the urge to jump off the barstool to escape. "I'm not in love with you, Liam. Not anymore. It's the truth, even if it's not what you want to hear. You broke my heart back then, and you've been breaking it repeatedly for the last five years, what with the money you borrow and the promises you make and break. I can't go back to that. I'm looking for someone who values me and wants to create a future with me. Not someone who lives above his parents' garage and is irresponsible with his money. I need stability, Liam. I crave it. You will never give me that. You never did."

Sasha stood up, grabbed her purse, and left quickly, ignoring the other customers' stares. This had been a terrible idea; she never should have agreed to sit down with Liam. Every time she did, she regretted it.

# Chapter 3

## SASHA

Sasha exhaled slowly as she walked down the hall to the conference room. Not knowing what to expect from the meeting made her nervous the whole weekend. She'd had a small part in the building's design, so small she couldn't fathom why she was being brought in over other junior associates who had also worked on the project. Maybe Eddie requested her help.

Edward "Eddie" Putnam was the project lead on the building design, as well as the on-site architect. Sasha suspected it was his idea to put her on the project.

Sasha stepped into the office outside the conference room. Clara Cleary, Eleanor's secretary, opened the door to the conference room and waved her in.

"Finally," she whispered as Sasha passed her, "they're waiting."

Clara's comment didn't help calm Sasha's nerves. She peeked at her watch. She was early, by five minutes. She steeled herself against any reprimands that might come her way.

Eleanor rose to her feet, a smile on her face. "Ms. Baker, thank you for joining us. This is Jerome Nelson, head of company expansion for Phillips Innovations." She gestured to the man sitting next to her, who gave Sasha a curt nod.

"Mr. Nelson," Sasha said, as she sat down. "How are you?"

"Irritated," Nelson responded, glaring at her.

Taken aback, Sasha stared at her pad of paper and gripped her pen. She reminded herself that his irritation was not her doing.

Eleanor cleared her throat. "There's no need to use that tone with Ms. Baker; she's not the project manager. I asked her to attend this meeting because I believe a fresh set of eyes on site will help get the project moving. Ms. Baker will be going down there in a couple of hours. She will report back to us in the morning. Isn't that right, Sasha?" Eleanor looked pointedly at her.

Sasha didn't know what her boss was talking about, but she wasn't about to admit that in front of Nelson. Instead, she forced a smile onto her face and nodded.

"If she isn't the project manager, who is?" Nelson asked.

"Edward Putnam," Eleanor said. "Unfortunately, he's running late. He should be here soon."

"I can't wait for him." Nelson shoved his chair back and stood up. "I came to discuss the Innovations building problems with the on-site architect. I'll return in the morning since he's not here. I expect answers." He marched out the door, leaving Sasha and Eleanor in stunned silence.

Eleanor sat down beside her. "That didn't go well, huh?" She gave Sasha a forced smile. "I apologize for taking you by surprise with all of this. But we've got enormous problems with this project. Nelson wants answers, and he wants them yesterday."

"What happened?" Sasha asked. "When we spoke on Friday, you mentioned something about the construction company?"

"Yes, it's the construction company," Eleanor replied. "No one has seen the owner in weeks. The foreman is trying to keep it together, but supplies aren't being ordered and people aren't being paid. They are over budget, and the project will not be done in six months."

Sasha stared at the top of the table. "I'm so sorry, Eleanor. I didn't know."

"Why would you?" her boss said. "Edward is the one in charge of this project, so the fault lies with him."

Sasha took a deep breath and nodded. "I thought Eddie had everything under control," she said.

"Apparently not," Eleanor muttered. She cleared her throat. "Sorry. I'm not happy with Edward right now. He waited too long to mention the issues. In fact, he didn't mention them. Jerome Nelson showed up unexpectedly to see how the project was going. The lack of progress puzzled him. Looking for answers, he emailed Edward, who emailed me. He has put my firm's reputation in jeopardy. This mess could have been avoided if he'd spoken up sooner."

Sasha sat up straighter, pulled her pad of paper close, and held her pen poised to write. "What do you want me to do?"

---

Sasha parked her late-model sedan in the dirt lot next to the construction site. She sat in the car, letting the cool air blow her dark hair away from her face. Sweat ran down her temple, thanks to the unseasonably warm Los Angeles weather. Sasha wasn't looking forward to summer, if spring was any sign of what was to come.

Through the window of her car, the skeleton of the ten-story building rose above her head. She couldn't see anyone working on the building. It didn't look like they would finish it in six months. No wonder Jerome Nelson was pissed.

Sasha shut off the car and climbed out. She grabbed the hard hat Eleanor gave her from the back seat, along with her notebook and pen.

"I can do this," Sasha muttered to herself. She spotted a group of men in hard hats near a trailer and headed in that direction.

Seven or eight men stood in a rough circle, coffee cups in hand, talking loudly. Sasha sighed. This would be fun. She steeled herself and stepped into the circle.

"Excuse me," she said. No one responded. She ignored her twisting stomach and forced a smile onto her face. "My name is Sasha Baker and I'm with McDonald and Skousen Architects. I'm here to check on the site."

"Too little, too late," one man said. He looked her up and down. "And I mean little."

Sasha rolled her eyes. Leave it to a man to comment on her diminutive height. She sighed. This was going exactly as she expected.

"Who's in charge?" she asked.

The guy who commented on her height pointed at two men standing close to the partially completed building. "Wyatt, the guy in the blue shirt. He's the foreman. Talk to him."

Sasha muttered her thanks. Maybe the other man was the owner of the construction company, though she couldn't be sure.

She steeled herself and strode purposefully across the site. She wanted answers and to straighten this thing out. It would be fantastic if she could report back that it was a successful day.

As she approached, she saw the shorter of the two men gesturing wildly, his voice high and animated. As she got closer, she overheard him.

"It's a mess," the man said. "I can't get supplies. The permits are going to expire soon, and I can't pay the men. I need help. Can you do anything? Or is it hopeless?"

"I need a minute to look at this," the other man said. He disappeared around the corner as she approached.

"Excuse me? Are you Wyatt?" she asked.

The man swung around. "I am," he snapped. "Who the hell are you?"

Sasha ignored Wyatt's terse tone. "I'm Sasha Baker from McDonald and Skousen Architects," she repeated. "I'm here to check on the site." She shifted her notebook to her left hand and held out her right. "I understand you're in charge here?"

"I'm the site foreman, if that's what you're asking," Wyatt said. He looked at her hand but didn't shake it.

The other man came around the corner. "Hey, Wyatt, I don't think this project is completely hopeless. We can definitely salvage it."

Sasha turned around and looked up, the sun temporarily blinding her. She squinted, trying to see, and gave the speech she'd practiced all the way to the site, hoping to meet the owner. "Well, sir, I recommend you do exactly that. Our client is very dissatisfied with the project's progress, and I see why. I heard you haven't been here for a while, but that changes now. This project is supposed to be done in six months, and you are going to fulfill your contractual obligations and get it finished. On time."

"Sasha?" the man said.

Sasha put her hand up to shade her eyes. Standing in front of her was someone she hadn't expected to see, not in the middle of a construction site in downtown Los Angeles.

Seth Mitchell.

Hands on hips, Sasha glared at the man. She last saw Seth two years ago at Sofia and Chris's wedding, where they were the best man and maid of honor. Her heart skipped in her chest. His boyish good looks, brilliant blue eyes, and dark brown hair that constantly fell in his face still took her breath away.

Sasha had known Seth owned a construction company in New York. She didn't know when or how he ended up in charge of the construction company whose inability to be professional and do their job might cost her firm their reputation.

Sasha knew Seth was a playboy and a goof-off. At first, she'd found him attractive, but then she discovered he was a playboy who used his good looks and friendship with a celebrity to his advantage. He didn't take life seriously. Like her ex-husband, he drank too much and partied too much. It explained why the project was in shambles.

"Seth? This is your construction site?" She shook her head. "Why am I not surprised?"

"Wh-what?" Seth looked so confused, it was almost comical. "What are you talking about?"

Sasha laughed and twirled her finger in a circle. "This. This mess of a construction site. You are over budget and out of time. You have been irresponsible and damn near destroyed this project."

"Whoa, whoa, whoa," Seth said. "I'll have you know, if this *was* my project—and it's not—it would be done. Ahead of schedule and under budget. This chaos wouldn't exist. I'm a professional who takes pride in his work. I would *never* let something like this happen."

Sasha took a step back. "This isn't your work?" she asked.

"No, it's not." Seth crossed his arms and glared at her. "I'm not even licensed to work in California. I came here because Wyatt is my friend, and he needed some advice."

Sasha exhaled. "I… I thought it was yours. When I heard you talking about salvaging the project, I assumed you were the boss."

Seth shook his head. "Not of this fiasco, that's for damn sure. Mitchell Construction takes pride in their work. Like I said, if this was my site, it would be done right."

Desperate to fix the construction site, she latched onto the first idea that came to her. "Then why don't you fix it?" she asked.

Seth laughed. "I'm sorry, what?"

"Fix it," she repeated. "If you're so great, you should be able to fix it."

"That's a great idea," Wyatt interjected.

"I can't just take over someone else's project," Seth said. "Especially one in a state where I'm not licensed to work."

"But you could." The wheels turned in Sasha's brain, the idea taking hold. "I can talk to Phillips Innovations and the head of company expansion. I can get permission for you to replace the other construction company. You can finish the building."

"It's not that easy," Seth interrupted. "My company is in New York. How the hell am I supposed to build something out here without a license?"

"My firm will help you with whatever you need—permits, business licensing, whatever it takes," Sasha said. "If you're as good as you claim, you can finish this building by the deadline in six months."

Seth rolled his eyes. "If you want me to finish this building, it is going to cost you."

"How much?" Sasha asked.

Seth snorted. "You can't afford me."

"I'll set up a meeting with Phillips Innovations and Jerome Nelson, and *they* can decide if they can afford you," Sasha said. "You come in and talk to them. Tell us what you can do."

Seth rubbed his forehead. "I don't know, Sasha—"

"It can't hurt to talk to them," Wyatt interjected.

"Please, Seth," Sasha added. "Give me one hour of your time. Please."

Seth threw his head back and stared at the sky for thirty seconds before he answered. "Fine." He yanked his wallet out of his pocket, pulled out a business card, and handed it to Sasha. "My cell is on there. Set up the meeting for tomorrow and call me with a time. I'll give them an hour at the most." He held up one finger. "One."

Sasha controlled her excitement. She nodded and agreed to call him as soon as she could set up a meeting.

Seth gave her a curt nod and turned to his friend. "C'mon, Wyatt. I need the full tour so I can put together some kind of plan. I'm also going to need everything you have." He glanced at Sasha. "I'm pressed for time."

"Wait? Can I come with you?" Sasha inquired. "I want to see how things are going."

Seth rolled his eyes. "Okay, but stay out of the way."

Sasha bit her lip and forced herself to keep quiet. She would put him in his place later, after he took the job and bailed her out. For now, she'd keep her mouth shut.

# Chapter 4

## SETH

Sasha followed as Wyatt led Seth around the site. Her pen flew over the pages of her notebook, the turn of those pages sounding like the flap of a bird's wings. She asked a million questions, jotting Wyatt's answers down in her notebook. She quizzed Seth, asking him repeatedly how he would solve the problems Wyatt pointed out.

It annoyed Seth, but Wyatt seethed, keeping his mouth shut by sheer force of will. Or maybe it was strength of character. Either way, if Sasha didn't leave soon, Wyatt might bury her in the concrete under the parking garage.

When they were done, Wyatt took them inside and spread the blueprints on the large table in the trailer office. Sasha stepped between them, notebook in hand, and stared intently at the plans in front of them.

"This isn't right," she muttered.

"What do you mean, 'it's not right'?" Wyatt asked. "These are the plans we've been using since the beginning."

Sasha huffed and shook her head. "These are old plans. There have been at least four or five revisions since this one." She took her hard hat off and dropped it on the table. "No wonder things are so messed up. You're working off the wrong plans. How could you *do* that?"

Wyatt raised his hands in surrender. "I followed orders. They gave me instructions, and I did as I was told. If we're working off old plans, that is on the owner."

"Damn right it is," Sasha snapped. "This is unacceptable. I should report this entire company for negligence."

"Look, lady," Wyatt snapped back. "I'm the foreman on site. The owner gives me instructions, which I then pass on to the men. I'm doing the best I can here. Why do you think I asked Seth to come out here and walk the site with me? Because I'm trying to fix it. Jesus Christ, give me a break."

Sasha's mouth snapped shut. She put her hard hat back on and marched across the room, her head held high, chin jutting out. She gave Seth a pointed look as she stopped at the door.

"I hope to hear good news from you tomorrow, Seth." She nodded at Wyatt. "It was good to meet you." Then she was gone.

Wyatt turned to Seth as soon as the door closed behind Sasha. "How the hell do you know her?" he asked.

"She's the friend of a friend," Seth said. "Actually, she's the friend of a friend's wife. Chris's wife. Sofia?"

Wyatt rolled his eyes. "I think everybody in L.A. knows Sofia Larson."

Seth cringed. Wyatt wasn't wrong. Everybody in L.A. knew Sofia, thanks to the tabloids destroying her life after she started dating Chris. The press was especially cruel after discovering that a well-known actor had begun a serious relationship with an escort.

"Sasha is Sofia's best friend," Seth explained.

"So, you met her at Chris and Sofia's wedding?" Wyatt asked.

Seth shook his head. "Six months before the wedding. Both of us helped Chris and Sofia move into their new place up north. We had an interesting, kind of flirty weekend, exchanged numbers, talked via text for a while, long-distance shit." He shrugged. "When I saw her at the wedding, she was kind of standoffish and kept her distance. Nice, but not the same as before. It was like she was intentionally giving me a 'not interested' vibe. I haven't seen her since."

"*You* couldn't get a girl?" Wyatt laughed. "Hard to believe."

Seth chuckled. "It happens."

"Not in my experience," Wyatt said.

"It's not a big deal," Seth said. "It's not like we're friends or dated or anything like that."

Wyatt shrugged. "Well, here's your chance to impress her. Salvage this project, and you might get her to date you." He laughed. "Or at least sleep with you."

Seth glared at his friend. "Can you drop it already? I've got a lot of work to do to get a proposal together by tomorrow morning."

"So, you're going to do it? You're taking over the site?"

"I'm going to put together a proposal," Seth said. "That's it. I doubt Phillips Innovations will even go for it. It's not going to be cheap. Completing this building on time will require a lot of work. For starters, we're looking at eighteen-hour days, which means two crews." Seth took his phone out of his pocket and opened his notes app. "Let's get to work. I don't have a minute to waste."

---

Three hours later, Seth was back at his hotel. Since he didn't have a lot of room, he'd covered the room's second bed with blueprints and papers. Seth sat on the other bed with his laptop balanced on his legs and twenty different tabs open. Wyatt had supplied him with everything he had, including the site–building plans—which were out-of-date—permits, supply orders, the names of the men and women on the crew, and the hours they worked.

Seth spent an hour on the phone with Anita, his administrative assistant in New York. He assigned her to work on the numbers, which included calculating the cost of a business license, his expenses for moving to California, and determining the potential financial loss if he were to leave his projects in New York with his foremen. Fortunately, he had an excellent team back home, a team capable of running his business without him. Now, he was brainstorming ways to get the Innovations project back on track.

He didn't bother to look at his phone when it rang; he snatched it off the table and hit the button to answer.

"Yeah?"

"I thought you were going to call me?" Chris said.

"Shit. Sorry." Seth dropped the papers in his hand on the table and rubbed his forehead. "I'm working."

"What do you mean, 'you're working'?" Chris asked. "I thought this was supposed to be a quick visit to give Wyatt advice."

"Well, it turned into a job offer because I can't keep my big mouth shut." Seth slammed his laptop shut, leaned against the headboard, and closed his eyes. "I may have stuck my foot in it this time, dude."

"What did you do?"

Seth described his conversation with Wyatt and his run-in with the architect at the construction site, omitting the fact that Sasha was the architect. He told Chris how he bragged about being able to finish the building on time and under budget.

"Please tell me you didn't," Chris said.

"I did," Seth said. "But I haven't told you the worst of it."

"It gets worse?" Chris asked.

"Yeah, a little. The architect is Sasha." Seth cringed, waiting for Chris's response.

"Sofia's best friend, Sasha? That Sasha?" Chris burst out laughing. "So, you were trying to impress her, started bragging, and backed yourself into a corner. Is that what I'm hearing?"

"Yeah, maybe," Seth muttered. "I didn't think Sasha would take me up on it, Chris. She challenged me to finish it. How could I say no?"

Chris laughed. "Easy. Say 'no.' Just like that."

"I never back down from a challenge," Seth said. "You know that."

"Especially if you feel the need to impress a woman." Chris laughed. "What are you going to do?"

"I'm crunching numbers to see if I can make it work," Seth said. "Wyatt is freaking out, excited that I might take the job. I don't want to let him down."

"Of course you don't," Chris said. "You're too nice, dude."

Seth sighed. "I know. I can't say no. Which is why I'm sitting here tearing my hair out, trying to figure out if I can do this."

"Why don't you take a break and grab dinner with me? We can hash it out over a couple of steaks."

Seth's mouth watered. He hadn't eaten since this morning, and he could use a break. "Man, that sounds great. Where at?"

They agreed on a place and time before ending the call. After Seth called an Uber, he looked over the mess of papers spread across the bed and sighed. It made his head spin, especially since he'd have to go back to work after dinner.

Chris was already at the restaurant when Seth's Uber dropped him off. Inside, Seth looked for Alex, Chris's intimidating bodyguard, but he was nowhere to be seen. He was hard to miss at six and a half feet tall, with thick muscles and covered in tattoos. He spotted Chris at the back of the restaurant, away from the crowds in a secluded booth. Sitting at the table with Chris was a guy who looked vaguely familiar, though Seth couldn't quite place him.

When the man jumped to his feet as Seth approached, he glimpsed a gun holstered at his hip, under his jacket. It had to be Chris's bodyguard. Chris grinned as Seth approached.

"You're here!" His best friend bounded to his feet and yanked his friend into a tight hug. "It's good to see you."

Seth hugged him back, slapping him on the back as he did. "It's good to see you, too. Where's Alex?"

Alex Peters had been Chris's bodyguard for years. Shortly before Chris got married, his company, Primetime Security, had assigned Alex to guard another actor, Miranda Putnam. According to Chris, it had been a harrowing, almost deadly experience, but in the end, Alex and Miranda fell in love and eventually got married.

"Miranda had her baby, so he's taking some time off." Chris said. He gestured for Seth to sit down and pointed at the man with him. "This is Rylan, Alex's brother. He works for Primetime Security, too."

That was why Rylan looked familiar; he looked like Alex. He wasn't nearly as huge as his brother, but he had a presence about him that screamed protective. Rylan and Seth shook hands.

"Congratulations on becoming an uncle," Seth said. "Boy or girl?"

Rylan smiled. "A little girl named Nicole. Nikki for short."

Seth chuckled. "Alex with a little girl? Oh, that is going to be interesting."

"Yeah, trust me, we can't wait to see how that goes," Rylan said. He smiled at both of them and excused himself.

Their server arrived a few minutes later to take their order. She seemed star-struck and unable to concentrate, but Chris was patient with her and let her take her time. When she finally got it straight and headed for the bar, Chris breathed a sigh of relief.

"Alright, now that our orders are in, tell me more about this construction project," Chris said.

Seth explained the project, outlining the steps and the estimated timeline for completing it. By the time he finished, their food had arrived, and he was on his second beer.

"What are you going to do?" Chris asked.

Seth shrugged. "I guess I'm going to put a proposal together and present it at the meeting tomorrow morning. I don't think it's going to be cheap. Phillips Innovations might not pay what I'm going to ask."

"Let's say they will pay it and you have to move, even temporarily. Where are you going to stay?"

"I don't know," Seth said. "A hotel."

Chris shook his head. "Nope. That will cost you a fortune. You can use my place. I'm only there when I'm shooting and most of the time, I'm sleeping. Weekends, I go to our place in the mountains to be with my wife. You can stay at my place for free."

Seth wanted to argue but couldn't. It was a great idea, and it would save him a fortune. Plus, he liked Chris's place; he had stayed there a hundred times.

"Thank you," Seth said. "That will save me a shit ton of money."

"Happy to help," Chris replied. "You should have asked, dude. You know I would have said yes."

"I didn't want to impose."

Chris threw his napkin at him. "You are never in the way. Jesus, we've been friends since elementary school. You shouldn't have to ask. I can't believe you're at a hotel this trip."

Seth threw the napkin back at him. "Whatever. I wasn't going to assume that I could stay at your place. And thank you. Again."

"Can you work with Sasha?" Chris asked.

"Yeah. She's just another architect."

Chris dropped his fork to his plate and stared at Seth. "She ghosted you."

Seth shook his head. "She didn't ghost me." Chris gave him a funny look, and Seth sighed. "Okay, maybe a little. Yes, we flirted and texted after I went home. And when I saw her at the wedding, she gave me the cold shoulder. I can work with her, though. I'm a professional." He finished his beer and signaled their server for another one. "Can we talk about something else?"

Chris nodded, so they ate their dinner and moved on to other topics. They talked about Sofia, Chris's show and movies, and Chris's dog, Oliver. The biggest surprise of the evening was when Chris said he and Sofia were trying to have a baby. Seth had never pictured Chris as a father, but now that he had Sofia, Seth could see it.

Dinner was over far too quickly. Seth hoped he could transfer to L.A. to spend some time with his best friend. Even if it meant the stress of taking on a half-assed construction project and working with an attractive woman who shot him down.

As he walked out of the restaurant with Chris, he realized he had decided he wanted to do this project. He could only hope that Phillips Innovations would accept his proposal. He knew he was worth it. Now he had to prove it to them.

# Chapter 5
## SASHA

Sasha chastised herself all the way back to her car. After challenging hotheaded Seth to take over the construction project, she wondered if she had screwed up again. She didn't know if he was good at his job or if he ran some fly-by-night company that couldn't build an outhouse.

After throwing her hard hat in the back seat, she started her car to get the air conditioner running. She dug her phone out of her purse and called Sofia.

Even though Sofia lived three hours away and was married to a hotshot celebrity, they maintained a close friendship. If anyone would be honest with her about Seth, it was Sofia. Her best friend answered on the first ring.

"Sasha!" Sofia answered. "Please tell me you are calling to say you're coming up for a visit."

Sasha laughed. "I wish. No, I ... uh ... I actually have a question for you. About Seth."

She pictured Sofia's eyes widening, and a grin spreading across her face. Sofia would think Sasha was interested in Seth. She was, once upon a time. That was until she realized he was a playboy known for dating a multitude of women.

"And it's not what you think," Sasha added. "It's about his construction business."

"His construction business?" Sofia said. "Why do you care about that?"

"There's a chance I might have offered him a job," Sasha muttered.

Sofia giggled. "You offered Seth a job? How the hell did that happen?"

Sasha explained what had transpired at the site. "I need you to tell me about his company, if you can."

"I can't," Sofia said. "Chris would be the one to ask. Seth is his friend. I can ask him if you'd like?"

Sasha shook her head, even though Sofia couldn't see her. "No, it's okay. I'll do some research myself. God, I hope I didn't screw up."

"Relax," Sofia said. "From what I understand, Seth is very successful. Try not to worry about it."

"Easier said than done." Sasha signed. "How about we talk about your next visit to town instead? I don't think I can get away soon, but I'm dying to see you."

They talked until Sasha pulled into the parking garage at her office. As she strode toward the elevator, they said their goodbyes. Once she was back at her desk, she opened her laptop and put Seth's full name into the search engine.

She got back exactly what she expected, article after article about Seth's escapades with his best friend, Chris Chandler. Sofia's husband. Of course, those escapades took place long before Chris and Sofia had gotten married.

Every article pointed out that Chris's friend Seth was a playboy, often seen with a variety of women, whether it was in California when he was with Chris or when he was home in New York. How did he run a business while seeing a new woman every week?

Sasha dropped her cursor in the search bar and stabbed the backspace button until Seth's name disappeared. She typed in the name of his construction company, Mitchell Construction, and hit enter.

She thought she would have to weed through a multitude of companies named Mitchell Construction before she found Seth's; his wouldn't be the only one in the United States. But at the top of the first page of her search results was a photo of Seth Mitchell in a hard hat standing in front of a high-rise building. Sasha clicked on the article.

*At thirty-three, Seth Miller is one of the youngest construction company owners in the state. While Seth has gained a reputation as a playboy and a perpetual bachelor with no desire to settle down, there is more to him than the reputation and the rumors would have one believe. Seth isn't afraid to go after the big contracts, the projects other companies are afraid to take on. His latest project, a high-rise in mid-town*

*Manhattan, has turned the construction world on its ear. The billion-dollar project is a high-tech marvel. In fact, it was so high-tech, Seth wouldn't share a lot of details with us, not even the name of the company behind the building. All we know is they are paying him big bucks to bring their dream to life.*

Sasha skimmed the rest of the article, garnering enough information to use her database to find the project and dig into the details. It only took her a few minutes, thanks to her knowledge of permits and business licensing, to discover who Seth worked for in New York. Seth Mitchell had snagged the bid to build the new headquarters for one of the largest car manufacturers in the United States—Encryption.

Encryption invested millions in a new building following a successful car company launch. Their line of electric vehicles had taken the world by storm, outpacing Tesla's sales by a huge margin and making Encryption's chief operating officer and owner, Genevieve Layton, a household name.

As she read, her doubts about Seth Mitchell slipped away. Building for Encryption would make this project easy for him. It was a third of the size and a fraction of the cost.

Sofia closed her laptop and smiled. She finally had luck on her side.

---

When Eleanor's secretary called and ordered her to report to Eleanor's office, a hard knot formed in the pit of Sasha's stomach, and her mouth went dry. She'd been nauseous all day, her stomach twisting and turning. Her lunch sat in the workroom refrigerator uneaten, and she'd thrown her iced coffee away after two sips.

Sasha's hands shook as she hurried down the hall. She had been anticipating this all day. Jerome Nelson agreed to meet with Seth and discuss the possibility of Mitchell Construction taking over the project. Sasha researched until two a.m. for Seth's company including business licenses, permits, and housing. She had everything in a folder clutched in her right hand. She had thought of everything; Seth wouldn't have an argument she couldn't counter.

Clara rose to her feet as soon as Sasha stepped through the door. She hurried around her desk and stopped in front of Sasha.

"Are you okay?" Clara whispered.

"I guess so," Sasha said. "I'm a little nervous."

Clara patted her arm. "There's nothing to worry about. Take a deep breath, go in there, and kick ass."

Sasha smiled at Clara before she entered the conference room. Two men sat at the long conference table with Eleanor. Her boss was at the head of the table with Jerome Nelson and Seth across from them. To her surprise, Nelson appeared to be happy—smiling and laughing.

Sasha took a deep breath, squared her shoulders, and opened the door. Eleanor rose to her feet, a bright smile on her face.

"Ms. Baker, thank you for joining us," Eleanor said. "We're waiting for Mr. Putnam. Have a seat."

Sasha slid into the seat beside Seth and smiled at him. "Thank you for being here." She reached over and squeezed his arm. "Are you ready for this?"

Seth nodded, a tight smile on his face. He looked away and fidgeted with the papers on the table.

Stunned, Sasha removed her hand from Seth's arm and sat back. Seth had always been sweet and somewhat flirty, even after she gave him the cold shoulder at the wedding. She must have offended him.

Honestly, she saw how it happened. She had been condescending and rude at the construction site. It was wrong of her to assume Seth was a goof-off. She knew nothing about his business, and everything she knew about him came from the gossip sites on the internet.

Sasha silently chastised herself. After everything that happened to Sofia, she knew better than to believe everything she read on the internet. One of the more popular gossip sites, *The Gossip Monger*, had nearly destroyed Chris and ruined Sofia's life. Yet Sasha was willing to believe the site's information about Seth.

*I owe Seth an apology.*

Immediately after the meeting, she would apologize and find a way to make it up to him. If things went well, they could get a celebratory drink.

Just as Sasha was about to ask Seth out, Eddie Putnam burst in. He dropped a rolled-up set of plans on the floor, reached down to grab them, then dropped the pile of papers in his other hand. Sasha jumped to her feet to help him.

"Thanks," Eddie whispered, as she crouched beside him to scoop up the papers.

"You're welcome," she replied. She straightened everything and set it on the conference table before returning to her seat.

Eddie gave her a grateful smile and sat down.

"Thank you for joining us, Mr. Putnam," Eleanor said. "What do you say we get started?"

Eddie nodded. "I'm sorry I'm late, ma'am," he said. "I was trying to reach Dreamland Construction. My intention was to offer them a chance to justify themselves."

"And?" Eleanor prompted.

"I left several messages, but I haven't heard from them," Eddie said.

"Let's get on with it," Jerome Nelson interjected. "I'd like to hear what Mr. Mitchell has to say."

Seth jumped to his feet. "Great, let's get started. You'll like what I have to say."

Sasha crossed her fingers under the table. *I hope he's right.*

---

The meeting lasted two hours. Sasha's confidence grew as she observed Jerome Nelson's grin and Eleanor's enthusiastic desire to work with Seth on future projects.

Eddie appeared to be the only one unhappy. Not that Sasha could blame him. Eleanor had put him in charge of the largest project the firm had ever undertaken, and thanks to a terrible construction company, he had botched it. He looked like he needed a hug.

As Nelson said goodbye to Seth and Eleanor at the door, Sasha slid into the seat beside Eddie. "Hey, are you okay?" she asked.

Eddie shook his head. "No. I screwed up."

"It's not your fault," Sasha said.

"Oh, but it is," Eddie argued. "I didn't keep on top of the construction company like I should have. I didn't visit every day to check on things. This is on me."

"I'll talk to Eleanor," Sasha said. "Maybe she'll go easy on you."

Eddie shrugged. "I don't know, Sasha. Maybe it's time for me to try something new." He shook his head. "I'm sorry you got dragged into this."

Eleanor and Seth returned to the table. "Here's the plan," said Eleanor. "Sasha, you'll lead the project. Seth has agreed to finish construction, and Phillips Innovations, via Jerome Nelson, has agreed to pay what Seth wants. Clara is drawing up the contracts as we speak. Sasha, your first order of business is to fire Dreamland Construction. I want it done today. Understood?"

"Yes, ma'am," Sasha replied.

"You will coordinate with Seth to get him whatever he needs. Take some time to work out the details. Sasha, I expect to hear from you after you take care of the construction company." Eleanor shook Seth's hand. "Thank you for saving my company, young man. I owe you."

Seth blushed. "My pleasure, Ms. McDonald."

Eleanor turned to Eddie. "Edward, would you walk down to my office with me, please?"

Eddie nodded as he got to his feet. He followed Eleanor out of the office without bothering to pick up the papers or blueprints on the table.

Sasha took a deep breath. "Thank you again for helping me."

Seth held up his hand. "I didn't do it for you, Sasha. Expanding beyond New York has been on my mind for a while. Despite my reluctance, I cannot pass up this opportunity. I'm doing this for my company, the people who work for me, and my investors."

Sasha ignored the obvious brush-off. "Well, thank you anyway." She opened her folder. "I think I have everything you'll need right here. I even researched some places for you to stay while you're here." She slid the folder across the table.

Seth took it and leafed through her notes. He smiled at her, but Sasha noticed it was tight and unfriendly. "This is great. I can use some of these. I won't need a place to stay, though. Chris offered me his place."

"Oh, um, okay," Sasha said. "Would you like to go for a drink with me? I owe you an apology for the way I acted yesterday. I made assumptions about your work and your professionalism based on what I know about you personally, and I shouldn't have done that."

Seth snorted. "What do you mean, 'what you know about me personally'? You barely know me, Sasha. We hung out one weekend over two years ago and again at our friends' wedding. I don't think that gives you any kind of knowledge about me."

"I'm sorry, I didn't mean to offend you—."

"I'm not offended." Seth gathered his papers together and stacked them in a leather folder before shoving the folder in a briefcase. "I don't appreciate being judged by someone who knows nothing about me. I could assume you're stuck-up, fastidious, and anal based on the few hours we spent together yesterday. That wouldn't be fair to you, right?"

Sasha shook her head because she couldn't speak. Seth had nailed her personality in three words, and he wasn't wrong.

Seth strode to the door and yanked it open. He turned back to look at her. "You have my business card if you need to get in touch with me. I'm flying home to New York tomorrow morning, but I will be back next week. Wyatt is shutting the site down until Monday. Once I have enough people for two crews lined up, we'll get started. I'll let you know if or when I need you."

Seth turned and left, leaving Sasha staring after him with her mouth open.

# Chapter 6

## SASHA

*Seth nodded in Sofia's direction, made a left turn, and jogged up the stairs with the box balanced on one shoulder. Sasha paused and leaned over the box she was unpacking to watch him go up the stairs.*

*Behind her, Sofia giggled. "Sash?"*

*"What?" Sasha feigned innocence and went back to the box of utensils she was unpacking.*

*"I saw that," Sofia said. "You totally eyeballed Seth."*

*Sasha shrugged. "He's cute."*

*"And sweet," Sofia added.*

*Sasha smiled, but it only took a few seconds before the memories of her divorce and all the painful reasons behind it came flooding back. She stared at the floor and willed her hands to stop shaking.*

*"Don't play matchmaker, Sof," Sasha said. "I don't know if I'm ready for that."*

*"He's not Liam," Sofia said.*

The sound of her ex-husband's voice filled the room, as if summoned by her memories. Sasha took a swallow of her tea and craned her neck to see if he had brought the construction company owner with him as she'd instructed.

She raised her hand and waved at Liam. He waved back and headed in her direction with one of his high school friends behind him. Sasha struggled to remember his name, but it wouldn't come to her. All she could remember was him hanging around Liam, drinking beer, shooting pool, and swimming in Liam's parents' pool.

When they reached the table, Liam kissed her cheek and pointed at his friend. "Sasha, you remember Travis, right?"

*Travis. That is his name. Travis Crowder.*

Sasha got to her feet and held out her hand. "It's good to see you, Travis."

Travis shook her hand and took a seat. He waved over their server and ordered a beer with a tequila chaser. "Keep 'em coming, too, sweetheart," he muttered as she walked away.

"So, what's up?" Liam asked. "I assume since you wanted me to bring Travis, this isn't a social call."

Sasha put her best, kindest smile on her face. "You're right, Liam; this isn't a social call. I have to talk to both of you about the Phillips Innovations building."

Travis held up one finger. "Give me one minute."

Sasha held her tongue while their server put the drinks on the table. Travis picked up the tequila shot and downed it, then he took a drink of his beer. He pointed at Sasha.

"Okay, go," he said.

Sasha sighed. This would not be easy. She sipped her tea and hoped Travis wouldn't cause a scene. She launched into the speech she'd prepared on her way over.

"The construction project is behind schedule—"

"We're working on getting back on track," Liam interrupted. "Our goal is to be ready by the end of the month."

Sasha shook her head. "I'm afraid that's not good enough. We are too far behind. Mr. Nelson from Phillips Innovations won't wait another month for the project to get back on track after seeing its current state. It should never have gotten off track." She took a deep breath. "Effective immediately, Dreamland Construction is terminated. We have hired a new construction company, and they will take over next week. They will be on-site next Monday. Phillips Innovations will pay your company for the work completed. I'm sorry to be the bearer of bad news, but this project is too important to our client to waste any more time."

Travis slammed his beer down on the table. It sprayed from the top of the bottle, splashing all over Sasha and Liam. "Are you kidding me?"

Sasha had been expecting this. She shook her head and kept her anger in check. "No, Travis, I am *not* kidding you. You must know about the issues at your site. When it came to our attention, they sent me down to look into it. It's beyond abysmal. You are in breach of contract. It clearly states that we can terminate your company and bring in a new one if the work is not progressing as promised. That is the case. Therefore, we are letting your company go and moving on."

Liam grabbed her hand and squeezed it. "Sash, give us a week. We'll get it back under control, I promise."

"No," she said firmly. "Like I said, effective immediately. Please clear out the office on site of any belongings." She took a business card from her purse and set it in front of Travis. "If you have any further questions, call the main number and ask for the legal department. They will help you."

Before either of them could protest any further, Sasha got to her feet. She squeezed Liam's shoulder as she passed him. Despite the issues with the company, Sasha didn't want to put her ex-husband out of work. She would wait a couple of days before calling to check on him. Maybe he would consider working at Seth's company.

She was standing next to her car when she heard Liam yelling her name. She contemplated pretending not to hear him, getting in her car, and driving away. Instead, Sasha stopped and turned around.

"What the hell, Sasha?" Liam raged. "You're firing us. Is this a joke?"

"Would I joke about that?" Sasha asked.

Liam stopped in front of her, arms crossed over his chest, a vicious scowl on his face. "This is bullshit. Give us some time to get back on track. Another couple of weeks, and I'll have Travis where he needs to be."

"We don't have another two weeks," Sasha said. "This project is supposed to be done in less than six months. According to the new construction company's owner, it is at least two months behind schedule right now. We can't push it out because your boss is too drunk to run his company."

"That's not fair," Liam snapped. "Travis is having a difficult time. His wife left him—"

"I'm sorry to hear that," Sasha interrupted. "But his personal life shouldn't interfere with his professional life. Especially when he is causing a problem for another company."

"What about me?" Liam asked. "Don't you care about me? What am I supposed to do?"

Sasha sighed. This was what she'd expected. The guilt trip. Liam used this ploy when backed into a corner. He would try to make her feel bad, or worse, responsible for his problems, which she would attempt to solve to make him feel better. Nothing was ever Liam's fault. It was also someone else's doing.

"You know I care about you," she said. "Maybe … maybe I can talk to the owner of the new construction company and ask if he has a job for you. I could do that, I guess."

Liam offered a half-hearted smile. "Do you know him well enough to ask him to give your ex-husband a job?"

Sasha shrugged. "Maybe."

Liam chortled and shook his head. "Whatever, Sash." He looked over his shoulder, then back at her. "I should get back to Travis. I'm worried about him." He took a step closer to her. "Can you do me a favor and think about talking to Phillips Innovations about us keeping our jobs? I can fix it with more time."

Sasha didn't want to argue with her ex-husband anymore. Exhaustion had taken her over and addled her brain. "Sure, Liam. I can try."

Liam reached out and took her hand. "You know I love you, right?"

She nodded. "Yeah, I do."

Liam stared at her until she fidgeted under the scrutiny and dropped her eyes.

"Why can't you tell me you love me, too?" Liam asked.

"You better go," Sasha whispered. "Go check on your friend." She opened her car door and climbed inside. As she drove out of the parking lot, in the rear-view mirror, she saw Liam staring after her.

---

This was the longest week of Sasha's life.

Sasha sat at her desk, her coffee in her hand, staring at the calendar on her computer screen. Was it really only Wednesday? It felt like it should be Friday, but it also seemed like a Monday. She prayed for the weekend to get here quickly.

While things at work had turned around for her, it had come at a price and cost people their jobs. She hadn't wanted to hurt Liam; despite their tangled, sad history, Sasha wished the best for her ex-husband. They both deserved happiness after what they'd gone through. She hoped he would find it.

Part of her also felt bad for Liam's friend Travis. The end of a marriage was tough. Sasha was sure the stress of working under a strict deadline hadn't helped Travis's situation. Hopefully, losing his job didn't push him over the edge.

Her cell phone chirped from the corner of her desk. She smiled when she saw it was Sofia and quickly answered it.

"How did you know I needed my best friend?" she said.

Sofia laughed. "Intuition?"

"You always could figure me out," Sasha said. "Are you calling to tell me you're coming down to L.A.?"

"No, I called to ask you to come up for the weekend," Sofia said. "Please?"

Sasha sighed. Seth was due back next week, and she had a lot to do. She'd already planned to work through the weekend to get caught up.

"I can't, Sof," she said. "I have too much to do. Permits, licensing, and I need to familiarize myself with the blueprints so I have answers if the construction company has questions."

"Work on that stuff for the rest of the week," Sofia said. "Come up Saturday morning, stay the night, and drive back Sunday afternoon. I haven't seen you in months, and now that you're some big-shot architect working on a multi-million-dollar building, it may be a while before I see you again."

"I'm not a big-shot architect. Not yet anyway. Hopefully soon, though."

"It's only a matter of time," Sofia said. "It's in your future."

Sasha giggled. God, she wanted to visit her best friend. A break would be nice before work took over and her social life disappeared.

Sasha closed her eyes and mentally calculated all she had to accomplish before next Monday. If she worked late tonight and tomorrow, she might swing it.

"Okay, I'll do it," Sasha blurted, before she could change her mind. "I'll come up for the weekend."

"Yay!" Sofia shouted.

Sasha winced and yanked the phone away from her ear. "Ouch," she muttered.

"Sorry." Sofia laughed. "I'm so glad you agreed to come up. I can't wait."

"Me either," Sasha said. "I miss you."

"Stop it," Sofia mumbled. "You'll make me cry. Okay, I'll see you Saturday."

"Yes. Bright and early. I'll try to leave before traffic gets bad."

"Drive safe," Sofia said. "Hugs."

"Hugs to you, too. Love you, Sof."

Sasha hung up and set her phone on the desk. Thank God for Sofia. Otherwise, Sasha might work herself to death. Getting away before dealing with Seth full-time was a good idea.

# Chapter 7

## SETH

The sun wasn't even up when Seth met with his lead foreman at the Encryption Building site on Thursday morning. Seth had a lot to get done before he left New York on Friday. Talking to Romeo was his top priority.

Romeo Gallo was in his fifties, closer to sixty than fifty. He was second-generation Italian, unmarried, and one of the smartest men Seth had ever met. He had worked for Mitchell Construction since its inception. There wasn't anyone on earth Seth trusted more with his business than Romeo.

Romeo stared at Seth. "Have you lost your mind?" he asked. "Six months to finish this project? From what I can see, it isn't even half done." The lead foreman for Mitchell Construction examined the blueprints in front of him, then he held up one of several 8x10 photos Seth had of the Phillips Innovations site.

Seth chuckled. Romeo was straightforward. It was one reason Seth kept him around. Romeo kept him grounded when he got his head in the clouds.

"Yeah, I know, Rome," Seth said. "But I couldn't say no. I mean, the money is phenomenal, and it will expedite the expansion of the business. For months now, I've been trying to figure that out. I was trying to get a foot in the door. This blows that door wide open and shoves me through it. It was too good to pass up."

Romeo sighed. "I agree. It's too good to pass on. I understand where you're coming from, *figlio,* I just hope you do, too." He adjusted his hat and sat back in his chair. "Tell me what you need from me."

Seth put a folder on the table in front of Romeo. "I think I've got it figured out." He tapped the folder. "You will run the New York site. Everything you need is in here. Look through it and you'll see. I promise."

Romeo opened his mouth, most likely to protest, but Seth cut him off. "You can do it, Rome. The building is damn near done. We have less than a month to work on it, and it could build itself, given the progress so far. I trust you to finish the project."

"Ms. Layton won't like it," Romeo said.

Seth shook his head. "I already talked to Ms. Layton, and she understands. I assured her we will complete the project on time and as planned. I also promised her that if any unforeseeable issues affecting the building were to come up, I would be here within twenty-four hours."

Romeo narrowed his eyes. "Ms. Layton is not a reasonable woman, *figlio*. She may seem understanding, but she will change her mind. I guarantee it."

"I don't think so," Seth said. "After I explained to her I wanted to expand my business, she seemed to understand." He patted Romeo's arm. "It will work out. You've got Anita for all the paperwork and bookkeeping, and Lewis to help you. It won't be any different from the times I've flown off to hang out with Chris and left you in charge."

Romeo gave Seth a wry smile. "It was for a weekend, or possibly three or four days. You're packing up and moving to California."

Seth chuckled. "I'm not moving, Rome. I am temporarily relocating. You can reach me anytime by phone 24/7. Once I get things off the ground, I can put Wyatt in charge of West Coast operations, and I'll be home. I could never leave New York."

Romeo nodded, though Seth could see his lack of conviction. Seth figured he would come around in a day or two. Once he read through the folder, he would see Seth planned for every contingency. He left no stone unturned.

As Seth got to his feet, he patted Romeo on the shoulder. "I called a meeting with the crew in an hour. I'll meet you outside."

Seth wouldn't leave without explaining to his crew. He had an open-door policy with his staff and crew. Transparency was the key to this job. The crew deserved to be kept in the loop. He didn't want anyone to worry they might lose their jobs because he was in another state. His goal was to help them understand he was doing this for all of them; his employees were also his investors, and he would not hide things from them. Seth believed it was the reason he had a low turnover and kept a top-notch crew working for him.

Honesty was the best policy, at work and in his personal life.

---

Packing for six months differed from packing for three days. Seth had never gone to California for longer than a week. His suitcases were full, but he had more to pack. After an hour, he threw his hands in the air and gave up. If he forgot something, he would have to buy it or borrow it from Chris.

It had been the longest week of his life. He hadn't realized how difficult it would be to upend his life and move across the country. He'd been so worried about his business and doing everything necessary to keep it running that he'd forgotten about his personal life.

His apartment would sit empty for the next six months. Seth considered subletting it, but he couldn't get it ready in less than a week. So, he left his keys with his assistant, who promised to stop by once or twice a week to check on it. At least he didn't have any plants that would die or pets that needed attention.

After he finished packing, he grabbed his phone to make the phone call he'd been dreading all night. He'd been dating Allison for over three months. After she had published her article about him, she had called and asked him out to dinner. He had agreed, and they had been seeing each other ever since. Seth wasn't sure they'd reached any kind of relationship status that could be serious, though Allison introduced him as her boyfriend. He still referred to her as his friend. She was fun and sweet, but he hadn't seen their relationship lasting long.

His move to California, even though it was temporary, was reason enough to end the floundering relationship. It was clear for the last couple of weeks that things were ending, but he thought he realized it more than Allison did. He loathed doing it over the phone; it was a shitty thing to do. But time had gotten away from him, and he either would lead her on for the next six months or end it over the phone. The second option was the best, if not the kindest. He didn't feel emotionally prepared for this situation, especially if she became upset with him.

Seth pulled her name up from his contact list, took a deep breath, and hit the button to call her.

"Seth!" Allison cooed. "I'm so glad you called, baby. I haven't heard a peep from you in a week. How about we get brunch tomorrow?"

"I can't," Seth said. "I'm going to L.A."

"L.A.? Like Los Angeles?" Allison asked.

"Yeah, Los Angeles," he said.

"Ooh, are you going to see Chris?"

Seth sighed. Nothing irritated him more than the women he dated inquiring about his best friend. Most of them wanted to meet Chris, and they weren't shy about asking. Over the years, he'd grown accustomed to women using him to get close to his famous best friend. Seth avoided serious relationships because of it.

Allison seemed different; Seth assumed it was because of all the people she met as a reporter, including celebrities. While Allison knew he was friends with Chris, she hadn't seemed to care. Unfortunately, things had changed and over the last couple of weeks, she'd started bringing up Chris's name more and more, hinting that they should travel to California to meet his best friend. Seth got the impression she'd been biding her time.

"Actually, no," he said. "I've got a job out there."

"What do you mean a job?" Allison asked.

"I'm taking over construction on a site in California. I'm temporarily moving out there to get the job done."

"You're moving?" Allison yelled. "Are you serious? When the hell were you planning on telling me?"

Seth gritted. "I'm telling you now," he said. "This came out of nowhere, Allison. I've had less than a week to get my shit together. I'm sorry I didn't call you sooner, but my business took precedence."

"So, what does that mean for us?"

"I'm sorry, but I don't think we'll be able to see each other anymore. I'm going to be gone for months. You'll be here—"

"Wait," Allison interjected. "We can talk every day. I can come out and see you. It doesn't have to be over."

"I'm afraid it does," he said. "I can't commit to a relationship, especially a long-distance one. It's best if we end things now before it gets too complicated."

Allison sighed loudly. "This is bullshit, Seth."

"I know, and I'm sorry, I really am. It's been coming for a while."

"What?" Allison snapped. "It's been coming for a while? Were you afraid to tell me earlier? You waited until you had an excuse, like moving, to dump me?"

"I will not fight with you, Allison, no matter what you say." He took a deep breath. "I didn't intend to hurt you. I'm trying to be honest with you. A long-distance relationship won't work, especially when only one of us is invested in it."

"Fine," Allison said. "Whatever."

"Take care of yourself, Allison. I should go. Goodbye." He disconnected the call and tossed his phone on the bed.

God, he hated breakups. Hated them. He repeatedly broke up with his girlfriends. They either dated him because they thought he could get them close to Chris or they wanted more than he was willing to give. He needed to find a girlfriend who understood his career came first.

Seth checked his watch, swearing under his breath when he realized it was almost midnight. He had to sleep as his flight departed at six a.m. He took a deep breath, shook off the unpleasantness of the breakup with Allison, and stripped off his clothes. Thirty seconds after his head hit the pillow, he was asleep.

# Chapter 8

## SETH

Seth closed his eyes and turned his face up to the sun. This had been an excellent idea. He would have to thank Chris for insisting he come up for the weekend. He didn't know when he could relax again.

The door behind him opened, though Seth didn't bother to open his eyes. It would be Chris with their beers. Oliver stirred between his legs, his head came up off Seth's knee, and he snorted before he laid back down.

"Did you bring the chips and salsa?" Seth asked.

"Um, no," a female voice said. "Sorry."

"Shit." Seth struggled to sit up with the fifty-pound dog between his legs. "I'm sorry, Sof, I didn't mean—." He stopped himself when he realized it wasn't Chris's wife standing next to him.

Sasha stood beside his chair with a sheepish grin on her face. "Hi." She wiggled her fingers in a half-hearted wave.

"What are you doing here?" He winced. He didn't mean to sound like such an ass.

"I could ask you the same thing," Sasha said. She crossed her arms and glared at him. "You said you weren't coming back to California until Sunday."

"I changed my flight after Chris invited me up for the weekend," Seth explained.

"Sofia asked me to come up, too. She thought I needed to relax." Sasha snorted. "Do you think they're playing matchmaker again?"

"God, I hope not," Seth muttered.

"Thanks," Sasha deadpanned. "It's nice to know you think so highly of me."

"That came out wrong," Seth said. "I didn't mean to sound like a dick." He took a deep breath. "Look, we're both adults. Can we be civil for two days?"

"I can if you can," Sasha said.

Seth detected a hint of haughtiness in her tone. Not that it surprised him. He deserved it after the snide comment.

"Then we agree," Seth said. "We'll behave ourselves and act like adults."

"Agreed." Sasha turned, took three steps, halted, and glanced back at him. "I just wanted to say hi." With that, she continued her trek back to the house.

Seth thought about stopping her but didn't know what to say. He should apologize for how they left things after meeting with Phillips Innovations. He had been an ass, but the stress of preparing a bid proposal in less than twenty-four hours had left him exhausted and irritated.

He didn't get up and follow her, though. Once he'd crossed the line into what his mother liked to call his "dickheadedness," there was no turning back. It was a full commitment to the attitude. It saved him a lot of pain and heartache when he broke up with his girlfriend for the week. As Chris's best friend, he'd honed the attitude over the years. It was useful when dealing with paparazzi, journalists, and the girl who wanted Chris instead of him.

*Go apologize, asshole.*

Why did the voice in his head telling him to be nice have to sound like Chris?

Seth patted Oliver on the flank and ordered him to get up. He obeyed immediately, though that didn't stop him from side-eyeing Seth as he jumped off the chaise lounge and plopped down in the grass with a heavy sigh.

Seth jogged up the small incline to the back porch. He steeled himself for the inevitable dirty looks from Sasha—and most likely Sofia—then opened the door.

"There you are!" Sofia smiled. "I expected you to stay out there all day." She laughed as she set a bowl of popcorn on the table and sat down beside Sasha. "We're going to watch a movie while you and Chris drive into town for pizza."

That wasn't the reception he expected when he came inside. Maybe Sasha hadn't told Sofia about their exchange in the backyard. He smiled and winked at his best friend's wife.

"Your wish is our command, ma'am," he drawled.

Sofia giggled and Sasha rolled her eyes, though he noticed the corners of her mouth turned up the tiniest bit. Chris blew past him with his keys in his hand and opened the back door.

"Ollie! Come on, boy. Let's go for a ride!" Chris yelled.

Ollie barked and came bounding into the house. He sat down in front of Chris with his tail wagging.

Seth followed Chris and Ollie out to Chris's BMW. Ollie waited until Seth got in, then he climbed in and perched on his lap. Seth muttered, "Oof," and groaned.

"Your dog is spoiled," Seth said.

Chris laughed. "Yes, he is." He put the car in gear, and they were off, flying down the road. Seth had one hand on the handle above his head and the other on Ollie.

"I'm sorry I didn't tell you Sasha was coming up," Chris said, his eyes on the road. "Sof told me yesterday, but I spaced it out last night."

"Why are you apologizing?" Seth asked. "You can invite anybody you want to your home."

"According to Sofia, there have been issues between you two since you took on this job," Chris pointed out. "Like, you don't get along. You called her anal?"

Seth sighed. "Yeah, I did. But, in my defense, she is."

Chris chuckled. "That doesn't mean you *tell* her she's anal."

"It just came out," Seth explained. "I was tired, stressed, and irritated. She's the one who suggested I take over the project—"

"You didn't have to do it," Chris interrupted. "You could have told her no, gone home to New York, and avoided all the stress."

Chris slowed the car at the only stoplight in the small town. He turned left and parked in front of the crowded pizza place.

"I could have," Seth said. "But I didn't. And I took it out on Sasha."

"At least you know you're wrong." Chris opened his car door. "I'll be right back. The two of you wait here since Ollie can't come in." He jumped out and hurried inside.

"I hate it when he's right," Seth mumbled. He patted Ollie on the side. "Don't you hate it when he's right?"

Oliver snorted.

Seth laughed. "Glad you agree with me."

---

Seth went to the kitchen after everyone was asleep. It had been a long day. He'd been at the airport at four this morning, flew into LAX, then caught a ride with Chris north to his home in the mountains. They'd stayed up late watching movies and talking, so by the time he went upstairs to bed, he'd been awake for twenty-one hours. He'd forgotten how much the three-hour time difference kicked his ass. While it was midnight in California, it felt like three a.m. to him.

He was exhausted. But he'd enjoyed his time with Chris and Sofia. Being around Sasha was not as painful as he expected. True to her word, Sasha had been civil, and he'd done his best to do the same. Lack of sleep and alcohol caused a pounding headache.

The kitchen was dark except for a small nightlight by the kitchen sink Sofia kept on for company. It was bright enough for him to find the glasses and a bottle of headache medicine.

Seth filled a glass with water and swallowed four pills. He went to the living room, sat on the couch, and put his feet up. He rested his head against the back of the couch and closed his eyes.

The tension drained from his body, and the headache faded. Sleep wouldn't come easily with everything on his mind. He was preoccupied with tasks to do on Monday, things he forgot in New York, and the Phillips Innovations construction.

A loud creak forced him upright. He looked over his shoulder and saw Sasha standing in the doorway leading to the basement. Her dark purple shorts and white pajama top clung to her curves, and her black hair cascaded down her back. She tiptoed across the floor, stopping short when she realized she wasn't alone.

"Seth? What are you doing down here?" she whispered.

Seth tapped his forehead. "Headache. You?"

Sasha pointed at her head. "Same. My head is pounding."

"Too much to drink?" he asked.

"Are you implying something, Mr. Mitchell?" she asked.

Seth got to his feet with a sigh. "No, I'm not implying anything." He walked around the couch, bumped into the side table in the dark, and cursed under his breath. He stood in front of her. "That's why *I* have a headache. That and a lack of sleep."

"Oh, um, yeah. Too much alcohol," she said, taking a step away from him.

He ignored the slight and gestured for Sasha to follow him. "Come on, I'll show you where the headache stuff is hiding." He led her to the same cabinet where he had found the ibuprofen and poured her a glass of water while she dumped pills in her hand.

Sasha took the glass he offered, popped the pills into her mouth, and drank half the water in three swallows. She closed her eyes and sighed. "Damn, maybe I needed water."

Seth stepped around her, pulled a bottle of water from the fridge, set it in front of her, and retreated to the other side of the counter, careful to give Sasha her space. The light from the moon illuminated her face, making her seem ethereal. It reminded him his attraction to Sasha still existed. Maybe he hadn't *stopped* being attracted to her, despite it being two years since he'd seen her. He crossed his arms over his chest to resist the urge to reach out and touch her.

"Better?" he asked.

"I'll know in thirty minutes," she mumbled. She squinted at the clock on the microwave. "Is it really after midnight? No wonder I'm exhausted."

"You should go to bed and get some sleep," Seth suggested.

Sasha shrugged, put her elbows on the counter, and rested her chin on her hands. "Can I ask you a question?"

"Sure." Seth mirrored her posture on the other side of the counter.

"Why did you agree to take the Phillips Innovations project? Why did you do it, besides the money and the desire to expand your business?"

Seth stared at the counter and pondered his answer. "I thrive on challenges. I know I could finish it and finish it right. And yes, the money is good, and it helps me expand my business faster than I expected, but when it comes down to it, it's the challenge of taking on something people think can't be done. I want to prove them wrong."

"Wow," Sasha said. "That's, um, really cool. I hope you can do it."

Seth chuckled. "Of course you do. It reflects well on you."

Sasha grinned. "Yeah, it does."

"Now I get to ask a question," Seth said. "Tit for tat."

She was quiet for a moment, then she nodded. "Go for it," she said.

"Promise to answer, even if you don't want to?" he said.

Sasha grumbled something incoherent under her breath, but eventually muttered, "Okay, fine."

"What happened to us?"

"Us?" Sasha whispered.

"Yeah, us, as in you and me," Seth said. "We were in a good place, texting and stuff. We seemed to get along great, but then out of nowhere, right before the wedding, you ghosted me."

"Seth—"

"You promised to answer," Seth said.

Sasha exhaled and stared at the ceiling. "Look, Seth, you're a nice guy."

"Don't give me the 'nice guy' line, okay? Tell me the truth."

Sasha leveled her gaze at him. "You want the truth? Fine. I don't think you're the kind of guy I want to date. I'm not interested in a casual fling or a one-night stand. That's all you want. You're not looking for a serious relationship. What did the *Times* say about you? You're a playboy who has no intention of settling down?"

Seth snorted. "You read that? It was a line for a journalist who wanted an interesting story. She wanted the story about the young, playboy bachelor who is conquering the world."

"So, you *are* looking for a relationship?" Sasha asked.

Seth hesitated. To be honest, he didn't know the answer to that question. He wasn't sure what he wanted. He kept hoping he'd figure it out.

"I didn't say I was looking for a relationship," Seth replied. "I don't know what I want."

"See, Seth, this is what I'm talking about." Sasha sighed. "I apologized for the assumptions I made about you and your business. I won't apologize for thinking you're just a playboy looking for a quick lay. You don't strike me as a guy who wants to settle down. You never have." She straightened up. "I don't want to talk about this anymore. I'm going to bed."

Sasha turned her back on him and walked away, leaving Seth speechless in the dark kitchen.

# Chapter 9
## SASHA

Sasha lay in the dark bedroom and stared at nothing. It was pitch black in the spacious basement bedroom, a room decorated in blues and yellows, accented with sunflowers and daisies. Since the room was windowless, she couldn't see anything.

*What did I do?*

She had gone off on Seth, that's what she had done. It hadn't been her intention when she stumbled on him sitting on the couch in the dark, but stress, exhaustion, and the headache had all combined to push her over the edge. If she was being honest with herself, it was the *us* question, that damn "what happened to us" question that had done it.

Liam asked her the "what happened to us" question all the time. It had been his mantra for two years after the divorce, and he still asked it almost every time he saw her. When Seth asked her the dreaded question, it set her off.

Sasha wasn't certain if she meant to say those things. His reputation made her hesitant to get involved with him. Sasha had learned her lesson with Liam. She wouldn't make the same mistake twice.

Her attraction to Seth was a problem. Seth was the opposite of what she wanted in a man. Unfortunately, he was also everything she wanted in a man. He was a paradox, and it drove her crazy.

She gave up trying to sleep at four a.m. and got out of bed. She went to the bathroom, brushed her teeth and washed her face, then she threw her things into her duffel bag. Sasha tiptoed upstairs, careful not to step on the squeaky floorboards or bump her bag against the wall. She wanted to avoid everyone. Her relaxing weekend had been a bust, thanks to her run-in with Seth last night. She grabbed the pad of paper beside the phone and scrawled a note to Sofia. She folded it in half and propped it against the coffee pot. Silently, she left the house, got into her car, and drove off.

It would hurt Sofia that Sasha had rushed off without talking to her, but Sasha needed space and time to think. She couldn't do that with Seth around.

The situation between her and Seth was the epitome of starting off on the wrong foot. They had both said things they shouldn't have; they'd been cruel to each other—intentionally or unintentionally—and sadly, they made the idea of working with each other awkward.

She didn't know how to fix it. Apologizing obviously wasn't the answer; they had both done it, and then one of them opened their big mouth and screwed everything up again. Maybe she would pretend nothing happened. It seemed like her only option.

Sasha didn't notice she had reached L.A. until her exit was only a few miles away. She slowed down in the middle lane and signaled to turn left.

Her phone rang. Sasha grabbed it off the passenger seat where she'd thrown it, expecting it to be Sasha, but the name on the screen said, "Mother." She sighed and hit the button, putting it on speaker.

"Hi Mama," Sasha said.

"Where are you, Sasha?" her mother asked. "Why does it sound like you're in a fishbowl?"

Sasha laughed quietly and shook her head. "I'm in my car. I just drove back from Sofia's."

"Aw, Sofia! How is she? And that handsome husband of hers! I watch his TV show every week."

"Sofia is wonderful," Sasha said. "She says hi."

"You should come see me," her mother said. "If you are already out, anyway. I haven't seen you in weeks."

Sasha sighed. It hadn't been weeks; it had been one week, but her mother—Ophelia—was prone to exaggeration. She glanced at the clock in her car. It was early and, honestly, she didn't have an excuse *not* to go see her mother.

She switched her blinker from left to right. "I'll be there in twenty minutes."

Sasha parked in front of her mother's retirement community ten minutes later. She sat in the car, pulled her hair into a ponytail, and checked her reflection in the rearview mirror. A haggard, puffy-eyed woman stared back at her. Sasha was sure Ophelia would say something.

With a sigh, Sasha climbed from her car. She hefted her purse onto her shoulder, locked the car door, and went in through the front entrance.

Three years ago, Ophelia reluctantly agreed to move into a small condo in the fifty-five plus community close to Sasha's apartment. While Ophelia initially balked at the move, once she was part of the community, she didn't want to leave. She had friends and activities to keep her occupied: she played golf and pickleball, Bunko on the weekends, and hung out with her friends.

None of this kept her from demanding Sasha's attention. After Sasha's father, Paul, passed away, Ophelia turned to her only child for companionship and solace. Sasha enjoyed spending time with her mother, but she couldn't be there all the time. Her mother wanted her around 24/7. Sasha's life became her mother's life. She had to stop it, which was when they decided Ophelia would move into the Sunnyvale Retirement Community.

Sasha signed in and exchanged pleasantries with the woman at the counter. She got a visitor's sticker, walked through the dining room, and made her way to the small condos.

Her mother must have watched her cross the courtyard, because the door flew open before she could knock. Ophelia threw her arms around her daughter and loudly kissed her cheek. She took her daughter's hand and pulled her inside.

"You looked exhausted," her mother scolded. Any time Ophelia spoke to Sasha, it sounded as if she were scolding her daughter.

Sasha sighed. "I didn't sleep well last night, and I just drove for three hours. I'm not surprised I look tired."

"What is wrong, Sashie Bug?" her mother asked.

Sasha shook her head. When her mother called her "Sashie Bug," it took her back to her childhood and all the times her mother had embarrassed her by using that horrid nickname. Her parents thought the nickname was cute. Sasha did not.

"Don't you dare shake your head. I know when something is wrong. Spill."

Sasha contemplated her choices for about 2.5 seconds. If ever she needed her mother, it was now. So, she said, "It's a man."

Ophelia sat on the couch and patted the cushion beside her. "Sit. Tell me about it."

Sasha dropped her bag on the floor and sat down next to her mother. She planned to give her mother the abridged version of her troubles with Seth, but as soon as she opened her mouth, everything spilled out, all the way back to when they first met.

Talking to her mother was cathartic. Getting everything off her chest to someone who didn't know Seth and wasn't familiar with him was exactly what she needed. Ophelia had no preconceived notions or opinions about Seth. She didn't scroll through the gossip sites on the internet or watch the programs that discussed Hollywood gossip. Seth was nobody to Ophelia Drakos.

"Let me ask you a question, Sashie Bug," Ophelia said when Sasha stopped talking. "Is this young man a bad person?"

"What do you mean, 'a bad person'?" Sasha asked. "Like, does he kick puppies and run down old ladies in the crosswalk?"

Ophelia laughed. "Well, if he does that, he is a bad person, and you shouldn't date him."

"Agreed. He's not the puppy-kicking type. In fact, Chris's dog, Ollie, loves him. So, I'd have to say he's not a bad person."

"That's good." Ophelia smiled and patted her daughter's hand. "Put things in perspective, sweetheart. He's not a bad person, or an evil man. He's made mistakes, which we have all done. Even you. You should give him a chance."

"I don't know, Mama," Sasha mumbled.

"I know what this is about," her mother said. "You're worried that you'll end up with another man like Liam, aren't you? A man who will break your heart?"

Sasha shrugged.

"Can I give you some advice?" Ophelia asked. "A tiny piece of advice from your old mother?"

"You're not old, Mama," Sasha said. "And I will happily take your advice."

Ophelia took both of Sasha's hands in hers and held them gently. "Push through the pain and move forward."

Sasha closed her eyes and let her mother's words sink in. *Push through the pain and move forward.*

"Wow, Mama, that's ... that's kind of cool." She squeezed her mother's hands. "Thank you."

"You're welcome, Bug." Ophelia kissed her cheek. "Why don't we see what's on the menu at the clubhouse?"

---

After spending the morning and into the afternoon with her mother, Sasha drove home, turned on the TV, got comfortable on the couch, and fell asleep. She slept through two true crime documentaries, almost four hours total. After waking up groggy and out of sorts, she stumbled to the bathroom, relieved herself, and washed her face. She needed coffee. The lack of sleep from the previous night had caught up with her.

Her phone pinged from her purse. She dug it out from beneath the tissues, gum wrappers, and various types of lip balm, all the time wondering how many notifications she missed while she slept.

*Twenty.*

More than half of them were from Sofia, both voicemails and texts, two texts from Eddie, and four emails. There was also a missed call from Seth's cell phone, but no message.

"I should text Sofia," Sasha mumbled. "She's probably furious with me."

[Sasha: I am sorry I left. I will call you later this week and explain. I did something dumb, and I needed to get away from Seth to figure it out.]

[Sofia: OMG! Did you sleep with him? That would explain why he has been acting weird all day.]

[Sasha: No, I didn't sleep with him. I said some pretty harsh stuff to him. Rude stuff.]

[Sofia: What did you say?]

[Sasha: I will call you later and explain everything, okay? I need to figure out how I'm going to work with him for the next six months after sticking my foot in my mouth.]

[Sofia: Call me if you need me.]

[Sasha: I will, I promise.]

Sasha sent one more text, a heart emoji, then she went into the kitchen and made herself an enormous cup of coffee with tons of cream and sugar. She closed her eyes and sighed as the first drop of the dark liquid hit her taste buds. She needed that.

Sasha wondered if she should call Seth, since he had called her. If she apologized for what she said, they could start over. She refused to do it over the phone. Tomorrow morning, she would go down to the site, apologize, and ask him if they could start from scratch.

Decision made, she opened her fridge and searched for something to eat. Who knew sleeping half the day away would make her so hungry?

# Chapter 10

## SETH

Seth parked in the dirt lot next to the trailer early Monday morning. While it excited him to start construction on the Phillips building, first he had to meet with the crew. He knew some men were loyal to the other construction company and wouldn't want to work with him. He had the difficult task of releasing those men.

Not only was he preoccupied with work, but also the uncomfortable exchange with Sasha on Saturday. It had unnerved him. He had to worry about the crew's opinion and work with someone who disliked him. It made his head hurt every time he thought about it.

Fortunately, his best friend had done everything in his power to make Seth's transition to California effortless. Chris asked Seth to take a walk after breakfast, instead of driving him back to L.A. as expected. They went to the garage, and Chris opened the immense door with a flourish.

"Ta da!" Chris exclaimed.

Parked in the garage was a brand-new Land Rover. When Seth saw it, he shook his head and laughed. "What is this?"

"Use this while you're in Cali," Chris said. "It's a loaner. You need it, because you're the boss, and you shouldn't be using an Uber or a Lyft to get to work every day."

Seth opened his mouth to protest, but Chris cut him off.

"Don't bother trying to argue with me because you won't win." He held out the keys. "Take it and enjoy it."

Seth pulled Chris into a hug. "Thanks, bro. I didn't consider how I would get to work every day. Everything happened so fast."

Chris shrugged. "What else is a best friend for? Especially one with more money than he knows what to do with."

Not only had Chris given him a car to use, but when Seth got to Chris's house in L.A., he found the refrigerator fully stocked, his room ready, and the bathroom full of his usual toiletries. Chris had thought of everything.

Wyatt opened the trailer door and waved, pulling Seth from his thoughts. Seth raised a hand in greeting, then he grabbed his briefcase and climbed out of the Land Rover.

*Time to get started.*

Wyatt ushered him inside and shut the door. Seth tossed his briefcase on the chair by the desk and looked around the trailer. It was a mess. Empty paper coffee cups were on every surface, papers were thrown haphazardly all over the desk, and the trash by the door overflowed. Seth grimaced. His father had taught him that keeping a clean work area would help him stay organized and efficient. He couldn't concentrate in a mess like this.

"I hope you're ready for this," Wyatt said.

Seth turned to his friend. "Do you think it's going to be bad?"

Wyatt shrugged. "Maybe, maybe not. The owner of Dreamland Construction, Travis, had an entire week to fill the crew's ears with a bunch of lies. He's been telling anyone who will listen that he got bumped because the new architect is sleeping with you."

Seth rolled his eyes. "How many of them bought it?"

"Not many," Wyatt replied. "They've been here. They've seen what we're going through. I ushered him out of here pretty damn quick. I let him get his personal effects and showed him the door. But he knows these guys. He talks to them outside of work. He got to a few."

Seth nodded. "I figured as much. I'll talk to them, tell them where we're at, and see who wants to stay." He turned to the door.

"One more thing," Wyatt said. "Liam showed up today."

"Who the hell is Liam?" Seth asked.

Wyatt flinched. "I thought you knew. Liam is Travis's friend. Rumor has it he helped Travis get this job because he has connections with the architect firm. According to that same rumor mill, he's Sasha Baker's ex."

"Shit," Seth mumbled. "Liam is probably here to cause problems. Which I won't put up with. If he starts anything, we'll be escorting him off site. ASAP."

"Yes, boss," Wyatt said.

"Let's get this meeting started," Seth said. "The sooner I get to know who will be on my crew, the sooner we can hire more people." He put his hard hat on his head and rolled up his shirt sleeves. Time to introduce the new boss to everyone.

Seth was prepared for whatever might come his way. This wasn't the first time he had taken over a flailing construction project—though he had never taken over one of this scale—so he was accustomed to meeting with crews distraught over the possibility of losing their jobs.

Normally, he wouldn't be nervous, but Wyatt's revelation that Liam was Sasha's ex knocked him off his game. On the outside, he might have seemed calm, but his insides churned like a tornado.

The crew gathered in a group at the base of the building. Seth strode confidently toward them, a smile on his face. He wanted them to know he was approachable and, hopefully, they would find him to be friendly. He needed them on his side.

Seth shouldered past two of the crew and stepped onto a stack of cinder blocks so he could see everyone.

"Good morning," he said. "I'm Seth Mitchell of Mitchell Construction. Phillips Innovations hired me to get this building finished."

Two or three of the crew scowled, but most of them had tentative smiles on their faces. Seth pushed on.

"Let's address the elephant in the room. I understand there have been a few rumors regarding how I got this job," Seth continued. "Let's get something straight. They are *not* true. I got this job based on the merit of my work. Period. Anyone who tells you otherwise is mistaken or blatantly lying. Is that clear?"

Several of the crew nodded, but Seth noticed one man in the back of the crowd whose scowl deepened with every word he said. He kept an eye on him as he talked.

"Feel free to Google me and my company. I have been working in construction since I was a teenager, and I have owned my company since I was twenty-seven. I have built six large commercial retail buildings in the state of New York. My team is about to finish construction on a billion-dollar high-tech building right in the middle of Manhattan. I can assure you, I'm not some asshole who doesn't know what he is doing. I'm not afraid to say I know my shit. That's the reason I got this job."

He looked over the group of men. It appeared he had gotten their attention. He pushed on.

"We have a lot of work to get done in the next six months," Seth said. "It's not going to be easy. I'm going to be running two crews in ten-hour shifts. So, if you know anybody who needs a job, send them my way. We are definitely hiring."

One man raised his hand. Seth pointed at him and nodded.

"You paying overtime?" the man asked.

Seth nodded. "You bet your ass I am. I will pay anyone who works overtime double their pay rate for their troubles. I know this isn't going to be easy, but I will compensate accordingly."

Murmurs of appreciation rippled through the group, and several of the scowling men now had smiles on their faces.

"Also, I want you to understand, I am not poaching anyone from Dreamland Construction. Want to work for me? That's great. No hard feelings, if not. I know some of you are loyal—"

"You don't know what the hell loyalty is," Seth heard from the middle of the crowd. "You took this job away from a good, hardworking man, and you got it because you're dicking the female architect in charge."

Seth clenched his fists at his side, but he kept the smile on his face. "Who are you?" he asked.

"I'm Liam Baker," said the man, as he stepped out of the crowd. "I am—was—one of the foremen on site. You took this job away from my friend."

Seth sighed. This would be unpleasant, but he wouldn't sugarcoat it. The crew deserved to hear the truth.

"I didn't take the job from anyone. Your friend lost this job on his own. You, as the foreman, should know this site is in shambles," Seth stated. "You are weeks behind schedule, over budget, and your permits are inadequate for the building inspectors' standards. I've heard the rumors that I got this contract because I'm sleeping with the architect. You shouldn't believe the rumors, Liam. If the rumors *I've* heard are true, your friend didn't know how to do his job."

"That's bullshit!" Liam shouted.

Seth took a deep breath. "It's not bullshit. Just look around." He gestured to Wyatt. "Please escort Mr. Baker off site, Wyatt."

Liam scurried back out of Wyatt's reach. "I know who you are, Mitchell. You are friends with that hot-shot actor who married the prostitute."

"You should stop talking, Liam," Seth warned. He wasn't about to let anybody call Chris's wife a prostitute. "That's my best friend's wife you're bad-mouthing."

"Yeah, well, she's my wife's best friend, so I can say what I want," Liam snapped. "I know you and Sasha were both at their wedding, so you know Sasha. I can only imagine what happened up there in the mountains. Sasha wouldn't have taken this job away from me, unless it was going to somebody she was fucking."

"That's enough," Seth said. "Your services are no longer required, Mr. Baker. Wyatt, get him out of here."

Seth was taken aback when a few men from the crew took it upon themselves to remove Liam. Liam threw his hands up in the air and stormed off. Wyatt glanced at Seth, who followed the former foreman to the parking lot.

Seth turned back to the crew. "I'm sorry you had to see that," he said. "Liam's accusations are baseless. I am here because I am qualified to do this job, and I plan on doing it right. We start on Wednesday. But I'm not going to force anyone to work for me. If you don't think you can work for me, you're welcome to leave. No hard feelings. But, if you choose to stay, I need you to understand that it is going to be hard work for the next six months, and I will expect a lot from you." He took a second to look at the crew members before continuing. "I'm not going to make you quit right here in front of everyone, and I don't expect you to give me an explanation. If you choose to leave, come see me in the office, and I will cut you a check for your back pay. If you have questions, you can come talk to me." He pointed at the trailer used as an office over his shoulder. "I'll be in there, cleaning up."

Seth pushed his way back through the crowd of men and returned to the office trailer. The rest of the day would be a waiting game until the crew decided what they wanted to do. He would wait and see.

# Chapter 11

## SASHA

Several times on Monday, Sasha considered heading down to the Phillips Innovations site. Every time she talked herself out of it with one lame excuse after another. Instead, she stayed in her office, working on inconsequential paperwork that could have waited for another day. For the first time in weeks, she left right at five p.m. and drove home.

All day, her mother's words had played like some kind of self-help guru's mantra in her head. *Push through the pain and move forward.* Despite her mother's wise words, Sasha couldn't bring herself to go talk to Seth. She might mess it up or say the wrong thing. Again. Sasha thought she might make things worse if she didn't plan her words and actions before going to the site. At least, that was the excuse she gave herself all day on Monday.

On her drive home, she called Sofia. After she explained what happened between her and Seth on Saturday night, she begged her best friend for advice.

"Talk to him," Sofia said. "I think your mother's advice is on point. Seth isn't a bad guy. He's made mistakes, but who hasn't?"

"So, you agree with my mother?" Sasha asked.

"Yes, for once I agree with your mother," Sofia said. "Promise me you'll talk to Seth."

"I promise," Sasha said. She didn't know when she would talk to him, but she would keep her promise to her friend.

She turned off her phone, changed, and made popcorn as soon as she got home from work. Just as she turned on her favorite show, someone knocked on her apartment door. She cursed under her breath as she got up and hurried to answer it.

Through the peephole, she saw Liam, arms crossed and a furious scowl on his face. He pounded on the door again.

"Just a minute!" she yelled.

Since she wasn't wearing a bra, she grabbed a sweatshirt from the closet and pulled it on, then she took a deep breath and opened the door.

"Hey, Liam. What are you doing here?" she asked.

"Are you screwing that guy, Mitchell?" Liam snapped.

"Well, hello to you, too," Sasha said. She glanced at her neighbor's door less than ten feet away, knew they would be listening to everything, and made a snap decision. She held the door open wide and gestured for her ex-husband to come in.

He elbowed past her and went into the kitchen. He yanked open the fridge and stared into it, wordlessly. After shutting the door, Sasha stood on the other side of the counter and watched him.

"You don't have any beer." He grabbed a bottle of water instead, slammed the fridge shut, and glowered at Sasha.

"No, I don't have any beer. I don't drink it. Why would I keep it in my house?"

"It would be nice if you had some when you have company," Liam said. "You know, like when your husband comes over."

"You're not my husband anymore," Sasha said. "I'm tired of reminding you of that every time I see you."

"It would still be nice if you kept some beer around for when I visit," Liam muttered.

Her patience was wearing thin. Liam treated her and her small apartment as if he still lived with her, even though it had been five years since the divorce. Any time he showed up at her apartment, he acted like he owned the place. She wouldn't have invited him in if she hadn't been worried that her neighbors would hear him shouting.

"Why are you here?" Sasha asked.

Liam rolled his eyes. "You didn't answer my question," he said. "Are you sleeping with that Mitchell guy?"

Sasha did her best to stay calm. "Why do you think I'm sleeping with Seth Mitchell?" she asked.

"I recognized him as soon as I saw him. He's friends with that guy that Sofia married, isn't he? The actor,

Chris something. I've seen pictures of him." Liam twisted the lid off the water bottle and tossed it on the counter.

Sasha took a deep breath before she spoke. "Yes, he is friends with Chris. But that doesn't mean I'm sleeping with him. Why would you think that?"

"How else would he get the job? You're the architect, and the two of you are friends. I did the math." He took a drink from the bottle and smacked his lips.

Sasha sighed. "You were never good at math, Liam. I promise you it is a coincidence that I know Seth. He got the job because he's qualified. In fact, from the research I've done, it seems he is quite good at his job. Phillips Innovations is lucky to have him constructing their building."

"He fired me," Liam stated. He stared at Sasha, as if he expected a reaction.

"No, Liam, I fired you," Sasha reminded him. "Wait, did you go down to the site today?"

Liam nodded. "I did. I wanted to give him a chance. Instead, the douchebag who stole my job escorted me off the site. What's his name? Wyatt. In front of everybody, too. I didn't even do anything."

Sasha shook her head. "I'm sure there's more to the story."

Liam slammed the water bottle down on the counter. Water sprayed all over the counter and dripped down the cabinets to the floor. "Why don't you ever believe me? Why can't you take my word for it? Mitchell embarrassed me in front of everyone. And you don't care. Of course, I think you're sleeping with him. You're defending him."

"I'm not defending anyone. I don't know the complete story. You come in and make accusations without proof, expecting me to listen. I know you, Liam. I know how you react in certain situations. There's probably more to the story than just being escorted off site for no reason."

Liam snorted. "You wanted me to get fired."

Sasha didn't remind him—again—that she had been the one to fire him. She forced a smile onto her face. "I think you should leave," she said. It surprised her how calm she sounded. Liam was hot-headed. Once he settled down, he would regret barging into her home and making accusations.

Liam opened his mouth, probably to protest, but Sasha shook her head again. "I want you to leave," she said. "Maybe we can discuss this when you're not pissed off. Maybe."

Her ex nodded. He dropped the water bottle in the sink and wiped his mouth with the back of his hand. He stopped beside her on his way to the door.

"What happened to us?" he whispered.

Sasha closed her eyes. There it was. That goddamn question again. She was so sick of hearing it come out of Liam's mouth. He refused to acknowledge his part in the end of their marriage. He lived in denial.

"Go home, Liam," she whispered. She didn't move until the door closed behind him.

Sasha cleaned up the spilled water with some paper towels. She wouldn't feel sorry for Liam. So many of their problems stemmed from her feeling sorry for him and giving into his wants and desires to appease him. It took her a long time to figure that out. He had a valid reason to be angry. He'd lost his job, and he felt like she was responsible. Once he calmed down, he would realize it wasn't her fault.

*At least, I hope it's not my fault.*

---

Sasha planned to go to the Phillips Innovations site on Tuesday morning, but she couldn't do it, not after Liam's accusations. Did the other men at the site think she was sleeping with Seth? It seemed likely, since her ex-husband ran in the same circles as the crew from the construction site.

Sasha avoided going to the site and worked in her office instead. She got the permits in order, talked with the building inspectors, and sat down with Eddie to get his input. By Wednesday, she had run out of excuses for not visiting the site.

Late Wednesday afternoon, her desk phone rang. It was Clara asking her to come down to Eleanor's office. Her boss wanted an update.

"I'll be right down," she promised.

Sasha stood up, grabbed her leather binder, straightened her skirt, and left her office. She kept a smile on her face as she marched down the hall to Eleanor's office. The glass door leading to her office stood open, and she saw Clara at the filing cabinet with a stack of papers in her hand.

# CHAPTER 11

Sasha cleared her throat as she stepped through the door. Clara looked up and gave her a friendly smile.

"Hi, Sasha," she said. "Ms. McDonald is waiting for you. Would you like a coffee or anything?"

"No, thank you," Sasha replied. She took a deep breath and entered Eleanor's office.

"Hello, Ms. McDonald, how are you?" Sasha asked.

"I thought I told you to call me Eleanor," her boss said with a smile.

"Yes, sorry. Eleanor." Sasha smiled.

"Tell me how things are going at the Phillips Innovations construction site," Eleanor said, taking a seat behind her enormous desk.

"I believe they're going well," Sasha replied.

Eleanor pointed at the chair in front of her desk and said, "Sit down, please."

As Sasha lowered herself into the chair, her boss folded her hands and leveled her gaze at Sasha. "What do you mean, 'you *believe* they're going well'?" she asked. "Have you been to the site?"

Sasha kept her eyes down, staring at her shoes as she spoke. "Not yet, ma'am."

Eleanor sighed. "Sasha, this is *not* what I want. I replaced Eddie because he wasn't cutting it. I expect more from you. I want you down at that site tomorrow. Do you understand?"

Sasha felt like a child in the principal's office. She didn't look up, but she nodded. "Yes, ma'am. I'll go down there tomorrow morning."

"Bring me a full report tomorrow afternoon. I'll have Clara put you on my schedule." Eleanor picked up a stack of folders and opened the one on top. "That'll be all."

Sasha took some papers from her binder as she stood and set them in front of Eleanor. "Here are the permits, building inspection notifications, and some of my notes. I'll see you tomorrow afternoon."

She was almost at the door when Eleanor called her name. She reluctantly turned around.

"Yes, ma'am?"

"I didn't mean to chastise you," Eleanor said. "This building has the entire firm on edge. It could literally make or break us. I know that's a lot of pressure on you, Sasha, but I am confident you can handle it. Feel free to come to me for anything. Okay?"

Sasha nodded. "Thank you, ma'am, I appreciate that. I'm sure I'll bring you good news tomorrow." She excused herself and hurried back to her office.

As she stepped through the door, her desk phone rang. She snatched it up and said, "Sasha Baker."

"Hi, Sasha, it's Seth." He paused for a moment. "Seth Mitchell."

Her heart skipped in her chest. His boyish charm oozed from him, even over the phone. If she closed her eyes, she pictured his crooked smile, his sparkling blue eyes, and the hair falling over his forehead. She shook her head, trying to clear the image from her brain. She couldn't fall under Seth Mitchell's spell.

It was like she conjured him out of nowhere because of her meeting with Eleanor. She took a deep breath and prepared herself to talk to him.

# Chapter 12

## SETH

By Wednesday, Seth still hadn't heard from Sasha. Monday and Tuesday he'd waited expectantly for her to show up on site, but she never did. He called her on Wednesday afternoon. Since he was attempting to remain professional with Sasha, he opted not to call her on her cell phone, even though he had the number. Instead, he called the front desk at McDonald and Skousen and asked for Sasha Baker. She picked up her phone on the first ring.

"Sasha Baker."

"Hello, Sasha, it's Seth." When she didn't speak, he added, "Seth Mitchell."

Sasha spoke after another moment of silence.

"Hi Seth. How are you? Are you all settled?" she asked with too much enthusiasm.

"I am," he said. "I wanted to ask you when you might come down to the construction site. We need to discuss some things."

Sasha sighed loud enough that Seth heard it through the phone. "Is this about my ex-husband?"

Seth nodded, even though Sasha couldn't see him. "I didn't bring it up because I handled it. How did you find out about it?"

"I spoke to Liam," Sasha explained. "According to him, you embarrassed him and had him escorted off site," Sasha said. "Is that true?"

Seth snorted. "If Liam was embarrassed, that was his own doing. He interrupted a meeting with my new crew and said a lot of crap he shouldn't have said. He made accusations I didn't appreciate about me and you. And he called my best friend's wife a prostitute."

"He did what?" Sasha snapped.

Seth jumped and held the phone away from his ear. For a second, he'd forgotten Sofia was Sasha's best friend. Sasha was a colleague now, not a friend. He never mingled his business with his personal life. It made his life easier to manage. Sasha complicated things.

Seth took a deep breath. "He called Sof a prostitute. Nobody badmouths my best friend's wife. He crossed the line in several ways, so I asked Wyatt to escort him off the site. Wyatt and some crew members were happy to do it."

"I'm going to kill him," Sasha mumbled. "Bastard."

"You know, I didn't call to tattle on your ex-husband," Seth said. "When are you planning to come to the site?"

"Um, how does tomorrow sound?" Sasha asked. "I need to drop off paperwork and get an update."

"Tomorrow would be fine," Seth said. "You have my cell phone number, right? Text me when you get on site, and I'll come meet you."

"Okay, sounds good. I'll text when I get there." The call disconnected.

Seth held the phone away from his head and looked at it. "Goodbye to you, too," he muttered.

---

[Sasha: Hey, Seth, it's Sasha. I'm here in the parking lot by the office trailer.]

Seth looked at the text message and excused himself, promising to return as soon as possible to answer any more questions the crew might have.

Today marked the first day of work on site. Seth had spent the last two days getting organized and getting the crew in place so they could get started. To meet the deadline, he had two crews working twenty hours a day. He also had a crew of ten men who agreed to work weekends for the foreseeable future.

Seth figured it would take sixty to ninety days—working weekdays and weekends—to get the project caught up to his standards. At least he hoped it would only take sixty to ninety days. It would be too expensive for him to exceed that.

Sasha climbed out of her car as he rounded the corner of the building. She didn't dress like she was at a construction site, not with her three-inch high heels and business suit. She looked like she might spontaneously combust because of the heat. Seth thought she wanted to look professional, which she did, working from the office. It wasn't appropriate for a construction site. At least she had a hard hat, though it didn't fit well over the top of her ponytail. She perched it precariously on top of her head. It appeared unstable and likely to fall off her head.

He sighed and picked up the pace, hurrying to meet her at her car. Sasha waved when she saw him.

"You're going to have to take your hair down if you want the hard hat to fit properly," Seth greeted her.

Sasha rolled her eyes, but she took off the hard hat and yanked her hair down. She slipped the hair tie around her wrist, ran her fingers through her hair, then put the hard hat back on.

"Come on, I'll show you around. You can use the office for your belongings." Seth turned toward the trailer used as a makeshift office for the site. It was fifty yards away, across a dirt lot. Sasha would be uncomfortable walking across it in her high heels. But he kept his mouth shut; he didn't think Sasha would appreciate it if he pointed out her attire. Instead, he walked slowly, pointing out various things on the building's construction he intended to fix. Some things were not up to code and hadn't been done properly or according to specifications.

"If anything is going to slow me down on this job, it's fixing other people's mistakes," Seth grumbled. "There are a lot of them. Wyatt and I have spent the last two days poring over everything, looking for issues. We found a lot. Hopefully, we can get them settled in the next three weeks. That's the goal, anyway."

Seth jumped up the stairs into the trailer, skipping the first two. He opened the door, stepped inside, and waited while Sasha climbed the stairs. As soon as the door closed behind them, she shucked off her jacket and sat in a chair at the long folding table Seth used as a conference table.

Sasha crinkled her nose as she looked around. Seth knew the trailer wasn't much. It had an A/C unit in one window, but it struggled to push cold air into the room. The odor of sweat lingered because of people coming in and out all day. They worked outside, and it was an unseasonably warm spring. He should get some air fresheners.

A new futon sat along one wall. Seth had it delivered the day before. Late nights with the crew meant catching a nap when and if he could. He'd thrown out the ratty, old couch that was in the office because it smelled like someone spilled a case of beer on it. He'd also bought the folding table and six padded folding chairs, stocked the refrigerator with cold cuts, condiments, water, and sports drinks for the crew.

"Cozy," Sasha mumbled.

Seth shrugged. "It's not much, but it's a place to cool off or grab some food if the crew needs it. I try to be accommodating."

Sasha smiled. "That's very kind of you," she said. "Can I see the rest of the site?"

Seth cringed. *Not in those shoes.*

Sasha's eyebrows shot up. "What?" she said.

"Please don't take this the wrong way, okay?" Seth said.

"Take what the wrong way?" she asked.

"Well, you're not exactly dressed for a construction site. I know you're a professional, but here, you'll need work boots, jeans or khakis, and a sensible shirt. Heels and a power business suit will not cut it."

Sasha stared at her feet. Seth was sure he'd upset her. Her shoulders shook, and the first thing he thought was that he'd made her cry. It took him a moment to realize she was laughing.

"I am such an idiot," she said. "I was so worried about impressing you, showing you I was in charge, confident, and competent, that I didn't even think about how inappropriate what I'm wearing is for a construction site. Oh, lord." A giggle escaped her, and she slapped her hand over her mouth. "You must think I'm an idiot."

Seth laughed. "No, not at all." He leaned forward and dropped his voice to a whisper. "I'll tell you a secret. On my first day in construction, I showed up in shorts, a T-shirt, and Vans. My boss took one look at me and sent me home. Told me to return only after I learned how to dress appropriately. I also weighed about 125 and looked like a string bean. Can you imagine?"

Sasha snorted and the next thing he knew, laughter burst from her lips. He couldn't help but join her. It took them a few minutes to get themselves under control.

When they finally did, Sasha folded her hands on the table and smiled at him. "Can you update me on the changes you made and your plans? We can save the tour for tomorrow. I'll be out here, bright and early, in the proper attire."

Seth nodded. "That sounds great."

---

True to her word, Sasha came through the door the next day at seven a.m. Instead of a skirt and high heels, she wore jeans, a sensible button-down shirt, and boots. She also had six boxes of donuts in her arms. Seth jumped to his feet to take them from her.

"What is this?" he asked.

Sasha made a face. "Um, donuts," she said.

"I know they're donuts," Seth said. "I'm wondering why?"

"Well, if I'm being honest, I'm hoping to distract the crew with donuts," she said. "Maybe they won't realize I'm the architect supposedly sleeping with you."

Seth snorted. "Trust me, I've been very clear that we are not sleeping together. I've made it clear that rumors won't be tolerated."

Sasha smiled. "I appreciate that."

"I'm not doing it just for you," Seth explained. "Rumors like that undermine my authority and my ability to do the job."

"Well, I still appreciate it," Sasha reiterated. "Put the donuts on the table. I've got coffee, too. I'll be right back."

Seth took the donuts to the table, opened the boxes, and laid out napkins. Sasha returned with a container of coffee and a bag of supplies.

Seth poured himself a cup of coffee, grabbed a glazed donut, and returned to his desk. Sasha busied herself with setting everything out. She held up a bottle of vanilla creamer and a sugar packet.

"Did you want cream and sugar?" she asked.

"No," Seth snorted. "I drink my coffee black."

Sasha rolled her eyes. "Why am I not surprised?"

"There's nothing wrong with black coffee," Seth scoffed. "Let me guess, you load yours up with cream and sugar?"

Sasha avoided eye contact. "Maybe."

Seth chuckled. "I thought so."

Wyatt burst through the door, his normal entrance to any room, freezing as soon as he saw Sasha.

"Hi," he said warily.

"Hi, Wyatt," Sasha said warmly. "Would you like a donut and some coffee?"

"Yeah, sure," Wyatt said.

Seth knew Wyatt was not a fan of Sasha's. She had rubbed him the wrong way at their initial meeting, when he felt like she blamed him for the issues at the construction site. While he'd been careful to keep his comments to himself, after a long time being friends, he could read Wyatt very well.

Wyatt grabbed a donut and some coffee and scurried to the door.

"Wyatt!" Seth called.

His friend turned to look at him. "Yeah?"

"Can you let the crew know about the donuts in the office?" Seth asked.

"Will do, boss." Wyatt nodded at Sasha. "Thank you, Ms. Baker." He hurried out the door, letting it slam closed behind him.

"Remind me to tell him to call me Sasha," she muttered.

"Grab a donut before the crew gets in here," Seth said.

Sasha took a maple bar and a cup of coffee. After a few minutes, the crew came in and attacked the donuts. They decimated them in short order, leaving behind one Boston crème and a jelly-filled. Most of them shouted "thank you" over their shoulders as they exited the trailer.

"Are you going to bring donuts every day?" Seth asked.

"Will they like me more if I do?" she retorted.

Seth shrugged. "Probably."

"Then, yes, I will bring donuts every day." She grinned and took an enormous bite of her donut.

# Chapter 13

## SASHA

Sasha wasn't sure how it happened, but she and Seth became friends.

It started her first day at the site, when he made her laugh and didn't give her a hard time about her inappropriate construction site attire. Then, the next day, they chatted and laughed over coffee and donuts. It reminded her of when they first met.

Their friendship only grew from there. Sasha made herself a fixture at the Phillips Innovations construction site. She and Seth fell into a routine: coffee in the morning, walk the site, and meet with the crew. The men and women who worked for Seth expected to see her with him and when she wasn't there, Seth said they asked about her.

There was a simplicity to their friendship, an ease she didn't share with many people. They could be in the same room without talking. Their silence never seemed uncomfortable, and their conversations always flowed.

Seth loved talking about his job, loved explaining things to her or anyone who would listen. There was joy in his voice when he talked about construction. His crew loved him, loved working for him and with him. Seth was always right there, working alongside the men and women he'd hired, getting his hands dirty, and proving to them how badly he wanted to get the job done and get it done right.

Most days, Sasha would go to the Phillips Innovations site early in the morning, have a cup of coffee with Seth, attend his morning meeting, and walk the site with him to take notes for Eleanor and Jerome Nelson. In the afternoon, she would handle paperwork and catch up with Eleanor at McDonald and Skousen. She preferred being at the site with Seth.

The first time someone thought they were dating was two weeks after Seth took over the job. They were on the seventeenth floor of the project with Gary, one of the city's building inspectors. Seth was explaining why he yanked out the electrical wiring and replaced it with better wiring. Gary nodded along, a smile on his face as Seth spoke. After Seth finished speaking, Gary snapped a few photos, signed off on his report, and shook both Seth and Sasha's hands.

"I'm glad to see things being done right around here," Gary said. "The previous construction company made me worry every time I had to come on site. That's not an issue anymore. Your professionalism is refreshing, Mr. Mitchell."

"Thank you," Seth said. "That's kind of you."

The smile on Gary's face widened. "You two are great together. Most couples working together are at each other's throats. You two aren't like that. Again, it's refreshing."

"Couple?" Sasha said.

"Yes," Gary replied. "It's obvious you two are together, though I completely understand if you don't want word to get around to the crew. That can make things awkward." He glanced around and lowered his voice. "Don't worry, I won't say anything. Look, you two have a great day. I'll head down on my own." He waved and went to the temporary elevator on the building's side.

Seth glanced at Sasha out of the corner of his eye.

"Dating, huh?" Seth said.

Sasha grinned. "According to Gary, yeah, we're dating."

They both burst out laughing.

It happened again two days later. Seth and Sasha stood next to the crane, Seth on his phone and Sasha making notes on her clipboard, when one of the crew, a woman named Jessie, walked by. She smiled at them and stopped next to Sasha.

"How long have you two been dating?" Jessie whispered.

"I'm sorry?" Sasha said.

Jessie laughed. "Oh, come on, everybody on the site knows. You two are an adorable couple. And can

I say, you are so lucky. Seth is quite the catch." She winked and walked away.

Seth ended his call and shoved his phone in his pocket. "What did she say?" he asked.

Sasha crossed her arms and shook her head. "She thinks we're dating, too. Apparently, everybody on site thinks we're dating."

Seth snorted. "Really?"

"Wait, do you think it's funny?" Sasha asked.

"Yeah, a little." Seth shrugged. "Don't you?"

"No," Sasha muttered. "It's ... I don't want people to think we're dating. I mean ... isn't that what Liam told everyone? That you got this job because we were sleeping together?"

"Yes, but they know that's not true. They know I got this job on my own merits. Would it be so crazy to think that after spending time together, we might start dating? Maybe that's what it is."

It was Sasha's turn to snort. "Who knows what anybody thinks anymore?" She grinned at Seth. "You probably left two or three women pining for you back in New York, anyway, right?"

Seth rolled his eyes. "Um, that would be a big fat no," he said.

Sasha's mouth dropped open. She gasped loudly and pressed a hand to her chest. "Wait? You don't have a woman in your life?"

Seth rolled his eyes. "I don't. In case you hadn't noticed, work is kicking my ass, and I'm a little busy."

"And you lost your wingman, too. Damn it anyway." Sasha giggled. She quickly composed herself and smiled at him. "Sorry. That was rude."

Seth chuckled. "No, it wasn't rude. It was accurate. I lost my wingman."

"Have you had a date since Chris and Sofia got married?"

Seth narrowed his eyes. "Okay, *that* was rude. Are you saying I can't get a woman without Chris's help?"

Sasha shrugged. "Maybe." She drew the word out and tried to hide her smile. She failed miserably.

"If you must know, Miss Nosy, I *have* had a date since they got married. Nothing serious, though."

Sasha wrinkled her nose. "Your choice or theirs?"

"A bit of both." Seth rubbed the back of his neck and gave her a sheepish grin. "It's hard to find a woman who wants the same things I do. Finding a woman who isn't eager to meet my famous actor best friend is even more challenging. It sucks."

"Is that … is that a thing? Are most of the women you date trying to meet Chris?"

Seth nodded. "It is definitely a thing. Before he got married, I'd say pretty much every woman I dated wanted me to introduce them to Chris. It was like I was a stepping stone or … or a task they had to get past before they got to the good stuff. Once they started bugging me to meet Chris, I ended it. Why do you think I've had so damn many girlfriends? A term I use loosely, I might add."

Sasha shifted from foot to foot. "I, well, I guess I believed the gossip sites when they said you were a playboy or something. A different woman every week, never wanted to settle down, not interested in anything long-term."

Seth gave her a tired grin. "Don't believe everything you read on the internet. You know that as well as I do."

Someone called Seth's name from high above their heads. Sasha saw Wyatt waving at them from the third floor. Seth raised his hand in response.

"I better go see what he wants," Seth said. "Excuse me."

Sasha watched him jog across the small lot to the temporary elevator and climb on. He didn't look back at her, but she watched him until the elevator stopped on the third floor.

"I'm an idiot," she mumbled to herself.

How had it slipped by her what Seth dealt with as the best friend of a famous person? Why was she so locked on the idea of Seth being exactly what the tabloids said he was that she couldn't see him as anything else? Her assumptions kept getting crushed by the truth.

Sasha hated to admit it, but her mother was right. Seth *was* a good guy, and he wasn't like Liam.

"Dammit," she whispered under her breath. "Dammit, dammit, dammit."

"Sasha!"

She looked up and saw Seth leaning out what would eventually be a window. She waved at him.

"Get up here!" Seth yelled. "I need to show you something."

# Chapter 14

## SETH

As far as Seth was concerned, Sasha could hold her own with any construction crew, even the ones in New York City. Every day for two weeks, he saw her at the construction site before sunrise. Unlike most architects he'd worked with, she didn't sit in the office pretending to work; instead, she donned the hard hat and walked the site. She asked intelligent, respectful questions, never interrupted when they were in the middle of a sensitive or possibly dangerous task, and always had a smile on her face.

The crew looked forward to seeing her, even when she didn't have coffee and donuts for them. Sasha knew her stuff, but she never made anyone feel inferior. When she didn't show up, they asked about her. For the first time since starting his company, Seth enjoyed working with the on-site architect.

Sasha was easy to work with, knew her stuff, and surprisingly fun to be around. He'd expected her to be stuffy, anal, and a pain-in-the-ass, but she proved him wrong.

Seth looked forward to seeing her, spending time with her, and talking with her. She was inquisitive and wanted to learn. Seth never considered himself much of a teacher and, more often than not, teaching people about his job annoyed him. He never felt like that with Sasha. He wanted to tell her everything about his job, and she seemed happy to listen.

By Thursday of his fourth full week in California, things were ahead of schedule. Seth was positive that he would exceed expectations by the sixty-day mark, and that the project would be complete by the deadline. It was one reason he decided he would spend Friday driving around L.A., visiting some of the interesting architectural structures he had researched online. He did it with every project.

Balancing two cups of coffee and a hard hat, Sasha walked into the office. Seth jumped to his feet and hurried to help her. He plucked both coffees from her hand and held the door. Once she was inside, he kicked it closed and set the coffees on the table. He opened one, saw it filled with cream, and closed it quickly. He gave it to Sasha and took the other back to his desk.

"What's on today's agenda?" Sasha asked. "Any luck finding a tile guy for the lobby?"

"Wyatt is working on it," Seth said. "He said he knows a guy. He's worked with him before; he's reliable and reasonably priced."

"That's great. Is there anything you need from me?"

Seth shook his head. "Have I mentioned that you've been great? I'm surprised this is your first time as the on-site architect. You really know your stuff."

Sasha fidgeted with a napkin on the table. "I don't know. I'm flying by the seat of my pants. Someone else would do a better job. But thank you for being so nice."

"I'm serious," Seth said. "I'm not being nice for the sake of being nice. Out of all the architects I've worked with, you're one of the best. Definitely one of the most professional."

"Well, thank you." Sasha cleared her throat.

"What are you doing tomorrow?" Seth asked.

Sasha narrowed her eyes. "Why?"

Seth chuckled. "Don't be so suspicious. I'm not asking you to help me rob a bank or anything. I plan to tour the city to see some of L.A.'s notable architecture. Would you like to go with me?"

Sasha grinned. "Oh my God, that sounds fun. Where are you thinking of going?"

"Do you have any suggestions? I mean, I have a list, but maybe you could help me narrow it down and figure out the best places to go?"

"Show me your list," Sasha said.

Seth turned his laptop around and showed Sasha the list he made. She hopped up from the chair she was in, grabbed another one, and pulled it over to

Seth's desk. She sat down, leaned over the laptop, and examined his list.

"These are all great places," she said. "Why are you doing this?"

"I do it whenever I'm on a job," Seth explained. "I try to go to interesting architectural structures in the area for inspiration. And I'm kind of a geek for cool buildings."

"Me too." Sasha clasped her hands in her lap. "Okay, here are my recommendations. Start at Union Station, early. It's in a central location, so it's a great place to start."

Seth picked up a pen and jotted "Union Station" on a Post-it© note. "Okay, what's next?"

"The Bradbury Building. It's close to Union Station. Then the Walt Disney Concert Hall, since it's in downtown L.A. Oh, next should be the Hollyhock House. Frank Lloyd Wright designed it. Been to the Griffith Observatory yet?" she asked.

"I went there with Chris, but it was a while ago," Seth said. "I would like to see it again."

"Perfect. We can end the day at the Griffith Observatory if we time everything right. The view is astonishing. It overlooks the city and the Hollywood sign."

There was something to be said for letting a real, live architect plan your sightseeing tour of interesting architectural structures. It would be an interesting experience.

"Great," Seth said. "So, how about we meet here tomorrow morning around eight, and we'll head to Union Station?"

"That sounds perfect," Sasha said.

---

"My feet hurt," Seth grumbled.

Sasha laughed. "You big baby. How about we grab a bite at the Café at the End of the Universe?"

Seth furrowed his brows and pursed his lips. "What? I'm not going to the end of the universe for dinner."

"It's over there," Sasha laughed and pointed to the café. "We can sit on the terrace and eat dinner."

Seth looked where Sasha pointed. He saw a terrace with chairs and tables. It overlooked the city and the Hollywood sign, exactly like Sasha said.

They got in line where Seth ordered a ham and cheese sandwich, and Sasha got the buffalo chicken wrap. They both ordered cold iced teas. When their food was ready, they went out to the terrace.

Once they found a table, Seth dropped into a chair with a loud sigh. He stretched his legs out in front of him and groaned. "Oh God, that feels good. My feet are killing me. I can't remember the last time I walked so much."

Sasha's triumphant grin had him laughing. "Was that your goal? To wear me down?" he asked.

Sasha shrugged. "Maybe."

"Well, it worked. I'm exhausted." He picked up his iced tea and drank half of it in three swallows. "And thirsty. Wow! That was a lot of walking. I made a mistake visiting these places with an architect." He winked at her.

"I know the best things to see," Sasha said. "You saw things with me that you wouldn't see if you were alone or with someone else, I guarantee it."

His mouth full of food, Seth nodded in agreement. She knew everything. The unusual blend of Spanish Mission and Art Deco style at Union Station was a surprise and stunningly gorgeous. Before checking out the forty-foot windows and hand-painted ceiling tiles, he and Sasha snapped a selfie in front of the clock tower.

Their next stop was the Bradbury Building. Seth stood in the atrium, staring up at the sky-lit walkways crafted from ornate ironwork. He was in love. They spent almost two hours exploring, and he didn't want to leave.

His least favorite stop of the day was the Walt Disney Concert Hall. He understood it was a landmark but felt it was too much and not his style. He appreciated it, but he believed there were more iconic buildings than the concert hall.

Sasha's favorite stop of the day was the Hollyhock House, designed by Frank Lloyd Wright. The look on her face as they explored the house made him grateful he had invited her. She was in heaven, bouncing around the property, spouting interesting facts about Hollyhock House and Frank Lloyd Wright.

"Did you have fun?" Sasha asked.

Seth nodded again. It was interesting hanging out with a woman who was his friend. The attraction remained, but now Seth wanted more than just a few dates with this woman.

He enjoyed spending time with Sasha; their relationship wasn't complicated. There were no ulterior motives for either of them. They enjoyed being around each other. He could laugh and talk with her.

"What about you? Did you have fun?" Seth asked.

A huge grin spread across Sasha's face. "Yes. It was the best day. I love doing things like this, but I can't find anyone to go with me. Liam always thought it was boring, my mom gets tired too easily, and I don't have Sofia anymore. Thank you for inviting me."

"Thank you for coming with me," Seth said. "It wouldn't have been the same alone."

"Well, you haven't seen the best part. Sunset at the Griffith Observatory." Sasha checked her watch. "After we eat, we can walk down to the park."

"Great idea," Seth said.

Thirty minutes later, they stood a hundred feet from the front of the observatory, staring at the sun setting over the city. Seth didn't usually care about things like that, especially growing up in the concrete jungle of New York, but he appreciated the subtle beauty of the sky at dusk.

Sasha bumped her shoulder into his. "Are you inspired yet?"

Seth looked down at her. "Only in about a million ways. Sometimes I wish I could be the architect instead of the guy in construction. I have too many ideas in my head."

Sasha whispered, "I had no idea. Have you ever thought about hiring an architect to put your ideas on paper?"

"No one can capture what I imagine." He shrugged. "Maybe someday."

They stood side by side, lost in thought. Seth longed to slip an arm around her shoulders and hug her to his side. He felt like a lovestruck teenager. Instead, he reached over and gave her hand a quick squeeze.

"Thanks for spending the day with me," he murmured.

"Thanks for letting me tag along." She rested her head against his upper arm and sighed. "I'll think of other places we can go."

"I'd like that." Seth closed his eyes. In fact, he'd like it far more than he would ever admit.

# Chapter 15

## SETH

When Seth woke up Friday morning, it was pouring rain. Seth checked his phone and saw that the forecast called for thunderstorms through the weekend. He had no other option but to cancel work for the day. He hated to do it when they were so far ahead of schedule, but it wasn't safe and, above all else, Seth put the safety of his crew first.

Seth sent out a group text canceling work for the day and, most likely, the weekend. Once he'd done that, he dropped to the couch, grabbed the remote, and started flipping channels. But he was restless. Being idle didn't sit well with him. He needed to be doing something. Hoping it would hold his interest, he attempted to watch a replay of a New York Giants football game, but thoughts of work crept in before the first half of the first quarter was over. He was grateful when his phone rang during the second quarter. He answered without checking who it was.

"Hello?"

"Seth? It's Sasha."

"Oh, shit." Seth shot to his feet. "Sasha! I forgot to call you."

How could he forget the woman he always thought about? Despite constantly thinking of her, he neglected to inform her the site was down for the day.

"Oh, you mean you forgot to tell me that, thanks to the rain, you shut the site down for the weekend?" she asked. "Did you forget to tell me that?"

Seth sighed. "Yeah, sorry about that."

Sasha giggled. "It's okay. I just wanted to give you a hard time. Wyatt texted me."

"Oh, really? Do you and Wyatt text a lot?" Seth's words were sarcastic to hide his jealousy.

The thought of Sasha and Wyatt exchanging text messages bothered him. He wondered what else he didn't know about them.

"So, what are you up to today?" Sasha asked, bringing his attention back to her.

"I was going to stay home and watch football, but I'm, uh, well, I'm actually thinking about going down to the site to do some paperwork." The thought had been circling in his head for the last thirty minutes. "What about you?"

"I'm at the office. I have work to do here since I can't go to the site. There are several stacks of papers on my desk that I've neglected." Sasha cleared her throat. "Hey, if you're going down to the site, would it be okay if I met you there? I have some paperwork for you to sign. Permits and stuff for your business license."

"Yeah, sure," he said. "Give me an hour and I'll meet you there. Bring your umbrella."

Sasha's laughter echoed in his ear as he disconnected the call. He shut off the TV and headed for the bathroom. He took a quick shower, brushed his teeth, and threw on some clothes.

Thanks to the rain, it took far longer than he'd expected to get to the site. People in L.A. didn't know how to drive in the rain. By the time Seth pulled into the lot at the construction site, it had been an hour and a half since he'd spoken to Sasha. He didn't see her car anywhere.

The dirt parking lot was a quagmire. Seth parked on the street and jumped out. He jogged over to a pile of planks, grabbed some, and used them to construct a makeshift walkway to the trailer. The rain soaked him and left him muddy by the time he finished. As he turned to go inside, Sasha pulled up and parked behind the Land Rover.

Seth gestured for her to get out of her car, which she did, umbrella in hand.

"What a mess," she commented, looking over the parking lot. Her eyes settled on Seth. "You're a mess. What happened?"

"I was putting down planks to walk on."

Sasha grinned. "I'd offer you my umbrella, but it looks like it would be pointless."

"You need it more than I do," Seth said. "I can't believe you're wearing a dress in this weather."

"It was sprinkling when I left my apartment. I thought it would let up." She looked up at the dark gray sky. "Guess I was wrong."

"Let's get inside. I need a cup of hot coffee." Seth pointed at the makeshift walkway. "Follow me and stay on the planks."

Inside the trailer, Sasha closed her umbrella and peeled off her raincoat. Seth excused himself, went into the small bathroom, and stripped off his wet clothes. He dried off with a small hand towel. He soaked it through before he finished drying his hair. Fortunately, he kept a full change of clothes in the cabinet, so he pulled them out and put on a dry T-shirt, jeans, and socks. He hung his wet clothes over the towel bar and picked up his muddy boots.

His T-shirt clung to his still damp torso, and his wet hair flopped over his face and into his eyes. He made a mental note to put large towels in the bathroom.

Sasha was at the table with a stack of papers when he returned. She glanced at him, then dropped her gaze back to the papers.

Seth dropped his boots by the door. "Coffee?" he asked.

"Sure," she murmured.

Seth could feel Sasha's eyes on his back as he stood over the coffeepot, but whenever he glanced her way, she was studiously looking over the papers or on her phone.

Once he had the coffee going, he crossed the room and stopped beside Sasha. With one hand on the chair and one on the table, he leaned down to examine the papers. His head was inches from hers. A spicy vanilla scent drifted over him. He resisted the urge to take a deep breath.

"What's all this?" he asked. Why the fuck did his voice sound high and squeaky? He cleared his throat and pretended it hadn't happened.

"It's the paperwork I told you about on the phone," Sasha mumbled. "Remember?"

"Yeah, yeah," Seth said. "Um, where do I sign?" He pulled out the chair next to her and sat down.

Sasha took a pen from her bag, handed it to Seth, then she pushed the paper in front of him and tapped the bottom of the page.

With his left hand, Seth took the pen. His elbow bumped her side as he turned to write. He muttered "Sorry" under his breath.

After signing everything Sasha required, he dropped the pen on the table. He stretched, his knee bumping Sasha's under the table.

"Sorry," he said again.

"You keep saying that." She shook her head and laughed. "Quit apologizing. I'm fine." She tipped her head to the left and smiled at him. "I haven't talked to you much since last weekend. Are you avoiding me?"

Seth chuckled. "No." He abruptly got up, went to the coffeepot, and poured himself a cup.

He had been avoiding her. His complicated feelings for her confused him and, rather than confront them, he avoided them. Work was a great way to accomplish that. He'd made sure he was busy whenever she was on site. Once he figured out how to deal with his feelings for Sasha, he wouldn't need to avoid her anymore.

"Can I tell you something?" Sasha asked.

"Sure," Seth replied. "Let me get our coffee first." He turned to the coffeepot, poured two cups, dumped a bunch of cream and sugar into one, then returned to the table and handed Sasha's cup to her.

Seth sat down beside her. "What's on your mind?"

"I hope you won't take this the wrong way."

Seth chuckled. "You know when you start like that, my immediate instinct is to take it wrong?"

Sasha giggled. "That's true. I thought it would be impossible to work with you."

"Ouch," he said, one eyebrow raised.

Sasha laughed. "I guess what I'm trying to say is I was wrong. You're fantastic at your job, better than most. You're also incredibly smart, and you're a good guy." She stared at her hands folded in her lap. "I'm sorry I ghosted you after we met. I'm sorry I was bitchy at the wedding and when we both ended up at Chris and Sofia's place for the weekend. Defense mechanism, I guess."

"Defense mechanism?"

"Your history with women—"

"Isn't so great," Seth finished. "Yeah, I'm aware. And thanks to the stupid tabloids, so is everyone else."

"The tabloids are garbage. We both know that, after what they did to our friends." Sasha sighed. "Anyway, I wanted to tell you I'm sorry I underestimated you." She gathered the papers from the table and shoved them into her bag. "I should go back to the office."

They stood up together. Seth wasn't sure what happened, maybe his knee hit hers or her foot bumped into his, or the universe decided it was time to quit fucking around, but the next thing he knew, their legs were together and they fell. As they headed for the floor, Seth grabbed Sasha by the upper arms and turned at the last second. He hit the floor first and ended up sprawled on his back, with Sasha in his lap.

"Are you okay?" Seth asked, his hand on her hip.

Sasha nodded. "Are you?"

"My tailbone is going to hurt for a few days, but yeah, I think I'm fine." He looked pointedly at his lap, then at Sasha.

"Oh, sorry." She climbed to her feet and held out a hand to him.

Seth took her hand and climbed to his feet. They stood hand in hand, gazing at each other.

Seth didn't know who moved first, whether it was him or Sasha. One second, they were staring at each other, and the next, they were in each other's arms.

Seth tangled his fingers in her long black hair and tipped her head back while pulling her close. Sasha moaned quietly. They kissed, and it shook him to his core.

When they broke apart, they stood a foot apart and stared at each other, both of them panting, the air thick with their desire.

"Damn," Sasha whispered. She licked her lips. "How long have you wanted to do that?"

"A long time," Seth murmured. "Though I didn't realize how much until it happened."

"I didn't either," she said.

"What are we going to do about it?" he asked.

Sasha dropped her head and stared at her feet. She took a deep breath, her shoulders rising and falling. Their eyes met, and he couldn't look away from her beautiful brown eyes.

"I live about fifteen minutes from here," Sasha whispered. "Maybe … maybe we need to get it out of our system. One time."

Seth nodded. "One time."

"Follow me to my place?" she asked.

Seth nodded again. Sasha grabbed her bag off the chair and headed for the door. She took a moment to look at Seth before leaving.

Seth exhaled, pulled his keys from his pocket, and followed Sasha.

# Chapter 16

## SASHA

Sasha used the rearview mirror to watch Seth pull into the parking lot behind her apartment building. He parked beside her, cut the engine, and looked at her through the window. She smiled at him and got out of her car.

Seth followed her up the sidewalk and into her apartment. She unlocked the door and stepped inside, with Seth right behind her. Sasha peeled off her coat as she walked across the room, then she tossed it and her bag on the couch and turned to Seth.

He took her hand and tugged, pulling her into his arms, his hands settling on her back. He stepped into her and caught her lips in a tentative kiss, attempting to gauge her reaction. Sasha kissed him back and ran her fingers through his hair at the back of his head.

The kiss evolved from cautious to passionate, filled with long-suppressed desire.

Kissing Seth was marvelous. Sasha lost herself in the closeness of their bodies—the feel of his mouth on hers as he explored her with his tongue and his hands ran over her body, making her squirm with need. She wanted more. She wanted him.

When they broke apart, Sasha's hands shook, and her lips quivered. A thin sheen of sweat glistened on Seth's forehead, and he gnawed on his lower lip.

Sasha shifted from foot to foot and twisted her fingers together. "Would you like a drink?" she asked hesitantly.

Seth shook his head. "No, thanks. I'm fine."

She pushed a hand through her hair and nodded. She looked everywhere except at Seth.

"Sasha, what's wrong?" Seth asked.

She laughed. "I don't know. I'm really nervous. I'm trembling, and my heart is racing."

Seth stepped closer and his scent overwhelmed her—a spicy musk scent that made her insides quiver with need. She swallowed, her throat clicking. Seth brushed his knuckles across her cheek, leaned over, and put his mouth against her ear.

"You're nervous because whether or not you want to admit it, this is what we've both wanted since we met," he whispered. He cupped the back of her head, guided her mouth to his, and brushed a kiss across her lips. "We need to get it out of our system. We have sex, we enjoy the hell out of ourselves, and we're good. One time, like you said. Right?"

"Right," Sasha agreed. "Let's get it out of our system and move on." She relaxed into his arms with a sigh, wrapped her arms around his waist, and rested her head against his chest.

Sasha wasn't opposed to hooking up with Seth. In fact, she'd been thinking about it for weeks. She found it difficult to not like him when she spent hours every day with him and realized what a great person he was. She knew Seth wasn't one for long-term relationships, which might be perfect for her. One incredible, memorable romp in the sack with a guy who wasn't interested in any kind of commitment, then she could walk away. It might even be possible for them to stay friends afterward.

For once, Sasha didn't want to overthink it. She wanted to forget about work, her ex-husband, and all the things that held her back from doing what she wanted. All she wanted in that moment was to kiss Seth.

Seth brushed his fingers through her hair and tugged gently. "Okay?"

Her answer was to take his hand and lead him through the small apartment to her bedroom. Now that her nerves had dissipated, she wanted nothing more than what she'd craved for months—Seth.

He took Sasha's hands in his and guided her to the bed, kissing her as they moved. He perched on the edge and pulled her down next to him. Seth let go of her long enough to kick off his boots, then he gathered her back in his arms. He kissed her neck and nipped at her collarbone and the soft skin behind her ears. Sasha kicked off her shoes and scooted backward to the middle of the bed, the skirt of her dress sliding up to the top of her thighs as she moved. She tossed her decorative throw pillows on the floor, laid down, and pulled Seth down beside her.

His hands were everywhere—her waist, her back, her hips, caressing her face or her inner arm. Sasha gasped when he slipped his hand under her skirt and into her sensible cotton underwear. Today was the worst day to not wear something sexy.

Seth sat up, got to his knees, and grabbed the bottom of her dress in his hands. He pulled it over her head, both of them laughing when it caught on her chin. She struggled out of it and tossed it on the floor. Seth hovered over her, his eyes running up and down the length of her body, sending heat coursing through her.

He sat back on his haunches, his hands resting on his knees. "Take them off."

Sasha sat up, her eyes never leaving Seth's as she unhooked her bra and slid it down her arms. She laid back, slipped her fingers in the sides of her underwear and slowly pushed them down her legs. When she reached her knees, Seth let out an exasperated growl, pushed her hands away, and yanked them the rest of the way off.

Seth dropped his head and took her breast in his mouth, his tongue circling the nipple before gently tugging it with his teeth. Sasha groaned and her back arched, pushing herself into his mouth. Seth wrapped his arm around her back, holding her as he moved back and forth between her breasts, paying equal attention to both of them. His lips drifted down her stomach and across her hips, then back to her breasts again. His touch was like a feather on her skin, making her squirm with unfulfilled need.

Sasha slipped her hand under the hem of his shirt and traced the defined muscles of his stomach. Her fingers danced along the waistband of his jeans until she reached for the button. She fumbled with it, muttering in frustration when she couldn't undo it.

Seth chuckled, stood up, yanked his T-shirt off, and hurriedly removed his jeans and boxers.

Sasha's breath caught in her throat at the size of him, and her heart pounded in anticipation. She swallowed back a moan and pointed at the bedside table.

"There are condoms in the top drawer," she said.

Seth took a condom out of the drawer, dropped it next to Sasha's head on the bed, and got back on the bed. He kissed her and put his hand between her legs, caressing her, the gentle pressure driving her crazy with desire.

Sasha took Seth's heavy shaft in her hand and stroked, hoping to give him back some of the pleasure he was giving her. His hips moved, thrusting into her hand, low moans emanating from the back of his throat even as he continued kissing her.

Two fingers slowly entered her, massaging her, opening her as he circled her sensitive nub with his thumb.

Sasha's ability to concentrate was gone thanks to things Seth was doing to her. He was incredibly attentive, attuned to her body and what she needed. Every touch from him inflamed her need for him until her body screamed for release. When she didn't think she could last any longer, she grabbed the condom and handed it to him.

"Hurry," she whispered.

Seth ripped open the condom and slid it on, then he eased into her with a satisfied sigh. He braced himself on his elbows and thrust deep into her. Sasha moaned his name and rocked her hips up to meet his. She dug her fingers into his ass and pulled him into her, wanting to feel every inch of him inside of her. He moaned as he moved, his cock buried deep inside her, plunging harder and deeper with every thrust.

Sasha was flying, rocketing toward orgasm, each thrust from Seth taking her closer to the precipice. When Seth moved faster, slamming into her, her hips snapped up to meet his and then she was gone, consumed by the sensations engulfing her as she came.

Seth caught her lips in a fierce kiss, devouring her, his movements becoming erratic and intense. He stiffened and groaned as he came, his face buried against the side of her neck. He collapsed on the bed beside her with a satisfied grunt.

"Wow!" Sasha giggled.

"I can't believe we didn't do that sooner," Seth added.

"Yeah, well, now it's out of our system." He looked at her. "Right?"

Sasha nodded. "Yeah. Yeah. Definitely out of our system."

"Where's your bathroom?" he asked.

Sasha pointed at the door. "Through that door, past the closet."

Seth climbed out of bed, scooped up his clothes, and hurried out the bedroom door. The bathroom door closed, and the water turned on a few seconds later. She got under the comforter and stared at the door. Five minutes later, Seth returned from the bathroom, fully clothed.

He leaned down, one hand by her head, and kissed her on the forehead. "Thank you," he whispered.

Sasha giggled. "I should thank you."

"I'll see you on Monday," he said with a grin.

Seth walked out without turning back. Once the front door closed, Sasha wrapped the comforter around herself and headed to the window. She opened the blinds and watched Seth trudge through the rain back to his Land Rover.

He got inside, but he didn't leave. He sat staring at the building for several minutes before he started the vehicle and pulled out of the lot.

# Chapter 17

## SETH

Seth put the Land Rover in gear and pulled out of the parking lot. Going back to the construction site was pointless. He wouldn't get any work done. He wouldn't be able to concentrate, not after the morning he'd spent with Sasha. It was all he could think about. *She* was all he could think about. Her scent, her taste, the way she sounded when she—

"Nope," he said out loud. "I can*not* go there."

Seth had done the one and done, get-it-out-of-our-system sex with other women, and it had worked. Every time. He didn't expect it to work this time. Not with Sasha.

He couldn't stop thinking about her.

Sasha had been on his mind for two years, ever since the day she rejected him.

---

*Seth caught Sasha's eye and smiled at her. She gave him a half-hearted grin and spun away. He'd been at Chris's home in the mountains for three hours, and he hadn't been able to get the maid of honor to even say hello to him. Before he could follow her and try to talk to her, Chris dragged him outside to talk to him about his speech.*

*Another hour passed, and the sun was down before Seth found Sasha putting the finishing touches on the table centerpieces. He sauntered up to her and bumped his shoulder against hers.*

*"Hi, stranger," he said.*

*Sasha took a step back. "Oh, um, hello, Seth." She scurried around the table away from him and fussed with the flowers in the centerpiece, while doing her best not to make eye contact with him.*

*"How have you been?" he asked.*

*Sasha shrugged. "Fine."*

*Seth exhaled. This was painful. Worse than a dentist pulling teeth. "The flowers look nice."*

*"Thanks," she replied.*

*"I haven't talked to you in a few weeks," Seth said. "You haven't returned any of my calls or answered my texts."*

*"Yeah, um, I've been busy," Sasha said. "New project at work."*

*Seth nodded. "Let's get drinks or dinner on Monday after Chris and Sofia leave. We can catch up. What do you say?" Seth asked.*

*Sasha glanced at him, then glanced away. She shook her head. "I don't think so."*

*"Did I upset you?" Seth blurted.*

*Sasha sighed and shook her head. "I'm not interested in dating you, Seth."*

*"Okay," Seth said, drawing out the word. "I guess I'm confused. I thought we got along well—"*

*"I'm not trying to be rude or anything," she interrupted. "But I am not interested in a relationship or a one-night stand." She shrugged again. "Sorry."*

*"Yeah, um, sure, I get it. I'm sorry if you feel like I pressured you or something," Seth said. He shoved his hands in his pockets and stared at the ground. "I'll see you around." He turned on his heel and walked away, hoping he didn't look as dejected as he felt.*

---

The blare of a horn from behind him startled him out of the memory. He waved his hand at the car behind him, stepped on the gas, and turned left. A few minutes later, he parked in front of Chris's house, shut down the engine, and stared out the window.

Seth told no one, not even Chris, how defeated he was after Sasha rejected him. He wasn't himself. He tried to resume his life in New York but felt off and not like himself.

Was it possible to fall in love with someone he'd only been with for one weekend? How else could he explain his lack of enthusiasm for other women, in anything really, unless it was because of a broken heart? Allison was the first woman he dated after returning to New York, and he constantly compared her to Sasha. He gave it a shot with her, but she wasn't the woman he wanted.

She wasn't Sasha.

Seth closed his eyes. He'd worked so hard to get over Sasha, and what did he do? He had sex with her. With a groan, he rested his head on the steering wheel.

"I'm screwed," he muttered.

---

Sasha breezed through the door bright and early Monday morning, set a cup of coffee on the desk in front of Seth, tossed her bag on the chair, and sat down.

"Good morning," she said.

"Morning," he mumbled.

She raised an eyebrow. "Are you okay?"

"Fine." He shrugged. "Why?"

Wyatt entered before Sasha could respond.

"We have a problem," he said.

"Shit, what is it?" Seth got to his feet and grabbed his hard hat.

"We've got flooding on the ground floor," Wyatt explained.

"Show me," Seth said.

He hurried out the door. His heart melted the second Sasha came through the door, and he'd had a hard time keeping himself from striding across the room, grabbing her, and kissing her senseless.

God, he wanted her.

"Are you okay, man?" Wyatt asked. "You've been unusually quiet all morning."

Seth rolled his eyes. "Why does everyone keep asking me if I'm okay? I'm fine."

Wyatt shook his head. "Sorry I asked."

"Good, because I don't want to talk about it," Seth muttered.

They were almost at the building when Seth heard his name being called. He saw Sasha jogging across the lot when he turned around. He and Wyatt stopped.

"Go ahead, Wyatt," Seth said. "I'll be right there."

Wyatt nodded, shot a look at Sasha, and walked away. Seth turned to Sasha. She stopped in front of him.

"I, uh, I have to go," she said.

"Go? Go where?" Seth asked.

"My office," Sasha explained. "Eleanor called, and she wants me down there ASAP."

"Did she say why?"

Sasha shook her head. "No." She pinched the bridge of her nose. "God, I hope she doesn't—"

"I'm sure she doesn't," Seth reassured her. "How could she?"

Sasha snorted. "That woman has an uncanny ability to know things she shouldn't. Anyway, I didn't want you to think I ran out on you. I'll call you or text you or something later tonight."

"Yeah, sure." He pointed over his shoulder. "I better go. I need to check the lobby."

Seth stepped closer, considered kissing her, shoved the thought away, and, instead, gently squeezed her upper arm. He gave her a smile and walked away.

He spent the rest of his day dealing with the flooded lobby area. Fortunately, it wasn't as bad as he'd thought. They could bring in a pump to get out all the water. After removing the water, they cleaned up the accumulated mud and filth.

Seth left the site after nine p.m., too tired to do anything but eat leftovers, shower, and fall into bed. He fell asleep before his head hit the pillow. He didn't realize until the next morning that he hadn't heard from Sasha.

# Chapter 18

## SASHA

Being summoned to Eleanor's office was disconcerting. While she had been to her boss's office plenty of times, the cryptic "get down here now" message from Clara had thrown her. Sasha kept her hands clenched by her sides as she walked down the hall and did her best to put a smile on her face. Her mind raced with the possibilities, but the one thing she kept coming back to was that somehow, Eleanor found out about her and Seth.

*She's going to fire you.*

Sasha ignored the voice in her head and stepped into Eleanor's office. Clara smiled at her from her position behind the desk, the gatekeeper of Eleanor's calendar and time.

"Go on in, Sasha," Clara said. "She's waiting for you."

"Thank you," Sasha mumbled. She took a deep breath and stepped into Eleanor's inner sanctuary.

Eleanor looked up. "There you are," she said. "Close the door and have a seat."

Sasha did as she was told. She eased into one of the brown leather chairs in front of Eleanor's desk, crossed her ankles, and folded her hands in her lap.

"I'm not going to waste your time with a bunch of nonsensical pleasantries and meaningless small chat," Eleanor said. "I called you here because we have a problem."

Sasha swallowed. "Problem? What kind of problem?"

"Eddie quit."

"Wait?" Sasha shifted in her chair and took a deep breath. "Eddie quit. Just ... just out of the blue? No notice or anything?"

Eleanor sighed. "I suspected he was going to," she said. "His boyfriend moved to San Diego last year. The separation has been hard on Eddie. I've been waiting for him to give notice and today, he did. Unfortunately, he wasn't able to give me two weeks. He applied for several jobs in San Diego, and he got one. They want him to start next Monday. He has a week to pack and move."

"Well, good for him," Sasha said. "I'm glad he'll be able to be with Robert. Maintaining a long-distance relationship must be difficult."

"I agree," Eleanor said. "That's why I can't be angry with him." She laughed. "Eddie's a good person and a talented architect. The problems at the Phillips

Innovations build were not his fault. Yes, he could have done a better job, but he couldn't have known what would happen." Eleanor exhaled. "You're probably wondering why you should care about this?"

Sasha grinned. "A little."

"I'm assigning you to all of Eddie's outstanding projects," Eleanor said.

Sasha's head snapped up. "I'm sorry, what?"

"I'm promoting you," Eleanor explained. "You are no longer a junior associate. I am giving you Eddie's projects."

"What about the Phillips Innovations build?" Sasha asked.

"I would like you to continue working with Mitchell Construction on that," Eleanor said. "You seem to have a solid working relationship with Seth, and I don't want to do anything to disrupt it. Most of your time needs to be spent here in the office for the next few weeks."

"That shouldn't be a problem," Sasha hurried to add. "Seth has that site running like clockwork."

"Good, I'm glad to hear it." Eleanor pointed to a stack of folders on the corner of her desk. "Those are Eddie's files. I will also get you access to all of his documents in the cloud. Just a heads up, it might take you a while to get up to speed."

"I better get started," Sasha said. She got to her feet, picked up the files, and gave Eleanor a smile. "I won't let you down. I promise."

Eleanor accompanied Sasha to the door. Before she opened it, she put her hand on Sasha's shoulder and squeezed gently. "I know you won't. You deserve this promotion, Sasha. You've worked hard. I'm excited to see what you can do."

Heat rushed to Sasha's cheeks. "Thank you," she whispered. If she spoke any louder than a whisper, she might burst into tears.

Eleanor opened the door and Sasha scurried out. She smiled at Clara, then hurried back to her office. After closing the door with her foot, she placed the stack of folders on her desk. She wasn't sure if she should call her mom or Sofia. The desire to cry, jump up and down, and do cartwheels in her office overwhelmed her.

She wanted to call Seth.

Sasha yanked her phone from her pocket and pulled up Seth's contact information. But before she hit send, she shoved her phone back in her pocket. Sasha sank into her seat and rested her hands on top of her desk. One slow breath in and one slow breath out.

*What are you thinking?*

"I'm thinking I want to tell Seth about my promotion," she said out loud. "There's nothing wrong with that."

What made her want to call Seth before anyone else? Telling Sofia or her mom should be her priority before the random guy at work.

Except she knew Seth wasn't just some random guy from work. He was *Seth*. She considered Seth a friend, even though they'd had sex. He would be happy for her, and she wanted to hear what he had to say about her new position. She took her phone out of her pocket again, fully intending to text Seth.

There was a sharp rap on her office door, and it immediately opened. Sasha didn't recognize the young man standing in her doorway.

"Ms. Baker?" he said.

Sasha set her phone in the center of her desk and got to her feet. "Yes?"

The young man entered with his hand extended. "Hi, I'm Alan. I'm on the Kittridge project. Is there was anything I can help you with?"

Sasha hurried around her desk to shake Alan's hand. "Hi," she said. "It's nice to meet you."

While they shook hands, another person entered her office and introduced herself as Mariah. She was also part of the Kittridge project and wanted to offer her help as well.

Overwhelmed, but eager to get to know her team, Sasha grabbed the stack of files off her desk. Her office was too small to hold a team meeting. It only took her a second to decide.

"Let's go to one of the conference rooms," Sasha said. "We'll have more room in there."

Both of the junior associates readily agreed. They followed Sasha out of the office and down the hall. Sasha's phone sat in the center of her desk, forgotten.

---

Sasha slammed her apartment door, dropped her things on the floor, and kicked off her shoes. She dragged herself to the bedroom, stripped off her clothes, and grabbed her pajamas. She checked the time on her way to the bathroom. It was almost ten.

For two weeks straight, she had worked anywhere from twelve to fourteen-hour days, getting up to speed on all of Eddie's projects. She'd also moved down the hall into Eddie's old office. It took her three days to get organized. The amount of work made her head spin.

Her phone pinged in the other room. With her eyes closed, she leaned over the sink and rested her hands on either side. She silently prayed that it wasn't one of her team asking another question. She needed a night off. Maybe if she ignored it, they would go away.

Another ping sounded from the living room.

Sasha pulled her hair into a ponytail, brushed her teeth, and washed her face. Only then did she go out to the living room and grab her phone from her purse.

[Seth: Hey! Long time, no talk. How have you been?]

Sasha sighed. She hadn't talked to Seth since she got her promotion. She hadn't had five minutes to go to the bathroom, let alone stop by the Phillips Innovations site. Seth texted her a few times, and she replied with emojis. She hadn't even told him about her promotion. She thought it would be better to tell him in person but wasn't sure when she'd have time.

Her promotion was the best thing to happen to her in years and everything she had worked for since her divorce. Unfortunately, it came at a bad time in her personal life. Things with Seth had taken a turn, and while she initially insisted that it be a one-time thing, she knew deep down she didn't mean it. She liked Seth, and she was interested in exploring the possibility of a relationship.

[Seth: Hello?]

Sasha quickly typed a reply.

[Sasha: Hi. Sorry. I'm swamped at work.]

[Seth: I've been worried about you. Are you okay?]

Seth's concern brought a tear to her eye. Exhaustion made her emotional. She had cried more than once in the last two weeks. She swiped at her wet cheeks and typed a response.

[Sasha: I am okay. Better than you can imagine. I'm sorry I haven't texted or called. That was shitty of me.]

[Seth: Are you coming down to the site soon? We've made a lot of progress in the last two weeks, and I would love for you to see it.]

Sasha sighed. That was the question she hoped he wouldn't ask. She took a deep breath before she answered him.

[Sasha: I don't know. Maybe next week, but I'm not sure. I promise you I have a good reason for being MIA, but I want to tell you in person.]

Her phone rang in her hand, Seth's name popping up on the screen.

"Hi," she answered.

"Go to dinner with me," Seth said.

Sasha laughed. "What?"

"Go to dinner with me this weekend," he said. "On Saturday. Tell me in person what's happening."

Sasha wondered if she should argue, tell him she was too busy and couldn't go, but that would be a lie. Things at work were coming together, and she had planned to take the weekend off after working for fourteen days straight. Besides, she *wanted* to go. She wanted to drink and laugh and enjoy herself, especially after the last two weeks. And she wanted to do it with Seth.

"I would love to go to dinner with you," she said.

"Great. How about Saturday? I can pick you up at seven," Seth said. "I'll make reservations at Blue Velvet."

"Really?" Sasha laughed. "That place is hard to get into. Impossible, from what I hear."

Seth chuckled. "I know a guy."

"Hmm, okay." She sounded skeptical.

"Trust me," Seth said.

"Okay," Sasha said. "Anyway, Saturday sounds great. Do you remember where I live?"

"Yep, sure do," he replied. "I'll see you on Saturday."

"Bye." Sasha set her phone on the coffee table and dropped to the couch. She stretched out, put her arm over her eyes, and promptly fell asleep.

# Chapter 19

## SASHA

At seven p.m. on the dot, Sasha stepped out of her apartment and locked the door behind her. She straightened her skirt and ran her fingers through her hair.

Sasha was grateful Seth invited her out to dinner. She needed to unwind and was excited to see Seth. She couldn't believe he got dinner reservations at one of the most popular restaurants in the Los Angeles area. He must have used Chris's name to get the reservation.

Sasha skipped down the steps and rounded the corner of the building. She scanned the parking lot until she saw Seth standing beside his white Land Rover. He waved when she caught his eye.

Sasha couldn't help but admire Seth as she approached. He wore navy blue dress slacks that clung to his muscular thighs and a somewhat too-tight light blue dress shirt. As usual, his dark brown hair fell over his eyes, and when he pushed it off his forehead, it immediately fell back into place, which made her smile.

"Hi," she said.

Seth stared at her, and she thought she might drown in his impossibly blue eyes. "Hello there," he said. "You look beautiful."

Sasha's heart thumped in her chest, and her hands shook. She looked down so Seth wouldn't see the blush heating her cheeks. She didn't know what to say, so she shrugged and mumbled, "Thank you."

Seth held out his hand, but Sasha hesitated to take it, afraid he might sense her uneasiness if he touched her. She finally took hold of it and let him help her into the car. She breathed a sigh of relief when he slammed the door.

Sasha hated the way her stomach twisted and turned, and her hands shook. Why the hell was she so nervous? She had worked with Seth for weeks, and they'd spent time together outside of work. For God's sake, they'd had sex. They had a great working relationship, which she believed extended to a strong friendship. She enjoyed going to the job site every day, not just to hang out with him, but also to learn the ins and outs of construction. Seth was a skilled teacher, and she enjoyed learning about the business from him. Maybe she would be okay if she approached tonight like it was one of the many lunches they ate together at work or their sightseeing trip to look at Los Angeles architecture.

Seth got into the Land Rover and started the engine. As soon as they pulled onto the street, Seth poked her in the arm.

"Alright, start talking. Tell me why you've been MIA for the last two weeks."

Sasha laughed. "Straight to the point, huh?"

"Yep. I'm dying of curiosity."

"I got a promotion at work."

"What?" A huge grin spread across Seth's face. "You're kidding me? When did this happen?"

Sasha hesitated, then muttered, "Two weeks ago."

Seth's face fell. "Two weeks. Why didn't you tell me sooner?"

Sasha placed her hand on his leg. "The only reason that matters is that I wanted to tell you in person. The promotion means a lot of work. I've worked twelve to fourteen-hour days, and I haven't been able to get down to the site to tell you. I'm so glad you asked me out tonight."

The smile returned to Seth's face. "I understand. I'm sure it's been a lot of work. Tell me everything."

Sasha launched into the story of her promotion, starting with her visit to Eleanor's office. She told him about her new projects, her office move, the raise in pay, everything. She talked until her mouth was dry and the restaurant loomed in the distance.

Seth pulled up in front of Blue Velvet, rolled down his window, and handed his keys to the valet. He got out, took a blue blazer out of the back seat, walked around the back of the SUV, and opened Sasha's door.

Sasha smoothed her skirt and took a deep breath. This felt like more than a casual dinner between co-workers.

Seth took her hand to help her from the Land Rover. He placed his hand on Sasha's back as they entered the restaurant. She ignored the sudden warmth that rushed through her at his touch. She wondered if he could sense how she felt.

Seth gave his name to the hostess. Less than five minutes later, she asked them to follow her to a secluded corner of the restaurant. They sat at a booth with high-backed seats rising above their heads, which kept the other diners from seeing them. Sasha felt like a celebrity, and it solidified her belief that Seth had used Chris's name to get them a table. The hostess probably thought the famous actor would show up at any moment.

"Isn't this place great?" Seth asked, breaking the awkward silence that had engulfed them since they arrived at the restaurant.

"It's amazing," Sasha agreed. "How did you get a table?"

"I told you, I know a guy," Seth said.

Sasha raised her eyebrows. "Chris?"

Before he could answer, a man in a white chef's jacket appeared at their table. "Seth!"

Seth jumped to his feet and embraced the man. "It's so good to see you," Seth said. "Man, there are so many people here," he said. "Busier than my last visit with Wyatt. Congratulations."

"Thank you. It's really taking off. Better than expected," the man said. "I'm glad you could make it in for a meal this time. Who's your friend?"

Seth smiled at Sasha. "Jake, this is Sasha. She's the architect for the building I'm constructing. Sasha, this is one of my high school buddies, Jake. This is his restaurant."

Sasha shook Jake's hand. "Your restaurant is wonderful. Thanks for getting us a table."

"Anything for Seth," Jake said. He patted Seth on the back. "I have to get back to the kitchen but wanted to drop by and say hi."

"Let's grab a beer next week when Chris is back," Seth said. "We can go to Harry's Bar and catch up."

"That sounds fantastic," Jake said. He turned to Sasha and bowed at the waist. "Sasha, it was nice to meet you."

"You too, Jake," Sasha replied. "And thanks for the table."

Jake saluted her before he headed back toward the kitchen. Seth sat down and picked up the menu.

"I think I owe you an apology," Sasha said.

Seth peered at her over the top of his menu. "Oh? Why is that?" he asked.

"I incorrectly assumed that you dropped Chris's name to get a table," she explained.

"Really?" Seth said. "Why would you think that?"

"A long time ago, I read some articles that mentioned you took advantage of your friendship with

Chris, you know, to get special favors and stuff." Sasha grimaced. "When you said you 'knew a guy' that would help us get a table, I thought you meant Chris. It kind of annoyed me."

Their server arrived to take their drink order. Seth ordered a beer, and she ordered a white wine spritzer. He turned to Sasha as soon as the server left.

"Look, you're not completely wrong," Seth explained. "I *used* to drop Chris's name all the time, especially in my early twenties. Being friends with a famous actor has helped me get dates and the occasional foot in the door at a club or something, and yeah, once or twice, I got an expensive hotel room at a discount, but I quit doing all that a long time ago. I felt like I used Chris, which isn't what our friendship is about. Chris is my friend, and he has been since we were kids. I didn't want to exploit the friendship. I still don't."

Sasha nodded. "Well, I was wrong, and for that, I apologize."

"Thanks, I appreciate that. I guess I can understand why you would think I used Chris's name to get a table. I kind of have that reputation, seeing as how he's my best friend." Seth took a sip of his beer. "Jake went to high school with me and Chris. He moved out here five, six years ago to work with some big-name chef. Next thing I know, *he's* the big-name chef and opening his own restaurant."

"California has been good to you guys," Sasha said with a smile. "Chris is a famous actor, Jake is a chef with his own restaurant, and now you are constructing a multi-million-dollar building."

Seth laughed. "It has been good to us. Unbelievably good. Now, what do you say we order dinner? And a bottle of champagne."

"Champagne? Why?" Sasha asked.

Seth smiled. "Well, I think we need to celebrate." He waved over their server and ordered a bottle of their best champagne.

"You don't need to do that," Sasha said.

"Yes, I do," Seth replied. "You deserve it." He leaned close to her and kissed her cheek. "Congratulations."

"Thank you," she whispered.

Their server returned with the champagne in an ice bucket and two champagne glasses. "What are we celebrating?" he asked.

Seth pointed at her. "Her."

Sasha blushed and looked down. Seth took the glasses and assured their server he would pour the champagne. He filled the glasses and handed one to Sasha.

"Congratulations on your promotion," Seth said. "Cheers to you *and* to working together for two months without killing each other." He tapped his glass against hers.

Sasha leaned close to Seth. "I enjoy working with you," she whispered.

"I like working with you, too, Ms. Baker."

Sasha giggled, grabbed the menu, and glanced at Seth out of the corner of her eye. He was so handsome.

When she caught him looking at her, she glanced down. Heat rose in her cheeks.

Seth wasn't anything like Sasha had assumed. He wasn't a womanizer who didn't take life seriously and used his friendship with a celebrity to his advantage. Seth was the complete opposite. He was hardworking, serious about his career, and he didn't have a girlfriend. Not to mention, he made her laugh; he made her stomach flutter uncontrollably, and she wanted to swim in those deep blue eyes of his. Sasha liked this Seth, and she wished now that she had been willing to give him a chance two years ago at Chris and Sofia's wedding.

"I'd like to make a toast," Sasha said.

Seth poured more champagne into each of their glasses and picked up his glass. "I'm ready," he said.

"To our invaluable partnership," Sasha murmured. "May it bring us both everything we've ever wanted."

"And more," Seth added, clinking their glasses together.

*Please let there be more,* Sasha thought. *Please.*

# Chapter 20

## SASHA

They ended up drinking two bottles of champagne between the two of them. Seth opted not to drive after consuming the alcohol, so he got his keys from the valet, left them with Jake, and called a cab.

As they walked out of the restaurant, Sasha put her arm through Seth's and smiled up at him. She had an amazing time.

The cab driver followed Sasha's directions to the parking lot behind her apartment building, pulled in, and parked at the end of the sidewalk. Seth jumped out and hurried around to her door, opening it before she even moved.

"Thank you," Sasha whispered as she stepped from the car. Her heart was in her throat.

Seth leaned past Sasha to speak to their driver. "Can you wait one minute? I'm going to a different destination."

"Sure," the driver said.

After slamming the door, Seth turned to Sasha, who had waited patiently. She didn't want to walk away without saying goodbye.

"So, here we are." Seth cleared his throat.

Sasha shifted from foot to foot, opened her mouth to speak, then she closed it. She wanted to invite him inside but hesitated.

"So, um, I guess I'll go," Seth said, pointing over his shoulder at the cab.

"Wait, do you want to come in?" Sasha blurted. "I could make a pot of coffee."

Seth nodded. "Yeah, sure. Coffee sounds wonderful. Let me pay the driver."

He took out his wallet, opened the cab door, and spoke to the driver. He handed him some money, slammed the cab door, and followed Sasha up the sidewalk to her apartment. As Sasha unlocked the door, Seth rested his hand in the middle of her back, sending a chill racing through her.

They stood awkwardly inside her apartment, staring at each other for a minute. Seth smiled at her, an adorable grin that made her heart melt.

"Let me, uh, put my stuff away, and I'll make that coffee," Sasha said.

Sasha swung around, suddenly uncomfortable, and yanked open the closet door. Inviting Seth to her apartment had been a spur-of-the-moment thing, and now she didn't know what to do. She hesitated to tell Seth she didn't want coffee. So, she busied herself hanging her purse in the closet, taking off her high heels, and shutting the door.

When she turned back around, Seth was right there, inches away from her, right up in her personal space, so close she could smell his spicy cologne and the mint gum he'd been chewing.

"I lied," he whispered. "I don't want coffee."

Sasha smiled. "I don't want coffee, either."

Seth slipped his arms around her and kissed her, a gentle, restrained kiss filled with all the pent-up energy and sexual tension they'd been keeping in check for the last few hours. It practically begged to be released and, good God, she wanted it.

Desperate to get her hands on him, Sasha kissed him back and pushed his navy blazer off his shoulders. Once it was off, she tossed it on the table by the door, where it knocked over a vase of fake flowers, sending it tumbling to the floor. For once, she didn't care about the mess, not when Seth's hands were in her hair, tipping her head back so he could kiss, suck, and lick her neck.

Seth stopped kissing her and stepped back to survey Sasha's small apartment. His last visit was brief. They hadn't been in the living room long enough for Seth to know where anything was. He took her hand and led her across the room to the couch, where he sat down and pulled her onto his lap. Sasha straddled him, her hands on the back of his neck, her body flush against his. He put his hand on her bare leg and slid it under the edge of her skirt as he drew her back into a kiss.

Seth's insistent kisses muffled Sasha's moans. The touch of his hands to her skin ignited a need deep inside her, which only Seth could fulfill.

Seth's hands were all over her. The straps of her tank top fell off her shoulders and her skirt rode up around her thighs. His kisses were teasing and slow, sweet, pushing her right up to the edge so her body thrummed with need.

Seth rocked his hips up and into hers, the hard line of his erection pressing into her, pulling a gasp out of her. Sasha pushed her knees into the couch, grinding herself on Seth, her body tingling with desire when he moaned.

"Do you want to move to the bedroom?" he whispered.

Sasha froze for a second, wondering what a second round of sex might do to their friendship. She chastised herself. She needed to relax and avoid overthinking. Because, oh boy, did she like to overthink things, especially sex. But it *could* just be sex. It didn't need to be anything else.

"Sasha?" Seth interrupted her train of thought. "You with me?"

Sasha opened her eyes and smiled at Seth. "Yeah, yeah, I'm with you." She wrapped a hand around the back of his neck and kissed him. "I ... I kind of got lost in the moment for a second."

Seth chuckled and squeezed her hip with one hand. "Are we going to the bedroom?" he repeated.

"God, yes," she whispered.

A giggle escaped her when Seth rose to his feet, taking her with him. His thighs flexed and his biceps bulged as he lifted her. Inside the bedroom, he set her on the floor and pushed her against the wall. His kisses were impatient, needy, and hungry. He nipped at her lower lip and his hips rocked into hers, his heavy cock rubbing against her.

"We both have too many clothes on," Seth muttered. He unbuttoned his shirt and yanked it off, then he opened his pants.

Sasha ripped off her tank top, followed by her bra. Her nipples hardened as the cool air hit them and goosebumps rose on her skin. In no time, their clothes were off, and their bodies were pressed close.

She clawed at his back to pull him closer, wanting him more than she'd wanted anyone in a long time. A low growl rumbled through his chest, and his hands clamped down on her waist. The next thing she knew, she was on the bed with Seth's head between her legs and his tongue sinfully deep inside her, along with two fingers.

Her legs opened, her hands twisted in the sheets, and filthy moans fell from her lips, all sense of propriety gone as she fucked herself on Seth's tongue. He flattened a hand on her lower stomach, holding her down as his thumb circled her sensitive nub, drawing sensations out of her she forgot existed. Sasha arched her back and moaned with pleasure, gripping the back of his head. Her body tensed and spasmed as she came.

Seth worked her through the orgasm until she was spent beneath him. He kissed her inner thighs, her hips, and her stomach as he moved along the length of her body, kissing her bare skin.

The sheer bliss rolling through her overwhelmed her, and it wasn't over. Seth rose to his knees, snagged his pants, fumbling in the pockets until he pulled out a condom. He slid it down his length, wrapped his arms around her, and eased into her, groaning as her warmth surrounded him.

Seth braced an arm against the bed by her head and flexed his hips, moving slowly, his lips on hers, his kisses tender, the intensity increasing as he moved faster. Sasha dug her nails into his shoulders and wrapped her legs around his waist, rocking with him as she rode out the insane waves of pleasure he elicited in her.

The experience was untamed, intense, and unlike anything she had ever felt before. Sasha gripped the slats in her headboard as Seth pounded into her. It wouldn't be long before she exploded; the coil deep in the pit of her stomach wound tight as Seth's cock dragged against her sweet spot with every thrust.

The orgasm swept through her like a fire rushing through a forest, consuming her, burning her, and sending electrifying tingles dancing all over her body. Her back bowed as she tried to push herself closer to Seth, to meld her body to his, to feel every damn inch of his perfect body. The headboard's wooden slats dug into her hands, the climax's intensity overshadowing the pain.

Seth buried his face against the side of her neck and let loose a deep, guttural groan. His body tensed and he came, a bone-deep shudder working its way through him.

Sasha let go of the headboard, and her arms fell to the bed beside her. "Holy shit."

Seth smirked and pressed a lingering kiss to her lips. "The feeling is mutual." He rolled onto his back and stretched.

Sasha rolled to her side to look at him. "So much for one time, get-it-out-of-our-system sex. I guess that didn't work."

"Fuck no, it didn't work." Seth chuckled. "I haven't been able to stop thinking about you since that day." He turned to face her with his head propped on his hand. "One time wasn't enough for me. I wanted more."

Sasha laughed. "Oh my God, so did I." She flopped onto her back and put her hands over her face.

Seth pried her hand off her face and kissed her. "I don't want this to end."

"Neither do I," she whispered.

Seth arched an eyebrow in an adorable comic-book-hero kind of way. It made Sasha's insides twist. "Okay, so we keep seeing each other, because obviously this," he gestured between them, "this is fucking awesome."

Sasha's long black hair fell over her face as she nodded. "I am so glad you said that. But I do have one favor to ask of you."

"Okay, what is it?"

"Can we keep it between us? If people find out we're having sex, it could reflect badly on me, maybe even cost me my job. I can't handle something like that."

Seth brushed a strand of hair away from her face. "I think that's a good idea. No use feeding the rumor mill. I doubt anyone would believe we didn't start having sex until after I got hired. Rumors can be vicious and, more often than not, completely untrue."

"Don't I know it," Sasha mumbled. She thought Seth was talking about Chris and Sofia and the rumors that almost ruined their relationship. She took a deep breath and smiled at Seth. "So, we keep it between us?"

Seth held out his hand. "I promise."

Sasha shook his outstretched hand. "Me too." When Seth let go, she straddled him, leaned over, and kissed him.

"One more thing. I'm not interested in a relationship, and neither are you. Can we have a 'friends with benefits' agreement? No commitment or long-term expectations?" she asked.

Seth tipped his head to the side, contemplating her request. After a few seconds, he nodded. "Sure. I can do that."

"Next question," Sasha said.

"You ask an awful lot of questions," Seth mumbled.

"You'll like this one," she said. "Do you need to leave?"

Seth shook his head. "Not right away," he answered. "Unless you want me to?"

Sasha laughed. "Oh no, I want you to stay. That was so much fun. We should do it again."

Seth laughed, wrapped his arms around her waist, and flipped her to her back. "Anything for you, Ms. Baker."

# Chapter 21

## SASHA

Sasha wasn't one of those "come awake with the rising sun" people. As soon as the sun reached her eyes, she was wide awake. The sun peeked through the curtains, and she was awake.

She sat up and looked to her left, expecting to see Seth stretched out beside her. The bed was empty. Sasha saw his clothes were missing from the bed's side. He must have left last night after she fell asleep. She hadn't asked him to stay, though she'd hoped he would. His departure felt like a rejection.

Dejected, Sasha got dressed and went to the bathroom. As she got dressed and brushed her teeth, she chastised herself, telling herself it was stupid of her to think Seth would stay over like they were boyfriend or girlfriend or something. Friends with benefits didn't mean sleepovers.

Sasha pulled her hair into a ponytail, yanked open the bathroom door, and stomped into the living room. She stopped short when she saw Seth coming through her front door, balancing two cups and a bag in one hand as he tried to remove her keys from the lock. Startled, she could only stand there staring at him.

"Little help?" Seth said, struggling not to spill the stuff in his hands.

"Oh, sorry." Sasha rushed over and took the cups and bag from him. The glorious aroma of coffee hit her nose, and the smell of fresh baked goods coming from the bag made her mouth water.

Seth pulled the key out of the lock and closed the door. He put her keys on the counter, took the bag, kissed her cheek, and headed to the small kitchen.

Sasha set the coffee down and leaned against the counter beside him. "I thought you left," she said.

Seth laughed. "I did. But only to get breakfast. I don't know about you, but I'm starving. I googled bagel places around here and found a little bakery down the street." He winked at her. "And I wanted coffee, but I couldn't find any in your cupboards." He grinned sheepishly. "Sorry, I went through your cupboards."

"It's okay." Sasha shifted from foot to foot. "It pissed me off when I thought you left."

"I left a note," Seth said, gesturing to a piece of paper on the counter.

Sasha looked at the note on the counter, sighed, and shook her head. "Sorry. I didn't see it. I feel stupid."

Seth stopped taking the pastries out of the bag, gathered her in his arms, and kissed her. When he let her go, her breath caught in her throat and her heart pounded. She rested her head against his chest.

"Is this a bad idea?" she asked, her voice muffled. "You and me, together?"

"No, I don't think it's a bad idea," Seth said. "I like you, Sasha. I had a great time last night. And I'm not just talking about the sex. I think we get along really well, and I *know* we had fun."

Sasha tipped her head back to look at Seth and smiled. "I had fun. And the sex was fantastic." She took a step back. "But you understand that I'm not looking for a serious relationship, right? Work is going well, and my personal life is okay. Getting involved in a serious relationship isn't in the cards right now."

Seth smiled and shrugged. "That's perfect. I don't have time for a serious relationship either. In case you forgot, I have a multi-million-dollar building to construct. I agree with the 'friends with benefits' thing."

"Great, we're on the same page," Sasha confirmed. She giggled and pursed her lips. "Except I'm not sure we're friends."

Seth's face scrunched up in a cute little pout. "Ouch," he mumbled.

Sasha reached around him and snatched the bag of pastries off the counter. "What's in here, anyway? It smells fantastic."

---

Sasha floated through the rest of the day. Seth stayed long enough for breakfast, then had to go. It was a perfect end to a perfect date.

She spent the morning straightening up her apartment and doing laundry. She was just settling down to watch a movie when her phone rang. To her surprise, it was Sofia.

"Sof! It's so good to hear from you! What's up?"

"Are you busy?" Sofia asked.

"No, why?"

"Let's get lunch," Sofia said.

"What? You're in town?" Sofia rarely came to Los Angeles. The paparazzi were relentless with her and Chris. Whenever she was in town, they followed her and provoked her, just to have a reason to display Sofia's face on the internet. She preferred the coziness of their mountain home.

"Only for the day," Sofia clarified. "I drove Chris down, and I'm going back tonight. But I wanted to see my best friend."

"Where can we get lunch the paparazzi won't find you?" Sasha asked.

"Chris has a friend, Jake. He owns the—"

"Blue Velvet," Sasha finished.

Sofia laughed. "Yeah. How did you know that?"

"I'll explain over lunch," Sasha said. "I'll meet you in thirty minutes."

---

Sasha breezed through the front door at the Blue Velvet exactly thirty minutes later. The hostess led her to a table overlooking a garden in the courtyard of the building. Sofia was already there, talking to Jake.

"Hey, hi!" Jake said. "Sasha, right? Seth's friend."

Sasha nodded. "Yeah, that's me."

Sofia's eyes narrowed. "You're 'Seth's friend'?"

"I think 'Seth's business associate' would be a better way of putting it," Sasha said.

Jake laughed and got to his feet. "Hm, if you say so. You guys looked a little more friendly than most business associates." He winked at Sasha. "If you ladies will excuse me, I have some cooking to do. Let me know if you need anything." He kissed Sofia on the cheek and excused himself. Sasha slid into the seat he vacated.

"Start talking," Sofia said.

"Hello to you, too," Sasha said.

"You're not getting out of explaining what I just heard." Sofia put her elbows on the table and propped her chin on her hands. "What's happening between you and Seth? Tell me. Now."

Sasha sighed. "Okay, okay. But I am swearing you to secrecy. You cannot tell anyone. That includes Chris."

Sofia looked taken aback. "I tell Chris everything."

"I know you do," Sasha said. "But you can't tell him this. Please, I'm begging you."

"Alright, I won't tell him." Sofia held out her pinky finger. "I pinky promise."

Sasha hooked her finger around Sofia's and squeezed. She trusted Sofia wouldn't say anything to her husband, not after extracting a promise. She inched her chair closer to Sofia's and leaned in.

"I slept with Seth last night."

Sofia's mouth dropped open. "You what?" she whispered.

"I slept with Seth," Sasha repeated. "We had dinner and when he took me home, I invited him in. The next thing I know, we're kissing and then, bam, we're in bed. It wasn't the first time, either."

"Holy shit," Sofia muttered. "Why am I just hearing about this? When was the first time?"

"A few weeks ago," she said. "Initially it was a one-time thing, but we had dinner and champagne." She shrugged. "And sex."

"How was it?" Sofia asked.

"Sofia!" Sasha shook her head and laughed. "Seriously?"

Sofia raised one eyebrow and stared at her. Sasha knew she wouldn't budge until she got an answer.

Sasha sighed. "Fine. It was unbelievable."

"So, are you two a couple now?" Sofia asked.

Sasha shook her head. "No. Neither one of us is looking for any kind of relationship. We decided it would be a friend with benefits thing."

"And you're okay with that?" Sofia asked.

Sasha looked around, leaned closer to Sofia, and lowered her voice. "Thirteen months, Sofia," she said. "It has been thirteen months since I had sex."

Sofia slapped her hand over her mouth and burst out laughing. "Oh my God, Sash, I didn't know."

"Yeah," Sasha said. "Not since I dated that guy that lived in my apartment complex."

"The one that moved to Texas?"

Sasha nodded. "Yes, that one." She grabbed her glass of water and took a drink. "Last night with Seth, it was ... Jesus, Sofia. It was the best sex I've ever had in my life. And you know what? He didn't jump out of bed and take off either. I mean, I thought he did, but I was wrong. He left to get coffee and pastries. Then he hung around to have breakfast with me. He kissed me goodbye when he left."

Sofia smiled. "I told you Seth was a sweetheart *and* a good guy." She rubbed her hands together. "This is so great."

Sasha laughed. "I knew you'd enjoy this."

"It's perfect, though! My best friend and Chris's best friend, together." Sofia giggled, vibrating with excitement. She grabbed Sasha's hand and squeezed it. "We can double date."

Sasha pulled her hand free of Sofia's tight grip and shook her head. "Sofia, stop. Seth and I aren't in a relationship. We're not in a double-dating kind of place."

"But—"

This time, Sasha squeezed Sofia's hand. "Sof, stop. I don't want to make this into something it's not. Give us time to figure it out, okay? If there's anything to figure out."

Sofia sighed. "Okay. I understand. Promise me I'll be the first to know if this works out."

"You will, I promise," Sasha said. "You'll be my first phone call." She grabbed her menu. "Now can we order? The food here is amazing."

Sofia grinned. "Nice segue and subject change."

# Chapter 22

## SETH

Seth swung by the construction site to check on the weekend crew and see if they needed anything. His weekend foreman, Butler, had everything under control, and it looked good so he stopped in the office to check his email and catch up on paperwork. Except he couldn't stop thinking about Sasha. He kept checking his phone to see if she had called or texted. She hadn't.

He gave up trying to work after an hour, locked up, and left for Chris's place.

When he opened the front door, Chris's dog, Ollie, shot out of the kitchen door and down the hallway to sit at Seth's feet. Ollie stared up at him, whining.

"Hey, Ollie," Seth said, crouching in front of the dog to pet him. "How are you, boy? Long time, no see. Is your dad here?"

"I'm in the kitchen," Chris called.

Seth patted Ollie's head and went to the kitchen. Ollie followed, right on his heels.

Chris stood in front of the stove with a cutting board loaded with mushrooms and onions, dumping them into a large stockpot. He grinned at Seth over his shoulder.

"Hey, dude, what's up?" Chris said.

Seth grabbed water from the fridge and sat down at the kitchen table. "I just came from work. What the hell are you doing? You don't cook."

"I do cook, just not like Jake does. I'm making my mom's sauce." Chris dropped the cutting board on the island in the middle of the kitchen. He paused and looked his best friend up and down. "Since when do you wear dress clothes to a construction site?"

"Um…" Seth took a drink of his water and cleared his throat, which turned out to be a mistake because he swallowed the water wrong and choked on it. He tried to catch his breath, but that only made it worse. He leaned forward, his elbows on his knees, and coughed, his throat burning. When he could finally catch his breath, he looked up to see Chris staring at him with his arms crossed over his chest.

"What?" Seth croaked. "Why are you looking at me?"

"You went on a date last night," Chris said. "And now you're doing the walk of shame in the same clothes you wore on your date. Alright, spill. Who was it?"

Seth shook his head. "It's not a big deal."

"Then tell me who the girl is," Chris said.

Seth sighed. "Okay, but you cannot freak out."

Chris made a face. "Why would I freak out?" He grabbed a large wooden spoon and stirred the mushrooms and onions in the pot, then he dumped in several cans of tomatoes and tomato sauce sitting open on the counter.

"It was Sasha," Seth said.

Chris dropped the wooden spoon and sauce splashed out of the pan, hitting the cabinets above the stove, the counter, the floor, and Chris. He swore under his breath as he grabbed the dishcloth.

"Did you sleep with her?" Chris asked.

"I did," Seth replied.

"Sofia is going to kill you." He tossed the dishcloth in the sink, dug the spoon out of the pot, and rinsed it off.

"Why would she kill me?" Seth asked. "I didn't do anything wrong."

"Sofia is protective of Sasha," Chris explained. "Sasha's ex is a jerk."

"Yeah, I've had the pleasure of meeting him," Seth said. "He is a jerk."

"I've only heard the stories," Chris said. "I never had the pleasure."

"Trust me, it's not a pleasure. He's a jerk." Seth took another drink of water. "Okay, so we established that Sasha's ex is a jerk. How is that related to me?"

"Sofia worries about the men Sasha dates, you know, that they'll hurt her like Liam hurt her," Chris said.

"So, Sofia thinks I'm a jerk who will hurt her best friend?"

Chris sighed. "I didn't say that. Look, don't take this wrong, but you're not known for your devotion to relationships. You have a reputation."

Seth snorted. "So do you."

Chris laughed. "You're not wrong. But I'm not like that anymore. I've settled down."

"So have I," Seth said. "And in my defense, I'm too busy for a relationship." He got to his feet and tossed his water bottle in the recycle can. "I'm not going to justify my relationship with Sasha to you *or* Sofia. We are both adults, and we know what we're doing. It's private and not anyone else's business. End of story. Now, if you'll excuse me, I need a shower and a change of clothes."

Seth rarely got angry with Chris. They argued over insignificant things like sports, movies, or music. They had never argued about Seth's love life before. There wasn't much to argue about.

He wouldn't hurt Sasha. He liked her more than she liked him. Rather than becoming angry with his best friend, he should have explained it to Chris first.

Seth emerged from the shower to a house that smelled like an Italian restaurant. It brought back memories of dinners with Chris's family when he was a kid. Chris's mom came from a big Italian family, and the woman could cook.

Chris was in the living room watching a college football game with Ollie's head in his lap. He gestured at the coffee table, where Seth saw snacks and drinks.

"Peace offering?" Seth asked, as he sat down on the couch.

Chris chuckled. "Yes." He scratched Ollie behind the ears. "I need to apologize to you. Whatever relationship you might have with Sasha is private and none of my business. I'm sorry for trying to butt in."

"I appreciate that," Seth said. "It would have been strange if you didn't butt in."

"It would have been," Chris mumbled. "Anyway, I'll talk to Sofia, make sure she doesn't try to kill you for dating her best friend. Be good to her, okay? Sasha's had it rough. Married right out of high school, divorced by twenty-two, but still has to deal with her asshole ex mooching off of her and using her like she's an ATM. Don't hurt her."

"I won't," Seth said. "I promise."

"Is this a purely sexual thing with Sasha?" Chris asked. "You said you don't have time for a relationship."

"I don't," Seth emphasized. "But—"

Chris laughed. "I knew there was a but."

Seth sighed and paused a moment before he spoke. "I like her, dude, a lot. I could be with this woman for a long time."

Chris picked up the remote and hit the mute button. "Wait? Are you saying you're considering a long-term relationship with someone? I thought you weren't interested in anything serious?"

Seth rubbed the back of his neck. "I'm interested if it's Sasha."

"Did you tell her that?" Chris asked.

Seth chortled. "No. She made it perfectly clear she was in this for the fun of it. For the sex."

Chris looked like he'd eaten a lemon. He snorted. "Too much information."

Seth laughed. "Sorry, dude."

"I will never look at Sasha the same way," Chris muttered under his breath. He cleared his throat. "So, what are you going to do?"

"Win her over," Seth said. "What other choice do I have? I'm going to have to do everything I can think of to convince her I'm boyfriend material."

"Husband material?" Chris asked, one eyebrow raised.

"Don't jump the gun," Seth said. "One step at a time."

Chris nodded. "I call best man," he said. He picked up the remote and unmuted the game. "Hand me a beer, will ya?"

Seth snorted and handed his friend a beer. He sat back and stared at the TV, though he wasn't paying attention to the game. Instead, he was thinking of ways to win over Sasha. It wouldn't be easy; it would take everything he had to convince her to give him a chance. But he would try.

# Chapter 23

## SETH

"Good morning," Sasha said, as she breezed through the on-site office door. "I brought you coffee. Black, like your heart." She winked, set the coffee in front of Seth, then she slipped into the chair that Seth thought of as "Sasha's chair."

Wyatt burst out laughing and shook his head. "Wow, she has your number, doesn't she, Mitchell?"

Seth narrowed his eyes and when Sasha wasn't looking, he flipped Wyatt off. His friend snorted and left the office, his voice raised to call the crew together for what he liked to call "his morning briefing."

It impressed Seth how far Wyatt had come in a short time. When Seth came to California, Wyatt was afraid to speak up about the messy construction site. Now, he was managing the crew, taking charge, and solving problems. Seth couldn't ask for a better foreman.

"How is it going?" Sasha piped up. "Any problems?"

Seth shook his head. "Not one. You should know that by now. My projects are drama- and problem-free. As they should be." He propped his chin on his hand and stared at Sasha.

"Why are you staring at me?" she asked.

"I enjoy looking at you," Seth said. "It makes me happy."

Sasha giggled. "What do you want, Mitchell?"

Seth feigned shock. "What makes you think I want anything? Can't I give you a compliment without there being an ulterior motive?"

"Not usually," she shot back. "What do you want?"

"I was wondering if you would like to go out tomorrow afternoon. I thought we could do something, I don't know, different. Fun." He grinned at her.

"Fun? What kind of fun?" Sasha asked.

"Why are you suspicious of everything I do?" Seth asked.

They had been secretly dating for almost three weeks. Since their dinner date at Blue Velvet and the subsequent sleepover, the only thing they'd done was hang out at Sasha's apartment. Seth longed for a fun and different adventure.

"Let's go to the Santa Monica Pier and check out the amusement park," Seth said.

"Pacific Park?" Sasha smiled. "You know what? That sounds like fun. I haven't been there in *ages*." Her grin widened. "Will you win me one of those ridiculously huge stuffed animals?"

Seth got to his feet. "I'll try." He grabbed his clipboard and hard hat. "I'll pick you up around two."

"I'll be ready," she said.

---

Seth couldn't stop looking at Sasha out of the corner of his eye. She wore a pair of tan shorts, a loose navy-blue T-shirt, and a simple silver necklace. Brown sandals adorned her feet, and she had painted her toenails a bright red. She pulled her long black hair up in a high ponytail, though a few tendrils had escaped and brushed against her face. Large, dark sunglasses, like the old movie stars had worn, adorned her face, along with a bright smile.

Sasha took his breath away.

"You're staring at me again," she murmured.

"Sorry. I can't help it." Seth focused on the road ahead. "You understand you are gorgeous, right?"

Sasha shook her head. "You're just saying that because I'm sleeping with you."

Seth rolled his eyes. "Not true. You're gorgeous. Breathtaking. Beautiful. Stunning."

"Okay, okay, you can stop now." She cleared her throat and stared out the window. "It's been a while since a man said something nice to me without some hidden agenda."

Seth reached over, took her hand, and squeezed it. "I have no ulterior motive, I swear. I wanted to tell you I think you're beautiful."

Sasha cleared her throat. "I think I see a parking spot over there."

Seth pretended not to hear the catch in Sasha's voice when she spoke. Instead, he followed her directions to the empty parking spot and pulled in. He shut off the engine and turned to Sasha.

"Are you okay?" he asked.

"Yes, of course I am. I'm sorry. I didn't mean to get all emotional." Sasha cupped his cheek in her hand and kissed him. When they broke apart, she pulled him close and pressed her lips to his ear.

"Get your ass out of the car. You owe me a stuffed animal."

Seth laughed. "Let's go."

He took Sasha's hand as they walked toward the boardwalk. The smells in the air took him back to his childhood and family trips to Coney Island—the salty sea air, fried bread, pretzels, and popcorn. Even the sounds were familiar—the clanking of the roller coaster and the screams of the riders as it dropped, crying babies and fussy toddlers, and the excited chatter of the people playing games.

"Are you hungry?" he asked.

"I would *love* a pretzel," Sasha said. "I haven't had one in forever."

"Okay, let's grab some wristbands for the rides and get a pretzel from that Wetzel Pretzel cart." He tightened his grip on her hand and pulled her after him.

Seth bought their wristbands so they could go on the rides, then they grabbed pretzel bites from the pretzel cart and a Coke.

They sat on a bench, eating and watching the crowds of people. Seth kept peeking at Sasha out of the corner of his eye. He loved how relaxed she looked, so different from the frazzled, on-edge woman she had been a few weeks ago.

When they finished their food, Seth took their trash and tossed it in one of the many cans along the pier. He pulled Sasha to her feet.

"Ready for some rides?" he asked.

Sasha nodded. "Nothing that spins like that, okay?" She pointed at a ride resembling spinning sharks.

Seth raised an eyebrow. "Oh, why not?"

"Do you want to deal with this?" Holding her stomach, she bent over and made retching sounds. She glanced up at Seth and burst into a fit of giggles. She could barely speak. "Oh God, the look ... the look on your face right now is priceless."

"Because you're fake puking in the middle of the Santa Monica Pier," Seth said. "I don't know whether to tell you I love you or run away screaming."

Sasha stood upright, her mouth hanging open, and her eyes wide. "What did you just say?"

Seth shook his head and laughed. He hadn't meant to use the dreaded "L" word. It was a joke that he now had to explain to Sasha.

"I'm joking, Sash," he said. "It's only been two, three weeks, right? While I do like you a lot, I'm not quite at the 'I love you' stage yet." He took her arm and tugged her close. "Believe me, you'll know when I am." He kissed her cheek. "Come on, I want to try the West Coaster. Or does that spin too much?"

"Nope, that's good," Sasha said. "I love roller coasters."

After riding the West Coaster four times, Sasha wanted a break. Seth agreed, because he was queasy after the fourth ride. He definitely didn't want to reenact Sasha's retching sounds for real.

The row of games beckoned them with bright colors and screams of delight from the winners. He and Sasha wandered the aisle trying to choose a game. Sasha gave Whack-a-Mole a try, taking the huge, padded hammer and slamming it repeatedly on the heads of the cute moles as they popped out of the holes. She smashed the most and walked away with a cute stuffed tiger.

"Okay, Mitchell, the pressure is on," Sasha teased. "Think you can win me a bigger toy than this adorable tiger?" She wiggled her stuffed tiger in his face and laughed.

Seth snorted. "Hell, yeah. Bigger and cuter." He dropped her hand and turned in a circle. A grin spread across his face as he pointed at the game that had caught his eye.

"That one, right there. The Goblet Toss." He turned back to Sasha. "Watch this." He walked backward, gesturing for her to follow him.

Sasha giggled, tucked her tiger under her arm, and skipped after him. They stopped in front of the Goblet Toss and listened to the woman at the booth explain how to play. When she was done, Seth dug his wallet out of his pocket and handed her some cash.

"You got this, honey?" she asked.

Seth nodded. "I got it."

The woman shrugged and handed over the wiffle balls. The object was to toss a wiffle ball into a colored goblet to win a prize. Seth's goal was to get it in the orange goblet for the large prize. He closed his eyes for a second and threw the first ball.

It hit the rim of a blue goblet, bounced out, and hit the ground. The next wiffle ball landed in a yellow goblet, not what Seth wanted. He threw the last ball. It hit a red goblet, bounced, landed on the rim of a purple goblet, bounced again, and landed in one of the orange goblets.

"Yes!" Seth shouted.

"Congratulations, sir," the woman said. "You get to pick one of these prizes."

"I'll take the brown sloth with the pink feet," he said.

The woman handed it over before moving to the next person. Seth handed the sloth to Sasha, grabbed her, and kissed her.

"What's next?" he asked.

They went on more rides—the Sea Dragon, Inkie's Scrambler, and the Seaside Swing. The Pacific Wheel, a huge, solar-powered Ferris wheel, ended up as their favorite ride. They rode it three times. They enjoyed sitting at the top, making out like teenagers, and looking at the ocean.

After the rides, they checked out the shops on the pier. Sasha bought three magnets for her refrigerator at home, and Seth bought T-shirts to send back to his family in New York. The smell of the funnel cakes next door made Seth's mouth water, so he suggested they get dinner before heading home.

They settled on Seaside on the Pier for dinner. Sasha ordered a giant salad, Seth got a burger, and they both got ice cold beers.

"I didn't know you liked beer," Seth said. "I've only seen you drink wine and iced tea."

"I prefer a cold beer after a day like today," Sasha said. "I had fun, by the way. A lot of fun."

"Me too," Seth said. "When I suggested the pier, I didn't realize we would have such a good time."

Sasha tipped her head to one side and gave him a funny look. "Oh, and why is that?"

He sighed. "If I tell you, you can't take it the wrong way, okay?"

She scrunched her nose and narrowed her eyes. "What was it you said? Saying that makes me assume it's bad or something like that? Anyway, I'll try not to," she said. "No promises, though."

"It's just that, not counting the first weekend we met, you come across as well, really ... serious. You don't let yourself have fun. This didn't seem like your kind of thing to me."

Sasha sighed and stared at the tabletop as she spoke. "Is that what you think of me? That I'm '*serious.*'" She used her fingers to make air quotations when she said the word serious.

Seth leaned across the table and grabbed her hands. Sasha kept her eyes on the table. "Hey, look at me," Seth ordered.

Her eyes came up, and Seth knew immediately he had hurt her feelings.

"What?" she asked.

"There's nothing wrong with being serious, Sasha. Nothing at all. Sometimes, it's good to let go and have fun. It's good for your soul to stop, take a breath, and let all the shit in your life go for one day. Enjoy yourself. Drink a beer instead of a glass of wine. Laugh like a little kid." He gave her a gentle smile. "Like we did today."

Sasha nodded. "I know that; I do. But it's hard. It's difficult for me to let myself relax and have fun." She exhaled loudly and shook her head. "I have a reason, but I don't want to talk about it now. I'll tell you about it sometime, but not today. This is one of the best days I've had in a long time, and I don't want to ruin it."

Seth grinned. "Oh, yeah?"

"Yeah," Sasha said. "Only one thing could make it better."

"What's that?"

Sasha looked around them, leaned over the table, and whispered, "Sex on the beach."

"Finish your dinner," Seth said. "I've got a blanket in the Land Rover."

# Chapter 24

## SASHA

Six days after her and Seth's date to the Santa Monica Pier, Sasha woke up feeling like crap. She got out of bed long enough to grab her phone and text Eleanor that she wouldn't be in because she wasn't feeling well. When she was done, she took the blanket and pillow off her bed, trudged out to the living room, and plopped down on the couch. She picked up the remote and found one of her favorite true crime shows playing on repeat. She pulled the blanket up to her chin and wondered why she never had cold medicine in the house when she needed it.

For a moment, Sasha considered calling her mother, but she squashed that idea. Her mother was exhausting and Sasha didn't have the energy to deal with her, not when she felt so lousy. Postmates was always an option, but she hated to pay those over-inflated prices.

Sasha dozed in and out for the next hour until her phone vibrated on the table. She reached over and grabbed it.

[Seth: Are you coming to the site today?]

Shit, she forgot to text Seth.

[Sasha: No, I'm really sick. Sorry I forgot to text you.]

[Seth: Do you need anything?]

[Sasha: Everything. Ha ha. Seriously, though, I just need to sleep. I'll talk to you tomorrow.]

She tossed her phone back on the table and closed her eyes. She refused to have Seth over while she was sick. Her hair was in a messy bun, her nose was red, her body ached, the apartment was a mess, and she felt like crap. She couldn't see Seth in this state.

Within minutes, she was asleep, though it was restless because her nose kept running, her head pounded, and she woke herself up coughing several times. She had two options—call Postmates or go to the store.

She was reaching for her phone when someone knocked on the door. Sasha considered ignoring it until her phone vibrated.

[Seth: Sasha, open the door, it's me.]

Wrapped in a blanket, Sasha went to the door. Through the peephole, she saw Seth's grin. Sasha unlocked the door and let him in.

"What are you doing here?" she asked.

Seth pushed past her and went into the kitchen. "I brought supplies: tissues, cold medicine, saltines, 7-Up, chicken noodle soup from that café by the construction site, cough drops, and ibuprofen. If I forgot anything, I can go get it. Otherwise, I am here to take care of you."

Sasha sat back down on the couch. "Don't you have to work?" she asked.

"I left Wyatt in charge and told him I was taking the day off." He must have noticed the panicked look on Sasha's face, because he added, "Don't worry, I didn't tell him why."

Sasha fidgeted. "How did you know I needed all that stuff?"

"I didn't. I assumed," he said. "Did you really need everything?"

She threw herself back on the couch. "Yes, I have nothing for a cold. You saved me." She put an arm over her eyes. "Now, go away."

"What? Why?"

Sasha moved her arm an inch and peeked at Seth. He looked genuinely hurt, which was not her intention.

"I'm sorry, but I am no fun to be around when I am sick," Sasha explained. "You're better off going back to work. Besides, you don't want to get sick, do you?"

"I don't care," Seth replied. "I also don't care if you aren't fun to be around. You don't feel good, and you need someone to take care of you."

"Hmmph. Whatever." She pulled the blanket over her head and curled into a ball. Maybe if she ignored him, he would leave.

Sasha listened to Seth moving around the kitchen, opening and closing the refrigerator and cupboards. After a few minutes, a hand rested on her hip.

"Sasha, can you come out from under the blanket for a minute?" he asked.

She moved the blanket enough to look at him. "Why?"

He showed her a small cup of vile-looking orange liquid. "Cold medicine."

"I don't need it," she muttered, followed by a coughing fit that lasted almost thirty seconds.

Seth rolled his eyes and waited for the coughing fit to end before he spoke. "Come on, Sash, take it, okay?"

"Fine," she grumbled. She threw the blanket off, sat up, and took the cup of medicine. She held her breath and swallowed it as fast as she could. "That was disgusting."

"I know," Seth said. He plucked the cup from her hand and returned to the kitchen. After he rinsed it out, he picked up the box of tissues and the bag of cough drops. He dropped them on the coffee table and sat down next to her.

"You're not leaving, are you?" she mumbled.

"No," he replied. "Get used to it. Why don't you lie down and try to get some sleep?" He put her pillow on his lap and patted it. "I'll watch TV while you rest."

"You're not going to put it on some sports program, are you?" Sasha asked.

Seth shook his head and pointed at the TV. Sasha waited for him to say something, but when he didn't, she lay down, and before she knew it, she was sound asleep.

---

Coming awake after taking cold medicine was not a pleasant experience. It disoriented Sasha at first. She heard unfamiliar voices in the room, and the light seemed wrong. She struggled to sit up and let out a startled squeak when a set of warm hands landed on her shoulders.

"Hey, it's okay," a familiar voice whispered.

"Jesus, Seth, you scared the crap out of me," Sasha snapped. "I forgot you were here."

"Sorry. Can I get you anything?"

"Something to drink?" she said. "I'm gonna go use the bathroom and brush my teeth."

Not only did she brush her teeth after she went to the bathroom, she also ran a comb through her hair and washed her face. Despite feeling somewhat better, she still had a headache and her throat felt as if she had swallowed glass.

A glass of 7-Up with a straw waited for her in the living room. As the cold liquid hit her throat, she let out a sigh. She scooped up one of the cough drops, unwrapped it, and popped it in her mouth. She sat down next to Seth and put her head on his shoulder.

"Sorry I was grumpy earlier," she mumbled.

Seth shrugged and slipped his arm around her shoulders. "You're allowed to be grumpy. You're sick. It's okay."

Sasha shook her head. "No, it's not okay. I'm miserable to be around when I'm sick. Nobody wants to be around me. My ex would leave when I was sick because I drove him crazy."

"Seriously? What an ass." Seth caressed her upper arm with the tips of his fingers. "I enjoy taking care of you."

"Thank you," she whispered.

They watched TV in silence for a while. While her throat still hurt and she had a slight headache, she found having Seth there with her made her feel better.

Sasha closed her eyes and talked. "Remember when I said there was a reason I'm so serious all the time?"

"I do," Seth said.

"A long time ago, back when I was in high school, I wasn't as serious as I am now. I could let loose, have fun, and I didn't take myself—or anything else—too seriously. I never planned ahead or cared about anything, just took each day as it came. I was a straight-A student, and I didn't even have to study. Volleyball, track, cross country, and softball were the sports I played. Having fun was all that mattered." She took a deep breath, which made her cough and her head hurt. "Could you get me something for my head?"

Seth nodded, got up, and got her some ibuprofen. He handed her the glass of 7-Up, another cough drop, and the tissues, then he sat down. Sasha swallowed the pills, blew her nose, and popped the second cough drop into her mouth.

"I had scholarships to San Diego State University, University of Southern California, and even Berkley. I could have gone to school for free. Everything was going my way. I was having too much fun to care. I partied hard every weekend, I fooled around with Liam, and I didn't give a shit about my future. And I drank. A lot. Looking back now, I realize I had a drinking problem. I thought I controlled the alcohol, but it controlled me. I figured my future would always be there, waiting for me. But I was wrong. God, I was so wrong. I graduated from high school, and I kept partying. I put off doing all the things I needed to do to go to college. I lost all three of my scholarships. God, when my parents found out, the disappointment in their eyes." Sasha shook her head and wiped her damp cheeks. "It about killed me to know I disappointed them. But, instead of apologizing to them, admitting I screwed up, and trying to fix it, do you know what I did? I went out with Liam, partied my ass off, and one long, drunken weekend, I ended up married to Liam."

"Jesus, Sasha, I never would have guessed," Seth murmured. "I've never known somebody who had their shit together like you do."

"Yeah, well, I haven't always had my shit together. Anyway, Liam and I were married for two years before I came to my senses. I was taking classes at the community college at night and working as a waitress during the day. Not that I was taking my classes seriously, I was barely scraping by, getting Cs and Ds, the occasional B. Then one night, right after I turned twenty, I stood in my parents' living room begging them for money to pay my rent, buy groceries, and pay my electricity bill. It hit me like a wrecking ball. I could do better. Not just that I could do better, but that I *needed* to do better. I was throwing my life away." Sasha stopped and cleared her throat.

Seth jumped to his feet and refilled her glass. "You don't have to finish if you don't want to," he said, as he sat back down.

"No, I want to," she said. "I *have* to. I went home and threw away all the liquor. The next morning, I registered for more classes before work."

"What did Liam say?" Seth asked.

Sasha laughed. "He wasn't home. Some camping trip with his buddies, which was really an excuse to sit out in the woods and drink himself into a stupor. When he came home, we got into a fight. A huge fight. He thought I was being stupid and overreacting. I begged him to stop drinking and go back to school with me. He said he liked our life the way it was. I should have left him, but I couldn't. I still loved him. Liam wasn't a good guy. I couldn't accept it. So, I pretended everything was fine with my marriage. I worked full time and attended school full time. I busted my ass while Liam jumped from job to job, partied on the weekends, and refused to take life seriously."

"Why did you stay with him?" Seth asked.

"I kept hoping he would change. He didn't. I came to my senses after my father died. After his death, I was distraught. Inconsolable. I'm an only child, and my father and I were close. I needed my husband. I needed someone to ... to just *be there*. Do you know what Liam did? He didn't go to the funeral with me or stay with me when I needed him the most. Oh, no, he didn't bother to take care of me, his grieving wife. Instead, he went to Vegas with his buddies for a long weekend." Sasha took a tissue from the box and wiped her nose. "I begged him to stay with me, begged him to go to the funeral with me. But he couldn't let down his friends, not for me, not for anyone." She blew her nose. "I filed for divorce the day after my dad's funeral. I'm sorry it took me four years to do it."

Seth hugged her and pressed his lips to her temple. "I'm sorry he hurt you."

"Yeah, me too. But it's in the past. Forgive and forget, right? But it changed me. I had to fix myself and my life. That meant taking things more seriously. I had to get back on track. Being me, I went too far in one direction." She turned to Seth. "But when I'm with you, I can let myself have fun. I think it's because while you know how to have fun, you also know when it's time to be serious. I really like that about you." Sasha put her arms around Seth and rested her head on his shoulder. "Thanks for listening to all that."

"Thanks for telling me," Seth said. "You didn't have to."

"I know," Sasha replied. "But I wanted to." She tipped her head back to look at Seth. "Did I hear you mention you brought chicken noodle soup?"

Seth grinned. "You did." He kissed her forehead. "I'll get it for you."

Sasha let go of him so he could stand up. Winking at her, he went to the kitchen and got the soup from the fridge.

"You're a good guy, Seth," Sasha said.

*Which is exactly what scares me.*

# Chapter 25

## SASHA

Sasha worried that her confessions to Seth about her life might scare him off. No one wanted a woman who couldn't enjoy life. Who knew how long her fun with Seth would last?

Her worries ended up being for nothing. Seth spent most of the weekend with her, taking care of her while she recovered from whatever crud she had. They cuddled on the couch, watched movies, and binged on true crime shows while she recovered. Sasha repeatedly urged him to go home so he wouldn't get sick, but he didn't seem to care.

On Monday, she was feeling better, so Seth could go to work. She took another sick day to make sure she was better.

Tuesday morning, she woke up feeling like a new person. Relieved that she was over her illness, she got ready for work. Before going to the construction site, she planned to check in with her boss and get some work done in the office.

Eleanor entered her office less than ten minutes after Sasha sat down. She shut the door and sat across from her.

"Good morning, Ms. Baker," she said. "Are you feeling better?"

"I am, thank you," Sasha replied.

"I wanted to talk to you about the Phillips Innovations project. It's been three months since Mitchell Construction took over. How are things at the construction site?"

"It's going well," Sasha said. "Exceptionally well."

"Would you be willing to sit down with Jerome Nelson and discuss it?" Eleanor asked. "He's asking for an update."

Sasha nodded. "Of course," she said. "When did he want to meet?"

"Tonight," Eleanor said. "He's only in town for one day, flying out early tomorrow morning for a conference in Australia."

"Um, okay," she said. "Do you want Seth to be there?"

"I think it would help," Eleanor replied. "Nelson is unwilling to come down here. Or go to the site. He said he doesn't want to spoil the eventual reveal. I can have Clara make reservations at a nearby restaurant for you if you'd like."

"I think that's a good idea," Sasha said. "Rudy's down the street is good."

Eleanor got to her feet. "I'll have Clara email you the details." Pausing at the door, she turned around. "I want you to know, Sasha, I am very impressed with you. Although I've asked a lot of you lately, you've more than delivered. I won't underestimate you again."

"Thank you, ma'am," Sasha replied. "I can't tell you how much I appreciate that."

After Eleanor left, Sasha grabbed her phone and dialed Seth's number. He answered right away.

"Hey, Sash, how are you feeling?" he asked.

"Much better, thanks," she replied. "Hey, are you up for dinner tonight?"

Seth chuckled. "I guess you are feeling better."

Sasha giggled. "We won't be alone," she said. "Jerome Nelson is asking for an update. Clara is making reservations for us. I could really use your help."

"I can't say no," Seth murmured. "Just give me the time and place."

Sasha's stomach did a lazy roll, and goosebumps rose on her arms. Damn him. His voice got her excited. She took a deep breath and exhaled in a half-hearted attempt to slow her racing pulse.

"I'll be at the site this afternoon," she said. "I'll fill you in then."

"Sounds good," Seth replied. "Talk to you soon."

Sasha disconnected the call and set her phone on the desk. She closed her eyes, but an image of Seth popped into her head, so she quickly opened them. He consumed every thought, and she wasn't sure she liked it.

*Except you do.*

"Shut up," she muttered to the voice in her head that sounded a lot like her best friend. "I don't need your crap today."

She turned on her laptop and forced herself to concentrate. She had work to do before seeing Seth, or else she wouldn't be able to focus on anything else.

---

The click of the lock on the trailer door was like a starter pistol, sending them into action. Sasha threw her hard hat on the floor and jumped into Seth's arms, nearly knocking him over. He tossed his own hard hat aside and slipped his arms around her waist.

She had been waiting for this moment for hours, the anticipation only heightening her need for him. Not being able to touch him, kiss him, *be* with him was agonizing. She hadn't realized how deep her desire for Seth ran until she had to hide her feelings day in and day out. It only strengthened their connection and honed their need for each other.

"Are you sure everybody is gone?" she asked.

"Yes," Seth said. "The parking lot is empty. Just my car and yours." He pressed her against the wall next to the door, his mouth covering hers, the kiss stealing the breath from her lungs.

Sasha twisted her fingers in Seth's hair and held him close, a soft moan leaving her as the kiss deepened.

"God, it feels like it's been weeks since I could touch you." His voice was thick with desire, damn near a growl.

Sasha giggled. "It's been four days."

"Four days too long," Seth mumbled. He picked her up and carried her to the futon on the other side of the room. After he set her down, he pulled her down beside him and kissed her. He took her in his arms and kissed her again.

Dizzy with desire, she wrapped herself around him, pulling him close. The heat emanating from his body surrounded her and sent ripples of desire down her spine. His hands roamed over her body, caressing her through her clothes. She needed his touch like she needed air to breathe.

"You're so needy," he whispered.

"And you're a tease." She gasped, as his fingers slipped under her shirt and grazed her bare stomach.

Seth chuckled and sucked at the spot where her shoulder met her neck as Sasha squirmed and moaned, desperate for more.

"I could kiss you all night," Seth whispered.

Sasha's cell phone rang in her back pocket. She pushed Seth away and yanked it free.

"Hello?" she answered.

"Ms. Baker?" Eleanor's secretary Clara said. "Is that you?"

Sasha sat up straight. "Uh, yeah, Clara, it's me."

"Are you okay? You sound out of breath. I know you've been ill—"

"Oh no, I'm ... I'm fine. What can I do for you?"

"Mr. Nelson called. He'll be half an hour late to the restaurant."

*Shit, I forgot.*

"Okay," Sasha said. "Well, thank you. I appreciate the update."

"You're welcome," Clara said. "Have a good evening."

Sasha hung up and turned back to Seth, who looked undeniably sexy with his messy hair and flushed cheeks. She leaned over and brushed a kiss across his lips.

"We have to go," she said. "We have that dinner meeting with Jerome Nelson from Phillips Innovations. Remember, he wants a progress report."

"Oh, shit," Seth muttered. "I forgot."

"So did I," Sasha said. "We better go." She looked around the office. "I need to go home and change."

"Change?"

"I can't go like this." Sasha pointed at her jeans, button-down shirt, and Doc Martens. "I need to swing by my apartment and change. We shouldn't show up together, anyway. I'll text you the address of the restaurant and meet you there." She kissed the corner of his mouth, grabbed her hard hat and bag, and slipped out.

---

Sasha checked her makeup and hair in the rearview mirror before she got out of the car and hurried inside. She prayed Mr. Nelson hadn't arrived yet. If he arrived before her, he would stare at her with a disdainful look that made her squirm and fidget like a five-year-old who had to go to the bathroom.

The hostess smiled helpfully when Sasha burst through the door. "May I help you?"

"Yes, table for Baker. Sasha Baker," she said.

The hostess consulted her computer and nodded. "Yes, ma'am. You're the first to arrive. Let me show you to your table, and we'll get you started with some drinks."

Sasha breathed a sigh of relief, then followed the hostess to the back of the restaurant. Taking a seat, she ordered a glass of sweet tea and a beer for Seth. She relaxed, knowing she had arrived before Mr. Nelson. She watched the front door, happy to see Seth come through the door a few minutes later. He waved at her, exchanged pleasantries with the hostess, and walked over to Sasha.

Their server set their drinks on the table as Seth got settled. He reached under the table, squeezed her hand, and gave her his best, most dazzling smile.

"You look a little nervous," he said.

"I am," she said. "Nelson is intimidating. I feel like a little kid when he glares at me. I'm pretty sure he's silently judging me while assuming I'm doing a shitty job." Sasha shrugged. "It's annoying."

"You know you're doing an amazing job, right?" Seth asked. "You're the best architect I've ever worked with. And I've worked with a lot of architects."

Sasha leaned closer to him and lowered her voice. "You're just saying that because we're having sex."

Seth's eyes widened, and he shook his head. "No, I'm not!" He sounded indignant.

"I'm kidding!" Sasha laughed and took a sip of her iced tea. "And thank you. You're very sweet. Could you maybe mention that to Nelson?"

Seth nodded. "Absolutely. I'll do it, even though I shouldn't have to. Stand up to him, Sash. Nelson doesn't have a right to treat you like crap. You got this project going again. He needs to understand that."

Sasha set her drink on the table. "There he is." She cleared her throat. "Showtime."

"Relax, Sash. You got this."

Jerome Nelson made for an opposing figure as he strode across the restaurant, a determined look on his face. He yanked out the chair, sat down, and turned to the hostess.

"Bring me a scotch, neat," he said.

"Your server will be right with you, sir," the hostess said. "She'll take your drink—"

"Scotch neat," Nelson repeated.

"Yes, sir." The young lady scurried away.

Nelson turned his glare on Seth and Sasha. "Mitchell. It's good to see you. I was hoping you would be here so we could discuss some materials being used and their environmental impact."

Seth put a smile on his face and stuck out his hand. "It's good to see you, too, Mr. Nelson. I'm happy to discuss anything with you, but I assure you Sasha can answer all the questions you have."

Nelson grimaced at the mention of Sasha's name as he shook Seth's hand. Then he turned his gaze on Sasha. She reminded herself not to squirm as she smiled at the head of development for Phillips Innovations.

"Mr. Nelson, how are you?"

Nelson snorted. "Give me a good update and I'll be better."

Sasha launched into a rundown of how the construction project was progressing. While she talked, the server arrived with Nelson's drink, which he downed before signaling their server for another.

"Sounds like things are good," Nelson said. "I'm happy to hear it." Not that he sounded like he was happy; he still sounded annoyed. "I was concerned things might not be progressing as we'd hoped. What with the initial setbacks and all."

Seth opened his mouth to defend her, but Sasha put her hand on his arm, stopping him. She had heard enough. She sat up straight, put her shoulders back, and her chin up. "Mr. Nelson, I understand we had a rough start to this project, and that you were extremely unhappy. But things are much better. We're back on schedule and miraculously under budget. Mr. Mitchell has turned things around. I believe your snide, pointed comments are unnecessary."

Nelson sat back, stunned. For the first time since she had met him, a smile spread across his face. "Okay, Ms. Baker, okay. I'm sorry if I've been difficult. I am under a lot of pressure, and I took it out on you."

Sasha nodded. "Apology accepted, Mr. Nelson."

"And for what it's worth, Ms. Baker, I know it wasn't just Mr. Mitchell who turned this project around. You have been invaluable in getting it back on track. Thank you."

"You're welcome," Sasha replied. "Now, why don't we order dinner, and then we can show you this month's expense report? We should also discuss some interior design issues that have come up."

Nelson grabbed the menu. "That sounds like a great idea. I'm starving."

Sasha glanced at Seth out of the corner of her eye, mouthed "thank you," and gave him a grateful smile. Knowing he supported her and thought she was doing a great job gave her the courage to speak up and emboldened her to take charge. After all, she *was* the architect in charge on site, and she wasn't going to let Nelson and his snide comments derail her. This was her project now, and she wanted to make sure everyone knew who was in charge.

# Chapter 26

## SETH

The dinner meeting with Jerome Nelson was a resounding success. Sasha was all smiles as they walked out of the restaurant.

"You were amazing," Seth said. "You really put Nelson in his place."

Sasha laughed. "I did. It felt amazing." She bounced on her toes, vibrating with excitement. "I never stand up for myself, Seth. Never. But I'm tired of Nelson treating me like the problems with this project are my fault. I *had* to say something."

They stopped beside Sasha's car. Seth leaned against it and pulled her into his arms. She wrapped her arms around his neck and looked up at him. "Thank you for coming with me."

Seth snorted. "You didn't need me. I was unnecessary."

Sasha shrugged. "I'm still glad you were here." She rested her forehead against his chest. "Do you want to come back to my place?" she asked in a muffled voice.

"You know what? Chris's place is only ten minutes away. Why don't we go there?"

Sasha's head popped up. "Seriously? Is ... um, is Chris there?"

Seth narrowed his eyes, and his back stiffened. "I don't know. Why?"

"Because I am not ready to run into Chris after having sex with you," Sasha replied. "What's wrong? You went all stiff as soon as I mentioned Chris."

Seth sighed and shook his head. "I'm sorry. I think it was an automatic reaction. Women have used me to get to Chris. When you asked about him, it reminded me of that. I got defensive without even thinking about it."

"Really? I still can't believe there are women who used you to get to Chris. That seems shitty."

"It is really shitty," Seth said. "But I'm best friends with a celebrity. It comes with the territory."

"God, I'm so sorry," Sasha said. "I never realized."

"I've gotten used to it over the years," Seth said. "Even now that he's married, I still get the occasional woman asking me all these questions about Chris, asking when he's going to be around and if they get to meet him." He smiled down at her. "Maybe that's why I like you so much. You don't give a shit about Chris."

Sasha threw her head back and laughed. "Yeah, he's definitely more Sofia's type. And once you meet him, you realize he's just an ordinary guy who is on TV and in movies. Nothing special." She looked up at him, her lower lip caught between her teeth and her eyes wide.

Seth's heart skipped a beat, and his breath caught in his throat. Her finger circled the button of his shirt in the center of his chest.

"I'm not those women, Seth," she whispered.

"No, you're not," he said. "Like I said, that's what I like about you."

"Let's go back to your place," Sasha suggested. "I heard the view from the backyard is amazing."

"It is," Seth said. "It's absolutely amazing." He opened her car door and helped her inside. "Follow me?"

Sasha curled her fingers around the back of his neck and gently kissed him. She nodded. "Lead the way."

---

Seth parked the Land Rover in the driveway and went in the front door. "Hello?" he shouted.

Silence.

"Chris, are you here?" he called again. Still nothing.

In the kitchen, he found a note on the counter from Chris. He and Ollie had gone home to see Sofia and would return on Monday. Seth had the house to himself.

Just as he dropped the note on the counter, he heard a knock on the front door. Seth hurried back down the hallway. He saw Sasha peeking in the side window and waving. He opened the door and let her in.

"This place is off the beaten path, isn't it?" she said.

Chris's house was at the top of a hill in Hollywood, at the end of a long road. It overlooked the city, and Sasha was correct; the view was spectacular.

Seth ushered her inside and took her through the living room to the backyard. "Why don't you make yourself comfortable, and I'll be right back."

Sasha nodded and headed outside. The nights had gotten warmer as spring turned to summer, so they wouldn't need jackets. Seth made a pot of coffee and set a timer on his watch to remind him to come back inside for it in ten minutes. He grabbed a blanket from the end of the sofa and joined Sasha outside.

She found the stereo in the cabinet under the window and turned on a soft rock station. She smiled at Seth when he came out the door.

"I peeked at the view. It's stunning. I would be here all the time if I lived here." She pointed at the pool. "Do you use this a lot?"

"I haven't had much time," Seth replied. "Too busy working. When Chris is here, he does laps every morning. He said it keeps him in shape."

"Is he here?" Sasha asked.

Seth shook his head. "No, he's with Sofia. Gone until Monday." He held up the blanket. "In case you get cold." He tossed it on one of the chaise lounges by the pool.

Sasha grinned. "Guess what I want to do?" she asked.

"I'm almost afraid to ask." Seth laughed.

"Let's go swimming," she said.

"You don't have a suit," Seth said. "I don't think I have one either."

Sasha shrugged, reached back, and unzipped her skirt. She let it fall to her feet and took a step back, leaving the skirt on the ground. She toed off her high-heel shoes as she pulled her blouse over her head and tossed it on top of her skirt. Without breaking eye contact with Seth, Sasha removed her bra and her underwear, grinning as she stood naked in front of Seth.

"I'm getting in the pool." She spun around, her long hair brushing against her naked back, and sauntered to the end of the pool. When she put her foot in the water, a sharp gasp left her, but within seconds, she languidly swam the length of the pool.

Seth couldn't take his eyes off her. Sasha never ceased to amaze him. The Sasha he worked with was not like this. While she was good at her job—better than good—she was always overly cautious, meticulous, and careful to a fault.

Both sides of her appealed to him.

The alarm on his watch interrupted his musings. He shut it off, took the watch off, and set it on a small table between the chaise lounges. Seth stripped off his clothes, though he left his boxers on, then he followed Sasha into the pool.

They played in the pool for almost an hour. They raced the length of the pool, floated side by side holding hands, dunked each other repeatedly, and kissed more times than Seth could count. Seth ached with need, the physical response to swimming with a naked Sasha ever present and demanding attention.

When they climbed out of the water, the temperature had dipped a few degrees. Seth grabbed towels from the cabinet under the stereo and led Sasha to one of the chaise lounges. She sat down, and he sat behind her, straddling the chair. He wrapped her in the gigantic, fluffy towel and dried the water from her skin.

When he was done, he slipped his arms around Sasha's waist. He kissed her neck as his hands roamed over her body. He cupped her breasts and circled the dark pink nipples with his thumbs, then he slid his hands down her stomach and between her legs.

Sasha arched her back and rested her head on Seth's shoulder. He kissed her, their tongues dancing across each other's lips. Seth slipped his fingers inside her and pressed his palm tight against her warm sex. She squirmed, and her legs opened wider. Her ass rose off the chaise lounge, one hand gripped the back of Seth's neck, and the other held tight to his wrist as he buried his fingers deep inside her. Her supple breasts bounced as she fucked herself on Seth's fingers, and her quiet gasps and faint curses filled his ears.

Seth licked her ear and whispered, "Cum for me, baby."

Sasha let go with a loud scream, her body tensing as the orgasm swept over her. Seth's cock, pressed between their bodies, jumped. He wasn't sure how much longer he could hold out.

Once Sasha's orgasm had worked its way through her, she smiled up at Seth, turned around, and pushed him to his back. She worked his wet underwear down his legs and tossed them aside, then she threw a towel on the ground, kneeled beside him, and took his cock in her mouth, swallowing him completely.

Seth groaned, pinched the bridge of his nose, and silently ordered himself not to cum. Sasha wrapped her hand around his shaft, sliding it up and down as she used her mouth on him. She seemed to enjoy it as much as he was; every twitch of her body, every gasp that came from her was an aphrodisiac, sparking a need in him that would have to be fulfilled soon.

Sasha released him and got to her feet. She grabbed his pants and dug through his pockets until she found the condom, then she came back to him. She tossed it to him and waited for him to put it on before she straddled the chaise lounge with her back to him. Seth held her waist and guided her as she lowered herself onto his thick shaft. They both moaned as he filled her. She put her hands on the chaise lounge between his legs and pushed back onto his cock, taking every inch of him.

Seth dug his fingers into her sides and held on tight as Sasha rode him. It was fucking incredible. Allowing her to control everything made the sex better.

Sasha's cries of ecstasy bounced off the surrounding walls, pushing him closer and closer to orgasm. When she pushed back against him one last time, her walls tightening around his cock, he let go with a loud cry.

Sasha collapsed between his legs, resting on her forearms, breathing hard. Seth rubbed her back and marveled at how goddamn fantastic this woman was. She stood and offered him her hand. He took it and climbed to his feet. He disposed of the condom and when he turned around, Sasha had her bra and panties on. Seth went to her side, took her in his arms, and pulled her back onto the chaise lounge. Sasha laid down between his legs and put her head on his chest. Seth covered them with the blanket from the lounger. He kissed the top of Sasha's head, then he closed his eyes.

"I made coffee," he mumbled after a few minutes.

"Mm," Sasha hummed.

Seth chuckled and hugged her close. He didn't want to move either.

# Chapter 27
## SASHA

Sasha hummed quietly to herself. It was a gorgeous morning, overcast and cool. Her shoes swung from her fingers as she tiptoed through the dewy grass outside her apartment building. She wanted to laugh, dance, or maybe sing.

*I'm falling in love.*

It scared the hell out of her, but she couldn't deny it, not anymore. Seth had won her over and proven himself to be the man she wanted in her life.

Last night was perfect—not only the meeting with Jerome Nelson, but dinner, drinks, swimming in the pool, making love, and cuddling on the chaise lounge afterward. She hadn't wanted to leave this morning; she would have gladly stayed the entire weekend if she wasn't supposed to spend the day with her mother.

Sasha squished her toes in the grass and giggled, then checked the time on her phone. It was just after eight a.m., and she was supposed to be at her mother's apartment by ten. She skipped up the sidewalk and around the corner of the building, stopping abruptly and freezing when she saw someone sitting on the ground in front of her apartment door.

Tentatively, she stepped forward until she could see past the stair railing. Leaning against her door, with his eyes closed, was Liam.

Sasha sighed and picked up the pace, hurrying to her door. She gently kicked her ex-husband in the leg until he opened his eyes.

"Hi," he mumbled. "I've been waiting for you."

"Obviously. What are you doing?" she asked.

Liam squinted at her. "I told you. I'm waiting for you."

Sasha rolled her eyes. "I heard you. I want to know *why* you're waiting for me."

"We need to talk," he said.

"I don't have time to talk to you," she snapped. "In less than two hours, I'm meeting my mother. I need to shower and change before I go. Whatever you have to say can wait until tomorrow." She stepped closer. "Can you move away from my door?"

Liam got to his feet with a loud grunt and stepped to the side while she unlocked her apartment door. She stepped inside and turned to shut the door.

"Five minutes, that's all I ask," he said.

"Fine." Sasha left the door open behind her. She dropped her shoes on the floor and purse on the coffee table, then she went into the kitchen and started a pot of coffee.

"Talk, Liam," she said. "You don't have much time."

Liam took a deep breath. "I know about you and the guy from the construction company. What's his name? Mitchell? Yeah, Seth Mitchell."

Sasha dropped the bag of coffee on the counter. Grounds spilled into the sink and onto the floor. She stared at the mess as she spoke. "What do you mean, 'you know about me and the guy from the construction company'?"

"You're sleeping with him, aren't you?"

"I don't think who I am sleeping with is any of your business anymore," she said. She grabbed the dishcloth by the sink, turned on the water, and busied herself cleaning up the mess she'd made. She didn't look at Liam. "Why do you think I'm sleeping with Seth, anyway?"

"I don't think it; I know it. I saw you last night outside of Rudy's. You were all over him." He crossed his arms and stared at her.

Sasha scrubbed the counter and contemplated her next words. That Liam knew she was sleeping with Seth shouldn't make her feel guilty. It wasn't like she was married to Liam anymore.

"I can be all over whoever I want, Liam. Or did you forget we've been divorced for five years?"

"God, Sasha, how could I ever forget? You remind me constantly. But you're always on my mind. I wonder what I could have done to keep us together. I never should have let you go."

Sasha slammed her hand on the counter. "Yeah, well, you did. You messed up, and the price you paid was losing me."

"And I've been busting my ass every day since to win you back."

Sasha snorted. "That is not happening. I've moved on."

"So, you are sleeping with Mitchell," he said.

"I told you it is none of your business," she said through her clenched teeth. She sucked in a deep breath and promised herself she wouldn't kill Liam.

He took a step closer to her and lowered his voice. "It is my business if you're making a mistake."

"I'm not making a mistake!" she shouted loud enough to make Liam jump back. "Jesus, please stay out of my business! Out of my *life*. I'm happy for the first time in ages. Why can't you let me be and stay out of my business?"

Liam shook his head. "I'm trying to protect you, babe. I don't want you doing something you will regret. That New York asshole isn't right for you. He's probably using you until he goes back to New York, you know, somebody to fuck while he's in a strange town. From what I hear, he's got that kind of reputation."

"You don't know what you're talking about," Sasha said. "I like Seth. He's ... he's my friend."

Liam snorted. "I'm sure he is. That's why you were all over him with his tongue down your throat and his hands up your—"

"That's enough," Sasha snapped.

"You know what, I bet your boss would love to know that you're fucking the owner of the construction company," Liam said. "Shit, I can convince her he got the job *because* you're fucking him. I mean, the rumors have already been going around. Maybe I should confirm them. I think your boss would agree with me it's extremely unprofessional."

A startled gasp left her, and her hands shook. "What are you doing, Liam? What are you trying to do?"

"I'm trying to save you from yourself."

Before Sasha could respond, he yanked open the apartment door and walked out, slamming the door behind him.

"Shit!" Sasha threw the dishcloth in the sink and raced after her ex-husband. He was gone when she opened the door and got to the sidewalk.

"Shit, shit, shit," Sasha muttered.

---

"I'm sorry, Mama," she said. "Something came up at work. Something I *have* to take care of today."

"You promised you would visit today," her mother said.

"I know, and I said I'm sorry. If I finish early, I will come by, okay?"

Ophelia was silent. Sasha pulled her phone away from her ear and checked it. Her mother had hung up. Sasha sighed and tossed the phone on the passenger seat. She would not hear the end of that for a while.

Saturday morning traffic was a bitch. Everyone was on the road. Sasha weaved back and forth across the lanes, intent on getting to her destination as quickly as possible.

She had considered trying to find Liam, to convince him not to screw up her life. She didn't know where Liam was headed, but she could find him and convince him not to screw up her life. He wouldn't answer her calls. She decided she would have to head him off.

At the next stoplight, Sasha snatched up her phone and dialed Seth. He picked up on the first ring.

"Hey," he said. "I thought you were spending the day with your mom?"

"Change of plans," she muttered. "Where are you?"

"At the construction site," Seth replied.

"You haven't seen Liam, have you?" she asked.

"Your ex? Why would he come down here?"

Sasha sighed. "It's a long story, one I'll have to explain later. Let me know if you see or hear from Liam."

"Okay. Do you need anything from me?"

Sasha turned into the parking garage and pulled into her parking spot. "No. I'll come down there in a little while and explain everything, I promise." She grabbed her purse and got out of her car. "I'll call you later." After ending the call, she switched off her phone and put it in her purse.

Since it was Saturday, she had no clue if Eleanor was in the office, but she had to try. She had to talk to her boss before Liam got to her.

# CHAPTER 27

The hallways were dark and silent when she stepped off the elevator. She hurried past the reception desk and headed for Eleanor's office. Clara wasn't at her desk, but Eleanor's office door was open, and Sasha could hear music. She dropped her purse on the chair by Clara's desk, took a deep breath, and stepped into Eleanor's office.

"Eleanor?" she asked.

Her boss looked up. "Sasha? What are you doing here? Working on a Saturday?"

"I was wondering if I could talk to you," Sasha said. "It's important."

"Sure," Eleanor said. "Come on in. Have a seat." She gestured to the couch by the wall as she got to her feet. "Would you like a cup of coffee?"

"I would love one. Lots of cream and sugar." Sasha perched on the edge of the couch with her hands folded in her lap.

Eleanor made coffee and placed one cup in front of Sasha before sitting on the other end of the couch. Eleanor was definitely dressed like it was Saturday. She wore jeans and an AC/DC T-shirt, her feet were bare, and her toenails were painted hot pink. It made her seem so normal.

"You look so serious," Eleanor said. "What's on your mind? What happened with Nelson at the meeting last night?"

After everything that had happened in the last two hours, Sasha had completely forgotten about the meeting with Jerome Nelson. She immediately shook her head. "No, no, everything was great. Mr.

Nelson is pleased with how the construction is going and the progress we've made. Next month, he plans to inspect the project personally."

Eleanor sipped her coffee. "That's a relief. Jerome is sometimes difficult to work with. I was worried he wouldn't take you seriously. He often does that with women. When he hired our firm, he wanted all of his meetings with Mr. Skousen. Every time I met with him, he'd ask me, 'Where is Mr. Skousen?' I finally had to tell him Skousen was my ex-husband and no longer a part of the firm. I thought he was going to fire me, but obviously he didn't."

Sasha nodded. "I can see that from him. I had to ask him to cut out the snide comments and take me seriously. He seemed to appreciate me being upfront and honest with him."

Eleanor smiled. "Exactly. He assumes the worst about people, especially women. But once you put him in his place, he gets over it. You did the right thing. You were the perfect fit for this job. Bringing Seth on board was a brilliant idea. He is nothing short of incredible at his job."

"Seth is good at his job," Sasha said. "Actually, that's why I'm here. I need to talk to you about Seth. And me."

Eleanor set her mug on the table. "You and Seth? What about you and Seth?"

Sasha cleared her throat and squeezed her hands together. "I … uh … Seth and I have been seeing each other. I guess you could say we're, um, well, a couple."

"Okay," Eleanor said.

"Um, okay?"

Eleanor leaned forward, the look on her face serious, though not angry or disappointed like Sasha had expected. "Is it affecting your work? Have you done something that would compromise the construction of the Phillips Innovations building or, God forbid, compromise my firm?"

Sasha shook her head, her hair flying around her face. "No, ma'am. Not even a little."

Eleanor picked up her coffee and sat back. "Then we don't have a problem."

"You're not angry with me?" Sasha asked.

"No." Eleanor laughed. "I'm not stupid, Sasha. I know workplace romances happen. As long as you keep it professional at work, then it isn't a problem. As long as you continue doing that, we're good."

"Wow," Sasha said. "This conversation didn't go as I imagined."

"Did you think I would be angry?" Eleanor asked.

"Yes," Sasha answered. "I thought you would be furious."

"Do you know how I met my ex-husband?"

"No, I don't," Sasha said. "You don't talk about him much."

"You're right, I don't. With good reason. Okay, well, I met him at work. We were co-workers at a small architectural firm in San Francisco. After we got engaged, we decided it was time to start our own firm. We named it using my maiden name and our married name. Things were good until my husband crossed professional boundaries at work. Except this time, it wasn't with me; it was with his secretary. That was the end of our story."

"I'm sorry, Eleanor; I didn't know," Sasha said.

Eleanor shrugged. "Eh, what's done is done. It's all in the past, and I'm over it. Long over it." She smiled, reached over, and patted Sasha's arm. "I appreciate you telling me about you and Seth. It was the right thing to do. Seth's a good guy—smart and ambitious. Just like you. You're a great couple."

Sasha released a shaky breath. "Thank you. I'm glad I told you. I feel a million times better."

"Don't be afraid to talk to me," Eleanor said. "What kind of boss would I be if my employees couldn't talk to me?" She got to her feet, picked up their coffee mugs, and went to the coffeepot to refill them. "Now, tell me all about your meeting with Jerome. Especially the part where you told him to cool it with the snide comments. I'm dying to hear about it."

# Chapter 28

## SETH

Seth worried all morning and into the afternoon about Sasha. Her cryptic "I'll explain later" only made him worry more. Fortunately, work kept him occupied for a few hours. After he finished helping the Saturday crew pour the cement for the sidewalks outside the front entrance of the building, he headed for the trailer. Once he cleaned up, he wanted to call Sasha and check on her.

The slam of the office door drew him from the bathroom, where he'd been attempting to scrub the cement off his hands. He peered around the corner and saw Sasha, fired up and ready to fight. She paced back and forth, muttering under her breath.

"What's wrong?" he asked.

Sasha froze, her gaze leveled at him. "It's Liam," she spat.

"I gathered as much from your phone call," Seth said. "What did he do?"

Sasha spun around, her ponytail whipping around and hitting her in the face. "He knows about us. He came to my place and threatened to tell my boss!"

"You're kidding? Why the hell would he do that?"

"He thinks he's protecting me," Sasha said. "Don't ask why because I don't know. I can't explain it."

"What are you going to do?" Seth asked.

"I already did something," Sasha replied. "I got to Eleanor before Liam did."

Now it was Seth's turn to freeze. "What did she say?" Seth asked. "She … she didn't fire you, did she?"

"No, thank God." Sasha sat on the futon, put her elbows on her knees, and her head in her hands. She exhaled before she spoke. "It went well. Eleanor isn't even mad."

"Really? Well, that's good." When Sasha didn't agree with him or respond to him, Seth trudged across the room and sat down beside her. "Isn't it?"

"Don't know," Sasha said. "It makes me angry to think about it. I think I deserve some of that anger directed at me."

Seth raised an eyebrow. "What do you mean?"

She glanced at him out of the corner of her eye, then glanced away. "I never should have put myself in this position," Sasha murmured. "I shouldn't have let myself get involved with you. It was stupid. *I* was stupid."

"Okay, wait a minute. Let's take a breath," Seth said.

Sasha glared at him. "Don't. Don't do that shit. I'm not in the mood for some bullshit 'calm down' lecture from you."

Seth straightened up and put his hands up, surrendering. "That's not what I was going to say. Or do."

Sasha screamed in frustration, cutting him off. "You know what? Forget it. Forget all of it. I knew this was a bad idea. I will not sacrifice my career for you. It's over, Seth. Over. Finish the building and go back to New York. We can say we had fun, but this wasn't what we wanted." Sasha jumped to her feet and headed for the door.

Seth quickly blocked her path to the door. "No, uh-uh, I don't think so. I'm not letting you push me away because you're pissed at Liam."

"This has nothing to do with Liam," Sasha clarified. "This is about you and me."

Seth dragged her close and looked down at her. "This isn't about us. It never has been. Liam has everything to do with this. You two may be divorced, but he has been standing between us every step of the way."

Sasha scowled and shook her head. "That's bullshit."

"No, it isn't. Liam hurt you."

"No, Liam *wrecked* me," Sasha snapped. "He destroyed me. I thought he loved me, but I wasn't as important as his friends, or the parties, or the other women. He threw me away."

"I won't do that," Seth said. "I know you think I'm going to hurt you. Or destroy the career you've worked so hard for. I won't. I would *never*. I am not Liam."

"I know that," Sasha mumbled.

Seth sighed. "I don't think you do, though. You keep pushing me away. We get close, and I think maybe this time we'll be able to move past this 'friends with benefits' thing we're doing, and then you pull back. You won't commit to more because you *are* afraid I will hurt you."

Sasha deflated, a defeated rush of air leaving her. "I can't do it again. I can't bear to go through that much heartache again. I can't be someone's second choice."

Seth pulled her into his arms. "Jesus, Sasha, you are not my second choice. I wish you could see that. You could, if you would let me in. Stop fighting it."

Sasha laughed, though Seth heard the fear and the pain bleeding through. "I don't know if I can. I've been fighting it for so long, I don't know if I can stop."

Seth tucked his finger under her chin and tipped her head back. "You have to want to stop. Tell yourself that you are done, that the pain will not hold you back anymore. It has to be your decision. No one can do it for you. Let Liam go."

Sasha swallowed, and her voice cracked when she spoke. "He won't let me go. He won't leave me alone and let me move on. No matter how hard I try, I can't say no to him when he comes back into my life. I've never been able to tell him no. Why do you think I married him when I was eighteen years old?"

Seth shook his head, confused.

Sasha closed her eyes and rested her head against Seth's chest. Her shoulders shook, and a muffled sob came from her. When she looked up at him, her cheeks were wet with tears.

"My marriage was not because of a drunken weekend, but a deliberate choice. I got pregnant the summer after graduation, so we got married. Three months into the pregnancy, I lost the baby."

"Oh my God, Sasha. I'm so sorry." Seth hugged her tight, his chin resting on the top of her head. "I didn't know."

"Nobody knows, except Sofia. I didn't even tell my mom." Sasha wiped her eyes. "I thought Liam would be there for me, support me, take care of me. Instead, he acted like it never happened and went on living his life, partying and drinking. He never mentioned our child again. It was like the baby never existed. It tore a hole in our marriage, a hole I tried to fill with alcohol." She released a shaky breath. "You know the rest."

Seth couldn't do anything more than gather her into his arms and hold her. He wanted to take away the pain, carry the burden of her past for her so she wouldn't have to, anything to make her whole again. No words could heal the pain of losing her child. He did the only thing he could think of. He hugged her tighter and held her close.

They stood in each other's arms until the sun shifted and the room darkened. The sudden darkness seemed to wake them up, and they broke apart.

Sasha kept hold of Seth's hand. "I need to tell you something," she whispered.

Seth nodded. "Okay."

"Before all of this happened, Liam butting in where he didn't belong, before that, I was … I was on cloud nine. Floating. Happy. Because of you. I want to hold on to that feeling. Forever." She squeezed his hand and stared at the floor between their feet. "You know, it's difficult to admit when you're wrong."

Seth laughed. "No, it isn't. Not for everybody."

"I was wrong about you. I've known I was wrong about you for a while now, but I didn't want to admit it, not even to myself. But I was. I underestimated you. Thank God I figured it out. I don't want this to end. Jesus, I don't even like to think about it ending. I can't bear the thought of you going back to New York."

Seth silenced her with a kiss. When it was over, he held her at arm's length and grinned down at her. "We'll figure that out when the time comes. Because I don't want this to end either."

Seth took a deep breath, and Sasha matched it with one of her own.

"I love you," they both blurted out at the same time.

Seth burst out laughing, and Sasha collapsed against his chest, giggling.

"Wow, it feels good to say that," Sasha said.

"Fantastic," Seth agreed.

"Thank you," Sasha whispered. "For talking me off the ledge." She pushed his hair off his face, where it had fallen over his eyes again.

"I should really get that cut," Seth whispered.

Sasha shook her head. "Don't you dare. I love it."

Seth chuckled. "Anything to make you happy."

"You know what would make me happy? Ask Liam to stay away from me."

Seth grinned. "I will if you want me to. I'll find him and tell him to stay away from you."

"No, no, I was joking." She put her hands on his chest. "Although I would love your help, I need to confront my ex on my own." She took a deep breath. "In fact, I think I need to do it sooner rather than later." She looked around the room. "Where is my phone?"

Seth pointed to her purse on the table. Sasha hurried across the room, took out her phone, and typed a text message. Within seconds, it pinged with a reply.

"He's going to meet me at my apartment."

Seth's heart jumped into his throat. "Are you sure about this?"

Sasha nodded and picked up her purse. "It will be fine."

"I don't know," Seth said, shaking his head. "I'm not comfortable with this."

Sasha stopped in front of him, kissed him on the corner of his mouth, and whispered, "I'll call you when he leaves."

Seth could only watch her go. He clutched his hands at his sides as the door closed behind her. He hated this.

# Chapter 29

## SASHA

Liam leaned against Sasha's door as she approached. He waved and gave her a half-hearted smile.

"Hi," he said.

"Hello," Sasha said. She needed to keep her emotions out of this discussion. The relationship with Liam needed to be put to rest. They both needed to move on.

Liam moved aside for Sasha to unlock the door. Once the door was open, she went inside, but to her surprise, Liam didn't follow her. He waited outside.

Sasha turned to look at him. "What are you doing?"

"Waiting for you to invite me in," he said with a shrug.

Sasha snorted. "Since when?" She made a sweeping gesture. "Come in."

Liam came in and closed the door. "Look, Sasha, I want to apologize for this morning. I flew off the handle, and I was jealous." He stared at the floor and cleared his throat. "Even if you are fooling around with that Mitchell guy, I'm not going to tell your boss."

"I already told her," Sasha said. She dropped her purse on the table and grabbed two bottles of water from the refrigerator.

"You told her?" When Sasha nodded, Liam narrowed his eyes and crossed his arms. "What exactly did you tell her?"

Sasha sighed. She'd known this was coming. Liam needed to hear it from her, or he wouldn't let her go. He could convince himself what he'd seen in the Rudy's parking lot wasn't real, that his eyes deceived him. Unless he heard it from her.

"I told her I was seeing Seth," Sasha explained. "I told her we were a couple."

Liam grimaced. "You are sleeping with him." It wasn't a question.

Sasha rolled her eyes. "There's more to it than sex, Liam. A lot more."

"What does that mean for us?" Liam asked.

"There is no us," she replied. "Why can't you see that?"

"Because it's you and me. It's always been you and me." Liam threw his hands in the air. "Why can't *you* see that?"

"Do you hear yourself? 'You and me' isn't a thing anymore. It hasn't been for a long time." She twisted the lid off the water bottle and took a drink. "It's been you and me since middle school. Sasha and Liam, Liam and Sasha. Everybody said we would end up together, that we would spend the rest of our lives together."

"Yeah, so," Liam snapped. "Why is that a problem?"

Sasha exploded, her voice raised. "Jesus, you don't get it. Everyone has been telling me for thirteen years that you needed me. For thirteen years, I've put you ahead of my wants and needs. I believed in Liam and Sasha. There's been no one else. Our lives are inexplicably intertwined, and I cannot separate them, no matter what I do. You won't let me. Every time I try to move on, you are right there, doing everything you can to keep us together."

"Is that so bad?" Liam interrupted. "I love you, Sasha. I've loved you since we were teenagers. That's something I'm not willing to give up. We're good for each other. We're good together."

A tear slid down Sasha's cheek. "No, we aren't. You can't compare us as teenagers to us as adults. There is no comparison. And after I got pregnant, things changed."

"Things changed because we were too young to have a baby," Liam interjected. "We weren't ready to take on adult responsibilities. Not at eighteen."

"No, *you* weren't ready for adult responsibilities. I was." The tears ran down her face. She didn't bother to wipe them away. They'd been a long time coming and damn it, she was going to let them flow. "I wanted our baby. That baby meant the world to me. I wanted to be a mom, and I wanted you to be the father the baby deserved. I wanted us to be a family. After we got married, I thought the partying and the drinking would stop. I was wrong."

"That's not fair," Liam muttered. "You never gave me a chance. Things changed after we lost the baby. You stopped trying."

Sasha put her hands over her face and screamed into them. "Jesus Christ. I tried for four years. Four years, Liam. You did nothing. You didn't help me heal, you didn't console me, you didn't do what a husband should do after his wife has a miscarriage. I grieved on my own."

"I was grieving, too!"

Sasha nodded. "I know. But instead of grieving together, supporting each other, and taking care of each other, we let the grief tear us apart. I turned to alcohol, and you pretended everything was great. You ignored our fights, the irritation building between us, and the inability to communicate. You spent all of your time partying, drinking, and cheating. I was a mess, and you were a mess, and being together was making things worse. After my father died, I realized I couldn't stay with someone as selfish as you. I left for a better life." She put her head in her hands. "And you let me go."

"I didn't know what to do," Liam whispered. "God, baby, don't you know I regret all the shit I pulled when we were married? I have apologized for everything. I don't know what else to say to you other than I love you. Please, give me another chance."

She shook her head. "No, it's too late. Don't you get it? You don't love *me*; you love the Sasha I was in high school. The girl who thought you were the sun and everything revolved around you. I'm not that girl anymore. I haven't been that girl in a long time." Sasha exhaled. "We need to move on, Liam. Both of us. You need to quit hanging onto the girl you loved in high school, and I need to stop hoping you'll change."

Liam sighed. "I don't think I can be Liam without Sasha."

Sasha laughed gently. "You'll figure it out. We both will. We have been divorced for five years."

"I always thought we'd get back together," Liam said.

"You *hoped* we'd get back together," Sasha clarified. "Don't you think it's time to accept that our relationship is over? Don't you think it's time to move on?"

Liam grimaced. "You mean like you've moved on with that jerk from the construction company?"

Sasha closed her eyes. "I will not fight with you, Liam. Seth is not a jerk. He's a good guy. This is going to sound cliché, but if you love me, if you want me to be happy, you'll let me go. Let me move on and love someone else. You need to do the same. Find someone who loves you. Because even though I love you, it's not the love a woman has for her husband. You deserve to find someone who loves you like that. That's not me."

"Jesus, crush my heart, why don't you?" Liam had a smile on his face, but his voice cracked, and the smile didn't reach his eyes.

"I'm not trying to hurt you," Sasha said. "That's not what I want. But I won't lie to you. I won't give you false hope. I should have done this a long time ago, except I … well, I couldn't tell you no. Letting go of the past was hard for me, too. I'm sorry."

Liam sighed, and his shoulders slumped. "I'm sorry, too." He cleared his throat and pointed at the door. "I'm, uh, gonna go."

Sasha nodded. "That's probably a good idea."

Liam paused at the door and turned back. "I'm going to miss you."

"I know." Sasha smiled. "You'll be okay. We both will."

Once the door closed behind Liam, Sasha let the tears fall. It hurt, even though it was what they both needed. Liam had been in her life for thirteen years; they'd gone through hell and back. After five years, it was clear she needed to move on. She couldn't take anymore of Liam borrowing money from her, begging her to take him back, then pushing her away, then magically appearing again. This would be good for both of them.

Her phone vibrated from her purse, an insistent, steady vibration, which meant it was a phone call, not a text message. Sasha took it out of her purse and saw that it was Seth.

"Hi," she answered.

"Are you okay?" Seth asked.

"Yeah, yeah, I'm good," she replied. "It was difficult, but it needed to be done. For both of us." She sighed. "I should probably go see my mother. I upset her this morning, and I've been ignoring her phone calls."

"Sasha, I have to go to New York," Seth said.

"What? What do you mean, 'go to New York'?"

"My lead foreman, Romeo, called," Seth explained. "The building inspector refused to do the last inspection unless I am there. I'm flying out tomorrow morning."

Sasha dropped to the couch, the air leaving her. "Shit," she muttered.

"Yeah, I know. Shit." He exhaled. "This is terrible timing, given everything that happened today. But I have to go. This is my business."

"No, no, I understand," Sasha said. "I wouldn't stop you from going. I just wanted to be with you." She closed her eyes and took a deep breath. "How long will you be gone?"

"At most, maybe four days," he said.

"Okay, that's not too long."

"Wyatt will run the site while I'm gone," Seth continued. "I'm only a phone call away if you need anything."

Sasha sat up straight. "We should be fine. Wyatt knows what he's doing. He can run the site, no problem."

"I know that, Sasha," Seth whispered. "I meant if *you* need anything. You should come to the house and stay the night."

"Why? Do you need a ride to the airport?" she teased.

"Yep." He laughed, then he dropped his voice to a loud, husky whisper. "Come to the house, Sasha. We'll eat dinner, swim in the pool, and make love. I want to see you before I leave."

Sasha's insides melted. How was she supposed to resist that?

"Let me throw some stuff in a bag," she said. "I'll be there in less than an hour."

---

Sasha propped the phone against a pillow and lay down beside it. She pushed her hair off her face and smiled at the screen.

Seth laughed. "You're sideways."

"I'm tired," Sasha mumbled. "Aren't you? Isn't it midnight in New York?"

"I'm on California time," Seth said. "Long day?"

"Yeah," Sasha whispered. "I was at the site early this morning, then I had a meeting with Mr. and Mrs. Kittridge about the plans for their house. It didn't go well. Mrs. Kittridge has very specific ideas and apparently, none of the boxes were ticked."

"That bad, huh?" Seth's face disappeared, and when he reappeared, he was sideways. "Tell me about it."

Sasha gave him a rundown of the meeting and all of her failings in it. It was good to get it off her chest.

"It's back to the drawing board, literally," she said. "I'm abandoning Eddie's plans and starting from scratch. I'm going to do the plans my way, with Mrs. Kittridge's specifications."

"I'm sure it will be perfect," Seth said. "I can't imagine you doing anything less for her."

"I hope you're right. Hey, tell me about your dream house," Sasha said. "If you could design it however you wanted, what would you do?"

Seth rolled to his back, his phone in his hand, held above his head. He took a moment before he spoke, then he launched into a vivid description of the type of home he would build.

Sasha closed her eyes and listened. Seth's descriptions were so perfect, so on point, she could picture the home coming together in her head. As he talked, she imagined every nook and cranny, every amenity down to the last detail. When he stopped talking, she opened her eyes and smiled at him.

"That's sounds perfect."

"Maybe someday we'll build it," he murmured. He put his hand over his mouth and stifled a yawn. "I need to get some sleep. I'm scheduled to meet Genevieve at the Encryption building tomorrow morning before heading to the airport."

"It feels like you've been gone forever," Sasha said.

"It's only been a week. Tomorrow night I'll be home, and I'll see you on Monday morning. I love you."

"I love you, too."

Sasha waved to him as she hit the end button. The wheels in her brain spun, so she climbed out of bed and grabbed a pad of graph paper. If she didn't get it down on paper and out of her head, she wouldn't be able to sleep.

She finished the last drawing and turned off the light at three a.m.

*Maybe someday we'll build it.*

# Chapter 30

## SETH

Seth took a deep breath and inhaled the smell of New York streets—exhaust, hot dogs, pretzels, a million different perfumes and colognes, and the underlying scent of body odor. He sighed as he pushed through the front door of the completed Encryption building. He missed Los Angeles.

Who was he kidding? He missed Sasha. This trip couldn't have come at a worse time, not when he had admitted his love for Sasha and she for him. Walking away from her now felt like running away. Fortunately for him, Sasha understood. In fact, she told him several times he was being stupid.

They'd talked every morning, FaceTimed every night, and texted off and on throughout the day. Seth was eager to get back to her, so he could figure out how she fit into his life. He didn't care what he had to do. Sasha Baker was going to be in his life.

Genevieve Layton stood in the empty lobby of her building, staring straight up at the modern marvel of glass and steel Seth had constructed. He couldn't take all the credit; Genevieve had hired a talented architect to design her building, and her vision was phenomenal.

Seth was clueless about why he was here. The inspection went well, and Seth was ready to catch a flight to L.A. He'd already spoken to Genevieve on the phone, filled her in on everything the building inspector had said, and thanked her for the opportunity to construct her building. Then, early this morning, he'd gotten a call from her assistant asking if he would meet Genevieve at the Encryption Building. He'd agreed.

"Ms. Layton," Seth said as he approached.

The Encryption CEO looked at him. "How many times have I asked you to call me Genevieve?" she asked.

"Several," Seth joked.

"How was California?" she asked.

"Warm," Seth replied.

Genevieve rolled her eyes. "Too warm. I prefer New York." She inched closer. "Thank you for meeting me. I have about thirty minutes before the interior design team arrives. I wanted to talk to you."

"What can I do for you?" he asked.

"Let me start by saying I cannot tell you how impressed I am with you. I thought no one could build my dream, but you did it." She touched his arm. "I owe you."

Suddenly uncomfortable, Seth took a step back. "I think those checks you wrote my company more than paid me what I'm owed." He cleared his throat. "As I explained on the phone, the inspection went well, and my work here is done. I found a landscape company to do the courtyard for you. If any issues come up, contact us. We can address any potential problems. I don't expect any, though."

Genevieve turned in a slow circle, her arms spread wide. "It's perfect. How could there be any problems?" She stopped and smiled at Seth. "Can I take you to dinner?" she asked. "As a thank you."

Seth shook his head. "I have to get back to California. I'm in the middle of a build."

Genevieve sighed. "Okay, Seth, look, I'm done dancing around this. I'm attracted to you. I've been attracted to you for a while, but you worked for me, and I wasn't willing to cross that boundary. Now that you're no longer employed by my company, I would love to spend more time with you. Join me for dinner, and let's see where it leads us."

Seth laughed and shook his head. "I appreciate the offer, Genevieve, but I have a girlfriend. Her name is Sasha." Saying "girlfriend" felt weird, but Seth loved the way it sounded when he referred to Sasha.

"Really? Somebody locked you down?" Genevieve grinned. "Lucky woman."

"I'm the lucky one," Seth mused.

"Tell me about her," Genevieve coaxed.

Seth told her about Sasha, though he didn't tell her she was the architect on his current build. It wasn't any of Genevieve's business. They chatted until the interior design team arrived with color swatches and catalogs filled with furniture, window coverings, and carpet samples. Seth promised to stay in touch, then he excused himself.

He was eager to go back to California. He missed Sasha.

---

It was still dark when Seth arrived at the Phillips Innovations site. He sat in the Land Rover, watching the sun come up on the east side of the building. He couldn't believe this was the same building he had agreed to finish four months ago. It was close to completion, no longer a skeleton in the sky.

The realization that the build was almost done was unsettling. When it was done, he was supposed to go back to New York, back to his life there while Wyatt ran the West Coast side of his business. That was the plan all along.

Until Sasha came into his life.

How was he supposed to leave her? He'd hated being away from her for a week. There was no way he could live on the other side of the country. Except his business, his life, were all in New York, waiting for him to return. He could never ask Sasha to give up everything she worked for and go to New York with him. He couldn't do that to her. It wouldn't be fair.

Seth scrubbed a hand over his face. Life seemed complicated. Love and money, money and love. The world's two driving forces caused his biggest headache. Choose one and you lose the other.

He gripped the steering wheel, and, for the briefest moment, he considered driving away, leaving all the complications behind. But then he blinked, and he could see Sasha's face behind his eyelids, hear her laughter ringing in his ears. He couldn't do that to her. He *wouldn't* do that to her. He needed to take charge of his life and make a decision.

Seth dragged in a deep breath. He knew what he had to do. It wouldn't be easy, and people might hate him afterward, but it was what he needed to do.

He shoved open the car door, grabbed his things, and crossed the lot to the office. With one hand, he balanced everything, unlocked the door, and turned on the light. A broad smile lit up his face when he saw Wyatt had kept the office clean while he was away. He left his stuff on the table and headed back to the Land Rover. A dozen boxes of donuts were in the back seat. He took everything inside, and by the time he had the donuts laid out and the coffee set up, the crew arrived.

After forty minutes, everyone finished the boxes of donuts, drank all the coffee, and Sasha still hadn't arrived. Seth sat at his desk, eating a glazed donut, sipping coffee, and watching the door. It opened, and Wyatt came in. He dropped into a chair across from Seth and crossed his arms.

"What?" Seth mumbled with a donut in his mouth.

"How was New York?"

"Dirty," Seth replied. "Why?"

Wyatt shrugged. "Just curious." He checked his watch. "Have you heard from Sasha? She's usually here by now."

Seth shook his head. "Maybe she's running late."

"When are you going to tell me?" Wyatt asked.

Seth dropped his donut. "Tell you *what*?" He brushed the crumbs off his desk.

Wyatt grinned. "That you and Sasha are dating."

Before Seth could answer, Sasha came through the door, a cup of coffee in each hand and a white plastic bag hanging from her forearm. Seth jumped out of his seat, darted across the room, and took her into his arms.

Sasha giggled, her arms spread wide, holding the coffee away from their bodies. Seth kissed her, then he released her and plucked the cup from her hand.

"Hi," she whispered.

"Hey, babe." Seth turned to Wyatt. "Yes, we're dating."

Wyatt chuckled. "I knew it." He took his clipboard off the table and hurried to the door. He opened it and yelled, "I was right!"

The door slammed closed behind him, and Seth could hear Wyatt yelling and the crew cheering and hollering. Seth shook his head and chuckled.

Sasha stared at him, her eyes wide and her mouth open. "Did you … did you just tell *everybody* we are together?"

Seth nodded. "You bet your ass I did. Well, technically, I told Wyatt, and *he* told everybody. I don't care.

I'm not keeping it quiet anymore." He took her coffee out of her hand, set it on the table, and pulled her into his arms. "I might climb to the top of the building and hang out a giant banner."

Sasha shook her head. "You're crazy, you know that, right?"

"Eh, maybe a little." He kissed her forehead, then he let her go. "Shit, I should have asked you first. I'm sorry."

"No, no, it's okay," Sasha said. "It's actually a relief. I didn't want to keep it quiet anymore. Now, there's no need for me to do it."

"Oh, thank God," Seth said. "I'm not so good at this relationship stuff yet."

Sasha grabbed his hand and held it tight. "You'll figure it out. We both will." She kissed the corner of his mouth, then she pointed over her shoulder. "Should we go out there and make sure Wyatt's not painting 'Seth hearts Sasha' on the building in spray paint?"

Seth laughed. "Yeah, probably." He took Sasha's hand, holding it tight. "Let's go."

# Chapter 31

## SASHA

Seth stood beside the Land Rover, hand on the door, eyes on Sasha. He let out a low whistle.

"You look amazing, baby," he said. "Absolutely stunning."

Sasha smiled and looked down. She felt amazing in a red, backless, calf-length dress and red high heels. It was the most money she'd ever spent on clothes, and she felt like a celebrity in it. The look on Seth's face made it worthwhile.

Seth opened the door and helped her inside. He kissed her cheek before he shut the door and jogged around the front of the Land Rover.

Once he was in the car, she poked his arm. "You look pretty damn good yourself, Mr. Mitchell."

Seth wore a navy blue, pinstriped suit, purple shirt, and a dark purple tie. He adjusted his tie and winked at her.

"Did you talk to Chris? Are he and Sofia okay to pick up my mom?" Sasha asked.

Seth grimaced. "Yeah, they're on their way there right now."

"What's wrong?" she asked. "You look like you swallowed a bug or something."

Seth snorted. "I'm kind of freaked out about meeting your mom. I'm not sure I can do it."

"Do what? Meet my mom?" Sasha rolled her eyes. "Please, my mother is harmless."

"You don't understand. I have never met the parents of a woman I was dating. Not once."

Sasha turned to stare at him. "Never?"

"I've never dated anyone long enough to meet her parents." Seth shrugged. "I always left the relationship before meeting the parents."

"So, my mother will be the first time you've met a woman's parents?" Sasha snorted, then burst into uncontrollable laughter. "Oh my God, you are in for a treat." She laughed so hard tears formed in her eyes. She took a tissue from her purse and dabbed the corner of each eye, praying she didn't mess up her makeup.

"Sasha, this isn't funny," he scolded. "I'm a nervous wreck. What if she doesn't like me?"

Sasha wiped her eyes and took a deep breath. She reached over and took Seth's hand and held it tight.

"My mother is going to love you. I promise. How could she not? I do."

"You're sweet," Seth muttered, "but that doesn't make me feel any better."

"It will be fine," Sasha reassured him. "Besides, you'll be too busy schmoozing all the Phillips Innovations bigwigs and making connections to worry about me or my mom."

Seth chuckled. "Schmoozing, huh?"

"Yes, schmoozing. I feel like you're probably superb at it, too."

"Oh, I am," Seth agreed. "How do you think I won Mrs. Kittridge over?"

"With that charming personality," Sasha said.

"Exactly."

Lola Kittridge met Seth at McDonald and Skousen late one afternoon when she was leaving the office after yet another meeting with Sasha. While Seth waited to take Sasha to dinner, he struck up a conversation with Lola's husband, Rick. Rick introduced Seth to Lola and the next thing Sasha knew, they hired Mitchell Construction's West Coast Division to build their home. After meeting Seth, Lola suddenly became a dream client. Everything Sasha showed her was "perfect," and everything Sasha did was "to die for." Seth swore he didn't say anything to Lola. He claimed it was all Sasha.

"Are you ready?" Seth asked. "You have a big night ahead of you."

Sasha shrugged. "I didn't do anything."

"Do not say that," Seth scolded. "Without you, the building would still be under construction. You stepped in and got it done. Don't discredit your contribution."

Sasha opened her mouth to argue, but Seth shot her a dirty look, so she snapped it shut. One thing she loved about him was how he never let her talk down about herself. If she did, he shut it down immediately. He encouraged her to be proud of her accomplishments, big and small. His support lifted her in ways she'd never thought possible.

Why did he have to leave her?

Sasha bit her tongue and refused to think about it. Seth had to go home to New York, back to his business. Wyatt would run the West Coast business, and Seth would visit when he could. They hadn't talked much about him leaving; it was a sore subject for both of them.

Seth parked in the newly paved parking lot in front of the Phillips Innovations building. Lights shined from every corner of the lobby and the front entrance. Cars filled the lot. They spared no expense in celebrating the project completion.

Seth took Sasha's arm and held her close as they walked inside. Sasha had to laugh as they entered the lobby; it was completely furnished and looked like the building was going to open tomorrow. She knew that everything above the lobby was empty. Anybody who walked in here would think the building would open tomorrow.

Eleanor spotted them as soon as they came in. She descended on them, took Sasha's arm, and whisked her away. Sasha waved at Seth as he headed for the bar.

"Mr. Phillips, I want you to meet Sasha Baker," Eleanor said to an older gentleman in his late fifties. "Sasha was integral in getting your building done on time."

Phillips shook her hand and spent the next five minutes gushing over what a wonderful job she had done on his building. She stood there and smiled.

Out of the corner of her eye, she saw Chris and Sofia come in with her mother. Ophelia looked starstruck, staring up at Chris as he escorted her inside. Sofia walked behind them with a knowing smile on her face.

"Will you excuse me, Mr. Phillips?" Sasha said. "My mother is here."

"Certainly, Ms. Baker." Phillips shook her hand. "I'll catch up with you later."

Sasha hurried across the room, meeting Seth halfway there. He kissed the back of her hand and smiled.

"Ready?" she asked.

"Ready," he said.

"Mama," Sasha kissed her mother on the cheek, then she hugged Sofia and Chris.

"You look beautiful, Sashie Bug," Ophelia said.

Sofia cringed, Chris bit his lip, and Seth snorted, then covered it by pretending to cough.

Sasha laughed, because honestly, it was all she could do. She took her mother's hand and led her to Seth.

"Mama, this is Seth," Sasha said.

Ophelia took a step back, eyeing Seth up and down with narrowed eyes and pursed lips. After a few seconds, she nodded once and held out her hand. "It's nice to meet you, young man. Sasha tells me some wonderful things about you."

Seth took her hand in both of his and squeezed it gently. "Thank you, Mrs. Drakos," Seth said. "It's so nice to meet you."

While Seth and Chris chatted with her mother, Sofia pulled her aside and handed her a cardboard roll.

"What is this thing, anyway?" she asked.

Sasha held it tight and smiled at Sofia. "It's a gift for Seth. Thanks for sneaking it in for me."

Sofia plucked it out of her hand. "I'm going to put it behind the reception desk over there."

"Thank you," Sasha whispered.

Wyatt appeared out of nowhere. "Sorry for interrupting, but Ms. McDonald is getting ready to say a few words. Seth, she'd like you and Sasha to join her."

They excused themselves, then they followed Wyatt to the other side of the room, where Eleanor stood with Mr. Phillips and Jerome Nelson. Seth and Sasha joined them and turned to face the crowd.

"I want to thank everyone for coming tonight," Eleanor said. "It thrilled me to be given the opportunity to work with Phillips Innovations to build their new home in Southern California. I *did* have that brief period of anxiety."

The crowd laughed, and Eleanor smiled. "Sasha Baker, an up-and-coming architect in my firm, and

Mitchell Construction completed the building on time and according to Mr. Phillips' specifications."

"Actually, it's better," Mr. Phillips piped up.

Another laugh from the crowd.

"Thank you again for joining us to celebrate the completion of this project. I can't wait to see where the future takes us." Eleanor raised her hands. "Have fun, everyone!"

Sasha was relieved Eleanor hadn't asked her to speak. She wasn't prepared for that. She stayed at the back of the group, accepting congratulations, shaking hands, and smiling her best smile.

An hour into the party, Sofia found her, took her by the arm, and whispered, "I need to talk to you."

They separated themselves from the crowd and found a quiet corner to talk. Sasha leaned against the wall with a sigh and looked at her friend.

"What's wrong?" Sofia asked.

"I don't know what you mean," Sasha replied.

Sofia crossed her arms and leveled her gaze at her best friend. "You're happy, but not *really* happy. It's like something is holding you back."

Sasha sighed and lowered her voice. "I can't be completely happy knowing Seth is leaving in a few days. The project is done, Sof. He has no reason to stay."

Sofia put a hand on her arm. "He has you."

Sasha's throat tightened, and it took her a minute to answer. "I can't ask him to stay," she whispered. "I can't ask him to give up his business for me. He wouldn't ask me to give up my career for him."

Sofia pulled her into a hug. "If you guys really love each other, you'll figure out a way to make it work."

"I know." Sasha sniffed. "You know what? I'd rather not think about it. Let's go have fun. You rarely leave the mountains, so this is a big deal. There aren't any paparazzi here to bother you."

They had fun. They ate, they drank, and they danced. Seth, Chris, and Wyatt took turns dancing with Ophelia; Jerome Nelson even danced with her. Ophelia was the life of the party. At least until ten, when she complained about her sore feet and how it was past her bedtime. By eleven, she was half-asleep at the table, her chin on her chest, her hands folded in her lap.

"We need to take my mom home," Sasha said.

"We'll take her," Chris volunteered.

Sasha shook her head. "You don't have to do that. Seth and I can take her."

"No, no, we got her," Sofia interjected. "We'll take her home. You stay here and have fun."

Sasha protested, but no one would listen to her. Instead, Sofia woke up Ophelia and helped her to her feet, while Chris excused himself to get the car. Sofia kissed Sasha on the cheek and assured her they would get her mother home safely.

"You stay here and talk to Seth," Sofia said. "Figure out what you're going to do."

Sasha walked Sofia and her mother outside, then waited while Chris helped everyone into the car. Chris kissed her cheek and gave her a one-armed hug while Sofia waved out the window, and Ophelia blew kisses at her.

Sasha found the cardboard roll behind the reception desk and went to look for Seth. She found him standing alone, watching the crowd.

"Hey," she said. "Do you mind if we talk in the courtyard?"

Seth nodded. "Sure." They went out the side door to the courtyard. Sasha led him to one of the concrete benches with a light pole beside it, and they took a seat.

"What's up?" he asked.

Sasha handed him the cardboard roll. "This is for you."

Seth opened it and slid out the roll of papers. He unrolled it and spread it across the bench between them. His eyes roamed over it, a smile dancing at the corner of his lips.

He glanced up at Sasha. "What is this?"

"It's the blueprints for the dream house you described to me," she replied. "On the phone, when you were in New York. I asked you what your perfect house would look like." She gestured at the blueprints. "Then, I drew it."

"Oh my God, Sash, these are amazing," Seth murmured. "I freaking love it. God, it's … it's perfect." A loud guffaw left him. "I really want to build this now, you know?"

Sasha grinned, but her heart broke.

"I have a gift for you, too," Seth said. He reached into his pocket, pulled out a small box, and handed it to her. "Open it."

Sasha glanced up at him through her lashes. God, she hoped it wasn't a ring. She loved Seth, but they had only been serious for a few months. She wasn't ready for a proposal. Not yet. She took a deep breath and opened the box.

Inside was a silver key.

"It's a key," Sasha said. "But, um, what is it for?"

Seth sat up straighter, his shoulders back, and a delighted grin on his face. "I bought a house. That's your key."

"What? You ... you bought a house? When? Where?"

Seth laughed. "Close to Chris's place in the hills. It's not as big as Chris's, but it's nice. Really nice. I signed the paperwork this afternoon."

Sasha exhaled. "Wait? Does this mean you're *not* going back to New York?"

"I'm staying here," Seth said. "I'll have to visit New York occasionally for business, but I have a lot of work here to do. Besides, the woman I love lives in California. How can I go back to New York when she's here?"

"I ... I don't know what to say," Sasha whispered. "I can't believe this is happening."

"Believe it, baby." He leaned over, careful not to wrinkle the blueprints, and stared into Sasha's eyes. "I want to be where you are."

Sasha stared up at the magnificent building she and Seth had built. It was a testament to her determination and everything she had to overcome to get to where she was in her life.

"You know what you did here is nothing short of extraordinary," Seth whispered.

"It wouldn't have happened without you," Sasha said. "You bailed me out when you didn't have to. Without your support and your dedication to finishing this project, it never would have happened."

"Taking on this project was the best thing that ever happened to me," Seth said. "I can't wait for our next project."

"It's scary, though, moving on to the next project. I've devoted so much of my life to this one and so much has changed since we started. It feels like I'm deserting it." She sighed and shook her head. "That sounds silly, I know."

Seth rolled up the blueprints and set them aside, then he slid across the bench and took Sasha into his arms.

"It's not silly," he said. "It is scary. But we'll take on this new future together. You and me."

"You and me." She took a deep breath. "And a cat. Let's get a cat."

Seth laughed. "I'm more of a dog person."

"It has to be a small dog," Sasha insisted.

"We'll talk about it. Now, will you shut up and kiss me?"

"Absolutely, Mr. Mitchell."

*The End*

# Book Club Questions

1. How does the author use the professions of architecture and construction work to set the backdrop for the romance between Sasha and Seth? In what ways does their work influence their relationship and character development throughout the story?

2. Explore the theme of personal growth and overcoming past heartbreaks. How do Sasha and Seth evolve as characters throughout the story, and how does their growth influence their budding romance?

3. Seth initially has a reputation as a partying ladies' man. How does this initial perception contrast with his true character and aspirations? Discuss the theme of appearances versus reality in the book.

4. Love and trust are central themes in the book. Explore how Sasha's past experiences with love and trust shape her approach to her relationship with Seth. How does Seth's history also impact his ability to trust and love?

5. Discuss the significance of the project that Sasha challenges Seth to take over. How does this project symbolize the challenges and growth of their relationship? What role does it play in the overall storyline?

6. How does the book depict the importance of friendship in the lives of Sasha and Seth? Discuss the impact of their friends on their decisions and actions, especially concerning their romantic relationship.

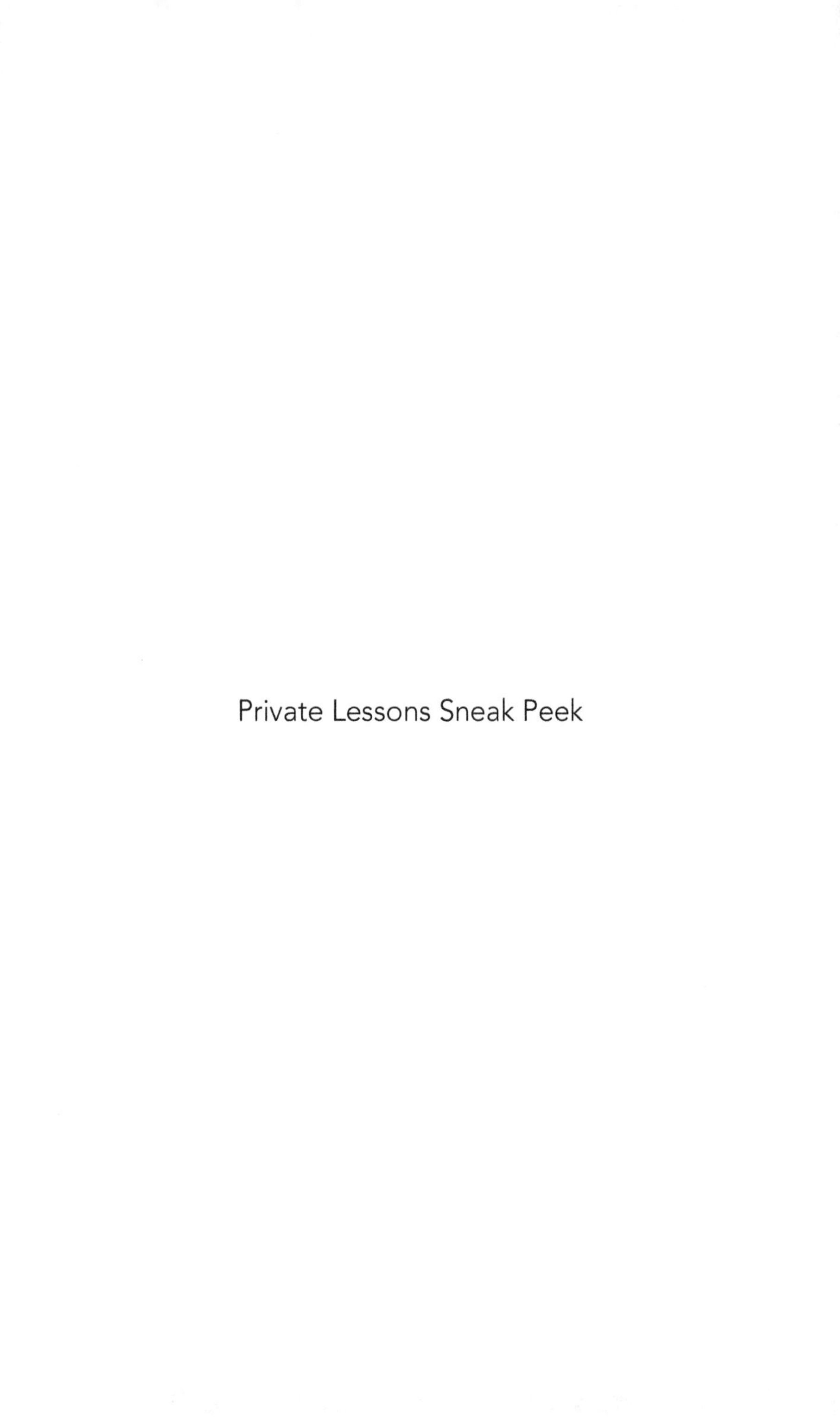

Private Lessons Sneak Peek

# Chapter 1

## WREN

Wren checked her watch as she rushed up the stairs. She only had an hour before she had to be back at the studio. Hopefully, her meeting with the owner of Primetime Security wouldn't take long. She worried about Maverick when she wasn't with him.

The Primetime Security offices were on the fifteenth floor. Wren didn't expect to step off the elevator into a tastefully decorated office with a pleasant young man at the front desk. Her research told her a group of ex-military men ran the company, which was why she chose Primetime Security. She'd expected bright lights, steel, and sharp corners.

Two minutes after she checked in, a distinguished older gentleman emerged from a long hallway and strode toward her. He extended his hand with a smile.

"Ms. Hansley? I'm David Westfield, the owner of Primetime Security. It's a pleasure to meet you."

Wren shook his head. "Thank you for seeing me on such short notice, Mr. Westfield."

"David, please." He led her down the hall to a spacious office and gestured for her to take a seat. He perched on the edge of the desk and smiled down at her. "How can we help you?"

"My son is Maverick Steele." When David didn't so much as blink, Wren continued. "He is the star of the children's program, *Junior Agents Unleashed*."

At this, David nodded.

"The show has become extremely popular in the last year, so popular that Maverick can't go anywhere without being recognized. At first, it was people waving at him or asking for the occasional autograph or picture, but now..." She trailed off.

"Let me guess," David said. "Now he can't leave the house without being accosted at every turn. People crowding him, trying to get his attention, pushing, shoving. Am I right?"

Wren nodded. "Yes. I reached my limit last week. Maverick takes weekly golf lessons. He loves the game and wants to improve his skills. But the last time we were there, a crowd of people gathered outside the clubhouse and ... how do I say this without sounding like a paranoid mother? They surrounded us, pushing and shoving, desperate to touch Mav, talk to him, or take his picture. We couldn't even walk to my car. It was chaos. Maverick tripped over something or someone because he couldn't walk, fell, and cut up his hands and knees. When we got home, I called the studio, and they provided temporary security, but I want something more permanent. Around the clock. The studio recommended you. You've worked with them before?"

"We have, frequently." David got up and sat down behind his desk. "I think I have someone who would be perfect for the job." He tapped a few keys on the keyboard and nodded to himself. "Let me explain how this works. We provide you with a team of bodyguards. You will have a lead bodyguard, and the others will work under him. This gives you one person to communicate with but provides you with the best protection. Your son will have two people with him at all times, one driver and one person who will follow your son around. They will rotate out as needed. Does this sound acceptable?"

"Oh my God, yes. That sounds perfect." Wren smiled. "I can't tell you how relieved I am. I've been so worried. Maverick thinks I'm being ridiculous, but he's thirteen. What does he know?"

"Once I talk to the bodyguard I have in mind, we should be in place by the end of the week." David opened a drawer in the desk and pulled out a folder. "I'm going to send this with you. It's an information packet. You'll need to go on the website, create a log-in, and fill out the new client paperwork." He tapped the folder. "This will help you."

Wren stood up, reached across the desk, and shook David's hand. "Thank you. I look forward to hearing from you. If you'll excuse me, I do have to get back to Maverick." She grabbed the folder and left.

Wren didn't allow herself to relax until she was in the elevator on her way downstairs. It was hard enough being a single parent, but being the single parent of a child star was even more difficult. Days like today made her miss her husband, Elijah. If he was alive, Maverick wouldn't need a bodyguard.

She looked through the folder as the elevator descended, wondering who they would assign to Maverick. She prayed it wouldn't be some huge, obnoxious, tattooed giant who grunted rather than talked.

Her nose buried in the folder, Wren stepped off the elevator and ran into a solid wall of muscle. She looked up into stormy blue eyes and a scowling face. It was as if he'd been conjured right out of her head. The man was a giant and covered in tattoos. There was something about his face, the jawline, and the eyes that seemed familiar.

Wren muttered, "Sorry," scooted around him, and raced to the door. She couldn't help but wonder if he worked for Primetime Security. With his size, he had to be a bodyguard.

"Please, not him," she said to herself. "He's too scary."

---

Maverick was with the other children in the studio classroom when she got back to the set. She grabbed some water and a pastry from the craft table while she waited for them to finish. Half an hour later, she heard Maverick's "Hi, Mom," behind her. Wren tucked her phone in her back pocket as she stood. She gave her son a one-armed hug, which he tolerated for three seconds before he stepped away.

"Where did you go?" he asked.

"I had a meeting," she explained. "I hired a security company."

Maverick rolled his eyes. He had only been thirteen for two months, and Wren was already tired of the teenage attitude. Affection from his mother was out of the question. Everything about her annoyed him. Her music sucked, her choice in movies and TV sucked, her ideas sucked, *she* sucked. She missed the sweet, little boy who thought his mother was everything.

Wren took a deep breath and lowered her voice. "Do *not* roll your eyes at me, young man," she chastised. "We discussed this. It's done."

"It's stupid," Maverick muttered. "Everyone is going to think I'm a baby because I need some jerk bodyguard babysitting me. It's not a big deal, Mom. It's my fans, fans of the show. They want to say hi. So what? I don't need someone to keep them away. They'll think I don't like them or something."

"No, they won't," Wren countered. "They'll understand it is for your safety. You could have gotten hurt last week. I can't have that happening."

Maverick crossed his arms and leaned against the wall. "Fine. Whatever."

Wren was about to get after him again, remind him who was speaking to, but the director's assistant arrived to take him to set. He grinned at his mother as he walked away.

Wren clutched her hands at her side and promised herself she wouldn't scream. She loved her son, but he drove her crazy.

With nothing to do but wait, Wren headed to Maverick's trailer. Inside, she pulled out her laptop and set to work. For three years, she had run a successful consulting company that helped parents navigate the ins and outs of Hollywood stardom for their children. She helped them find quality agents and managers; she showed them how to set up trusts; she helped them arrange for voice, singing, and dance lessons. The things she had to figure out on her own when Maverick first started acting.

People didn't always understand why she worked. After all, her son made a lot of money working on *Junior Agents Unleashed*, especially now that it had become so popular, and he had emerged as the main character. But Wren refused to rely on her son's income to sustain them like other parents did. Aside from necessities like this trailer, tutoring, and, now, a bodyguard, she put Maverick's money in a trust for use when he was older.

Wren answered emails and posted to her blog, a brief post highlighting her son's need for a bodyguard and the steps she took to make it happen. She did not name the company—she wanted David's permission first—though she dropped a few hints. She concluded the post with a description of the man in the elevator and her hopes that not all bodyguards looked like him.

After she finished the blog post, Wren navigated to the website for Primetime Security. She spent the next hour filling out their new client paperwork and describing Maverick's day-to-day activities. When it was complete, an email arrived in her inbox, informing her someone would be in touch with her soon. She closed her laptop and rested her head against the back of the chair.

Hiring a bodyguard was the right thing to do, despite her son's irritation. It would be an adjustment for both of them, but it would work out in the end. Everything always did.

# Chapter 2

## RYLAN

Rylan always got the shitty jobs.

Guarding a politician older than his grandfather, setting up cyber-security for a high-profile website, or sitting in his sister-in-law's bookstore slash bakery while his brother Caleb signed autographs. The latest, and probably his least favorite, was providing security for a thirteen-year-old child star.

"You get to guard one of the most gorgeous women in the world, and I get this kid," Rylan muttered.

"I heard that," his brother said.

"I wasn't trying to be quiet," Rylan snapped. "Why the hell do I keep getting these crappy jobs?"

Alex stacked the papers on his desk and set them aside. Ever since his wife Miranda had their baby six months ago, Alex stayed in the office, behind the desk, taking care of assignments and issuing orders.

He sat back and crossed his heavily tattooed arms over his thick chest.

"Because you're the best," Alex said.

"No, you're the best," Rylan corrected.

Alex chuckled. "Okay, then you're the second best. But I won't hold that title long, now that I'm a desk jockey. No more field work. I promised Miranda."

"It's a kid, Alex," Rylan said. "How dangerous can it be? Keep him from getting swarmed by the teeny boppers at the park or the ice cream parlor—."

Alex laughed. "Do you know how old you sound right now?"

"I feel old. Can't someone else do it?"

Alex shook his head. "David wants you."

Rylan grumbled under his breath. He took one more shot. "What about Chris? Who's taking over Chris's detail? Or Caleb?"

Alex glared at his brother. "Tiny is taking over for Caleb, and David hired a new guy who will work for Chris. It's covered. Stop trying to get out of it. It's a done deal." He slid a folder across the desk. "Here's the info. Kid's name is Maverick Steele. His daily schedule is in there. Donald and Jill are your backups. Todd is your driver. Phoenix Studios knows you're coming. Just show your ID at the gate, and they'll point you in the right direction."

Rylan gave Alex a dirty look. "I hate you."

"No, you don't."

Rylan snatched the folder off the desk and stomped to the door. As he headed out, he heard Alex yell, "See you at Mom's on Sunday!"

Rylan stopped a petite blonde wearing a headset, introduced himself, and asked her where he could find Maverick Steele.

"Maverick is on set," she explained. "Can I help you with something?"

"I'm Rylan Peters from Primetime Security."

"Oh, Mr. Peters! Yes, the studio told Mr. Quill—he's the producer—you would be coming. I'm Rachel, his assistant. If you follow me, I can take you to set."

Rachel mumbled something into her headset and gestured for him to follow her. They entered a large soundstage and walked down a back hallway until they reached a door labeled *Junior Agents Unleashed*. They walked past an extensive set that looked like an elaborate control room and stopped in front of a door labeled Maverick Steele. Rachel pushed the door open and pointed to the other side of the room, where a young man sat on a couch reading a book.

"That's Maverick," she said. "Sweet kid, though sometimes he's surly. Teenagers, you know?" She laughed as if she wasn't only a few years older than him.

"Are his parents here?" Rylan asked.

"Parent. His mom. She's around somewhere. Make yourself comfortable, and I'll see if I can find her."

Rylan thanked her and strode across the room. Maverick looked up, one eyebrow arched, his head tipped to the side. He was a small kid, approximately

5′ 4″ tall, thin, blond hair cut short and spiked in the front. He wore jeans and a Def Leppard T-shirt.

"Who are you?" Maverick asked.

"I'm Rylan, your bodyguard."

"I told my mom I didn't need a babysitter," Maverick grumbled.

Rylan sighed and perched on the couch next to the young man. "I'm not a babysitter. I'm not going to make sure you eat lunch or go to the bathroom or do your homework. I'm not here to watch movies with you or put you down for a nap."

At least that got a laugh out of the kid. He closed his book and looked Rylan up and down. "What do you do, then?"

"My job is to make sure you're safe. Period. People are worried about you. They want to make sure you don't get hurt. I'm here to do that."

Maverick nodded. "Okay. That doesn't sound too bad." He sat up straight. "How long have you been a bodyguard?"

"Seven years," Rylan answered. "After I got out of the military, I joined the firm where my brother works."

"Have you ever guarded anybody famous? I mean, besides me?"

Rylan snorted. He liked this kid. "Do you know Chris Chandler? Or Miranda Putnam?"

"Holy shit! Yeah. They're like famous *famous*. That's cool. Anybody else?"

"Have you heard of Caleb Peters?" Rylan asked.

Maverick rolled his eyes. "Who hasn't? He's like, even more famous than Chris or Miranda. I've seen all his movies. I want to be like him someday. You guarded him?"

"Oh yeah. He's my little brother."

Maverick's jaw dropped open. "O.M.G., dude! That is so cool. Do you think you could introduce me to him sometime?"

Rylan laughed. "I'll tell you what. If you don't make my life difficult, I'll see what I can do. I might even introduce you to Miranda."

"What?" Maverick's cheeks turned red and shook his head. "No way. She's so hot. I would kill to meet her."

"Kill to meet who?" a female voice asked from behind them.

"Mom!" Maverick jumped off the couch and darted across the room. "This is Rylan, my bodyguard. His little brother is Caleb Peters. Can you believe it? He said maybe I could meet Miranda Putnam, too. And he knows Chris Chandler. He's so freaking cool!"

Rylan got to his feet and turned to introduce himself to Maverick's mother. His eyes landed on a familiar face, a face he hadn't seen in years.

Wren Hansley.

Her eyes widened as they locked on his. "Rylan?" she whispered in a shaky voice.

There was a moment of silence filled with a rush of unspoken words and unresolved feelings. Maverick sensed the tension and took a step back, confused.

Wren came to her senses first. "You're Maverick's bodyguard?" she asked.

Rylan nodded. "Yes, ma'am," he whispered.

"Mom?" Maverick interjected. "You okay?"

Wren turned to her son. "Yeah, baby. Um, sorry. It surprised me to see Rylan. We went to high school together."

"Cool," Maverick muttered.

"They want you in wardrobe," Wren said. "You better hurry."

"Okay," Maverick said. "See you later, Rylan!" The young man bounded out of the room.

Rylan shifted from foot to foot. He needed to go with Maverick, but his mother blocked the door. He took a step closer and cleared his throat.

"I, uh, should go with him," he said.

"Oh, sure. Sure. Sorry." She stepped out of the way. "We'll chat later."

"Sounds good," Rylan said. He hurried out the door with his head spinning.

Wren had been Rylan's high school girlfriend. He hadn't seen her in sixteen years, not since the day she broke his heart. Somehow, fate brought the only woman he had ever loved back into his life.

Fate named Alex. He yanked his phone out of his pocket and sent a quick text to his big brother.

[Rylan: Did you know?]

[Alex: That Maverick's mom was Wren? Yes. But not when I gave you the assignment.]

[Rylan: Why didn't you tell me?]

[Alex: Because you wouldn't have taken the job, and David wanted you to do it. Are you okay?]

[Rylan: I will be after I kick your ass.]

[Alex: LOL. Go work. I'll buy you a beer tonight, and you can yell at me.]

[Rylan: Deal.]

He shoved his phone in his pocket as he caught up with Maverick. "Wow, kid, you move fast."

"I thought you were staying with my mom," Maverick said.

"I'm your bodyguard," Rylan said. "I go where you go."

Maverick grinned. "Cool."

# Author Bio

Mimi Francis is a sassy and confident romance writer known for her steamy tales of passion that leave readers breathless. Her creative writing style is filled with vivid imagery and bold characters that make her stories come alive. Born and raised in Montana, Mimi has always had a passion for writing and storytelling.

Mimi's love for writing began when she was a teenager, and she honed her craft by penning countless short stories and journaling. As an adult, she turned to fan fiction as an outlet for her need to write. But it wasn't until she started writing romance novels that she truly found her niche. Her books are filled with sizzling chemistry, well-developed characters, and laugh-out-loud humor.

When she's not busy crafting her latest heart-stopping romance, Mimi can be found sipping margaritas and indulging in her favorite Marvel movies. She's a self-proclaimed fangirl who can't get enough of superheroes and epic battles. But her true obsession lies with the TV show *Supernatural*, which she has watched from beginning to end more times than she cares to admit.

Mimi is also a wife and mother as well as a loving dog mom to four adorable Shih Tzus named Sebastian, Sadie, Sasha, and Sophie. Her furry companions keep her company while she writes and provide endless entertainment with their playful antics.

You can connect with Mimi on Instagram and Facebook at @author.mimi.francis, on X at @author_mimi, on TikTok at @authormimifrancis, or on her website mimifrancis.com.

# More books from 4 Horsemen Publications

## Romance

### Ann Shepphird
The War Council

### Emily Bunney
All or Nothing
All the Way
All Night Long: Novella
All She Needs
Having it All
All at Once

### KT Bond
Back to Life
Back to Love
Back at Last

### Lynn Chantale
The Baker's Touch
Blind Secrets
Broken Lens
Blind Fury
Time Bomb
VIP's Revenge
Chef's Taste
The Gold Standard

### Mandy Fate
Love Me, Goaltender
Captain of My Heart

### Mimi Francis
Private Lives
Private Protection
Private Party
Run Away Home
The Professor
Our Two-Week, One-Night Stand
Can't Fight the Feelings

**Discover more at 4HorsemenPublications.com**

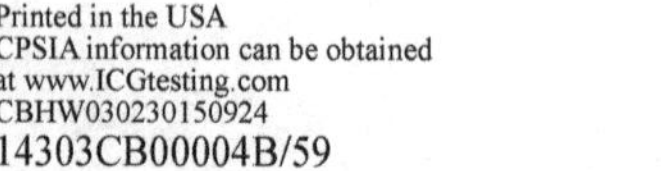

Printed in the USA
CPSIA information can be obtained
at www.ICGtesting.com
CBHW030230150924
14303CB00004B/59

9 798823 204033